I0721418

COLLEEN SNYDER

Knights of the Octagon:
MIA

Colleen Snyder

SADIE AND SOPHIE CUFFE

A Candle Island Cozy
Book #2

Devane's Rip

Miss Understood

by
Sadie & Sophie Cuffe

DEDICATION

To Dad, Bubba E., Gregg A., and all the Coast Guardians who go above and beyond to find the lost and bring them home.

ACKNOWLEDGEMENTS

To our church families and friends in the many coastal island communities of Vinalhaven, North Haven, Swans Island, Arrowsic, Five Islands, Georgetown, Islesboro, Deer Isle, Isle au Haut, and Lubec, Maine; and Deer Island (NB) and Campobello (NB), Canada. Our lives are so much richer because of our island connections.

To Cynthia Hickey, Winged Publications, for all the writing opportunities (and the great covers!).

To Jenny V. for her sharp eyes and even sharper wit.

To our Lord and Savior Jesus Christ, without Whom there would be no words, no music, and no happy endings.

PROLOGUE

I stepped off the ferry into a Candle Island hornets' nest. Shrill accusations salted the breeze from a trio of locals going at it twenty feet or so to my right. It appeared there were more than enough waspish personalities to go around on both the mainland *and* the island. I stood my ground while the tide of disembarking passengers eddied around me. I craned my neck, searching for the beat-up pickup I knew would be there to collect me and my two bags, and did my best to ignore the battling threesome staking their place between me and the parking lot.

My fellow passengers shouted and waved at folks swarming toward them. The nearby argument ebbed, or at least was eclipsed by the laughter and chatter of friends meeting. The happy groups drifted away toward the cars. Trunks and doors slammed. Vans and trucks roared off down the road until only two vehicles remained, neither of which looked familiar.

Face it! No one's waiting for you. It wasn't the end of the world, but it was an inauspicious start to my new life in this new world. I was a stranger among the clannish islanders, and there was no guarantee that status would ever change no matter how long I lived here. I tried to ignore the thought, but it chewed its way into my brain like those nasty little worms that always managed to burrow into my

Cortland apples. *It's not an omen.* I've never believed in omens, good or bad.

There was time enough to find a ride up to Blind Man's Bluff. I could always call my niece, Tasha. For now, I tried to enjoy the moment's anonymity. The gulls wheeled and cried overhead in the deep blue sky, as cars inched by me and bumped onto the waiting ferry. Everyone had somewhere to go this Labor Day weekend.

I turned and watched the crew load the deck for the trip back to the mainland. I breathed in the ambience of my new home—the air off the harbor, ripe with a mixture of diesel fumes, sun-warmed spruce, and the pungent funk of seaweed and flats with the outgoing tide.

CHAPTER ONE

The world of Candle Island. I closed my eyes and my imagination flooded with possibilities … my home-at-least for the next brief chapter of my life.

"A fresh start," I murmured, and as much as I longed to hug my personal fantasies closer, I shook them off and again hefted the two bulging duffle bags, both heavier than sin. My shoulders drooped at the load. That's what I got for packing heavy and assuming someone would be here to help me. It's always true what they say about those who assume, and I felt every ounce of my assumptions.

I might have only myself to blame, but after pack-muling up the rise to the main road, my arms burned, and my heart sank. I repositioned my load, my disappointment weightier than my stuff. *Don't be stupid. Scotty did not forget you. He's late or got tied up somewhere.*

My "caretaker," who came with the mansion I'd recently inherited from the late Vance Jones, was a busy man. Everyone turned to Young Stinson Sullivan Scott when they needed help, but in the short duration of our friendship—at least I thought of it as friendship (I wasn't exactly sure what name he attached to our relationship)— Scotty never forgot anything, and he was never late. I had a feeling both human flaws were blocked from his DNA.

I shrugged the strap of one bag onto my left shoulder, gripped the other by the handle, gritted my teeth and plodded ahead.

"Hey, you're Gwen, right?" A rough hand tweaked on my elbow. I spun around and the hand fell away. It was one of the arguers.

I gave him my best school-teacher-voice and stare. "I'm Gwen McPhail. And you are...?"

I must be losing my intimidation skills, or else they only work on five-year-olds. This guy couldn't have cared less.

Grizzled stubble thrust out at me from his angular jaw. The light blue eyes narrowed under the bowed bill of his stained Red Sox cap as the stranger gave me a once-over. We locked eye to eye and neither of us flinched until he drew back his lips and grinned. He had a gap the size of Devane's Rip where several front teeth were missing, but the rest, I'm happy to say, were clean, and the smile softened his sharp features and prickly advance.

"Of course, you are!" He thrust out a hand. I dropped my bag, and he clutched my hand in a vise clamp. "Kendall Jones. Scotty's cousin?"

When I didn't respond to the question, he released my hand just before my fingers went numb. "I'm the one who fixes stuff?" I shook my head.

"I can't believe he never mentioned me. Anyway, he asked me to run you up to Vance's place."

"Oh. Okay."

Kendall snatched up both bags and headed toward a green pickup nearby. "Anything breakable?" He threw the question over his shoulder, and it flew by before I could process it.

"Uh, no. Wait ... Yes!"

Kendall spun around, his laugh like the bark of a harbor seal. "Which one is it?"

"I do have a few breakables."

"Yeah, I got that. Which one are they in?" He hefted one bag, then the other, as if lifting dumbbells, but it was obvious I was the dumbbell here. *Get your brain in gear!* Kendall never missed a beat. "Knowing me, which it don't appear you do," he made a face, "I'd pick the wrong bag, chuck it in the back of the truck, and bust whatever it is into a thousand pieces. But then I'd fix it for you."

"The blue one is a bit more fragile. Here, let me help you."

A tinkling laugh punctuated my remark. "Help her out, Luke, Honey." The melodious voice was as Southern genteel as the speaker. She was the type of female that made me feel Amazonian. It wasn't because she was younger or that much smaller than I; it was everything about her from her perfectly cut strawberry blond hair, to her infomercial makeup, to her boutique skinny jeans and delicate gold-heeled sandals, to the faint scent of roses floating in the air as she approached.

If I'd thought my lavender T-shirt with the little flowers that I'd just purchased to impress Scotty was chic, this woman's feminine mystique tidal-waved my outfit to washout status. The kicker was, she didn't even notice what I thought of as upscale clothes or my attempt at pretty, simply because she eclipsed everyone around her.

She gave me a cool smile as if she knew just how lackluster I felt but, trust me, she'd never been like me a day in her life. "Anything Kendall touches is destroyed. I swear that man invented bad luck."

Luke, Honey trod past me in silence, but Kendall laughed, and I admired his easy grace. "You know the old saying, 'If anything can't possibly go wrong, it will anyway.'" He flashed his gap-toothed grin.

"Murphy's law," I said.

Kendall shook his head. "Kendall's Law. Murphy stole it. Whenever I'm involved, things usually get off the rails. But my friends don't hold it against me, eh, Luke?"

Luke grunted.

The younger woman shot me a pained rose-between-two-thorns smile. I was pretty sure she had both men wrapped around her finger and they were the ones in pain.

She nodded her patrician nose toward the dark-haired brute loading my luggage into the bed of Kendall's truck. "We haven't been properly introduced. Olivia Faraday, and that's my husband, Luke." She put forth a small, nail-painted hand glittering with more rings than a jewelry store. "You're the new schoolteacher. Is that right?"

"In a manner of speaking, yes."

She made a brief fluttering contact with my fingers before she withdrew her soft hand from mine. She didn't give me the blatant once-over I'd gotten from Kendall, she was too classy for that; but her cool assessment went much deeper than his. I felt her pitying eyes saw past my T-shirt and capris to my muffin top and cellulite.

I raised my chin a notch to hide my mental flinch. "I'm here to help Laurel Jones with her class."

Olivia shook her head and a birdlike "Tsk-tsk," popped from her pursed lips. "Then you haven't heard?"

I raised one eyebrow to convey my contempt for gossip, but she either ignored it or couldn't stop her lips once they got moving. I suspected it was a deadly combination of both. "They took Laurel to the mainland today." She leaned closer and her rose-garden scent wafted around me. "Complications with the pregnancy."

"Oh, dear."

Another "tsk" cut me off. "So, I suspect you'll be teaching in her place. Do you think that's a reasonable conclusion?" Her green eyes pierced me with ... contempt? Suspicion? It was definitely something nasty and I didn't even know the woman.

My earlier qualms came back to bite. Olivia might be from away, but she fit in. This was her turf, not mine, not yet. I squared my shoulders and countered her fierce gaze with my own. "I'm not sure what's happening. I just arrived." I gestured toward the loaded luggage. "I haven't heard anything yet from Principal Gray."

"Delia Gray's off to the mainland today as well." A

satisfied smirk graced Olivia's coral pink lips. Was she the Candle Island travel guru, or just a nosy so-and-so? I had my suspicions.

Luke Faraday returned to Olivia's side, his barrel chest and stocky build accentuating her feminine form. She smiled up at him, bright as sunlight bouncing off the rough water beyond the harbor, and he wrapped a protective anchor-tattooed arm around her shoulders. "My granddaughter Jacey's in kindergarten this year." His warm husky voice took me by surprise and belied his grim mouth. "She's right attached to Laurel."

"She absolutely *adores* Laurel. Doesn't she, Darling?" His wife's eyes dared me to contradict.

"I'm sure Laurel will be there to teach for the first several weeks to help the students and me get to know one another. We'll do our best to make it a smooth transition. That's why I'm here early, to help out and learn my way around." I smiled at them.

"I don't know how you can say that." Olivia's pursed-lipped *tsk* punctuated her words. "She went over to the hospital just this morning. You have no idea what's going on with her."

And neither do you! "You're right, Mrs. Faraday, but I'm hoping and praying for the best."

"Well, of course *we* are, too, but we don't know, do we? And this is so upsetting for Jacey. For our whole family, really. Jacey's so attached to her Grampie. She gets upset, literally makes herself sick, if she has to be away from him. You have no idea how disturbing that is for both of us." Olivia ran her bejeweled fingers over her husband's ample waist. "Luke hates to see her cry."

"She's shy. Don't take to newcomers. Don't know if she should go to school if Laurel won't be there." Luke frowned and rubbed his tanned forehead with his large hand.

"I understand. A lot of young children experience separation anxiety when they start school." Where was Jacey at this moment? Obviously not attached to Grampie's pant leg today. After meeting her grandparents, I had a feeling she'd save her wailing separation-anxiety bouts just for me.

"You don't know Jacey." Luke's wide face was as shuttered and unwelcoming as the cliffs of Blind's Man's Bluff on the far side of the island.

"No, I don't, but I look forward to meeting her. Perhaps we could get together before school starts, if that would make you feel better. Or maybe you'd like to consider helping out in the classroom."

"Can't. I gotta be out on the boat, if I can keep it running." Luke shot an accusing glare at Kendall.

"Maybe you'd consider it, Mrs. Faraday. We can get together with Principal Gray and Laurel and find the best solution for Jacey and you."

Olivia held up a glittering black-nailed finger and butterflied it through the air. "Oh no. It absolutely wouldn't work. Jacey doesn't care for me."

"But as her grandmother, I'm sure..." I let the encouragement dangle, mostly because I had one foot in my mouth and my brain needed to come up for air. *What are you doing? This isn't Bookerton or Brier Elementary. It's not even your classroom!*

My brain wasn't the only one suffering from any spark of intelligence. Bickering with strangers? I imagined we all knew better; it was just the *doing* better that escaped us.

"Neither Jacey nor I consider myself her grandmother, although Luke would have everyone believing differently. Besides, being at the school is *your* job, not mine or his." She cut me off at the ankles, but that made it so much easier to stuff the other foot in my mouth. She sighed. "One big happy family. That's Luke's dream, but I find I don't have anything in common with young kids, especially step-grandchildren, as I'm nowhere near mature enough to have any of my own."

I agreed with the immaturity assessment. As for her

aversion to kids, I'd met her kind too many times to count, but each new encounter evoked the same intolerant revulsion in me. What Olivia Faraday meant was, she had a makeup table mirror, a clothes closet and jewelry box where her heart should've been. For all her sugarcoated honeys and darlings, she had no emotional capacity for the tears, dirt, hugs, and kisses—all the messy stuff of life that comes with allowing the little ones to capture your heart and build their sandcastles and mud pies there.

The ferry horn tooted. She smiled, lowered her lids and ran her hand up Luke's brawny forearm. "We're at the stage where it's *me* time."

I had a feeling it had always been, and always would be, *me* time for Olivia.

"At least that's what Luke and I thought. Just the two of us. Sell the boat and spend our winters down in Florida. We weren't expecting to get saddled with parenting. We're still in the honeymoon phase of our marriage. Aren't we, Darling?" My eyes stared at her hand as she squeezed his arm but, when I flicked my gaze to her husband's face, his stony expression remained unchanged.

"Well, I guess the best thing we can do for now is wait and see." I hated it when I lapsed into chirpy trite isms, but I'd run out of conversational landscape and needed an out. "We should know more about Laurel's condition and Principal Gray's plans in a few days."

Luke jerked his strong jaw and looked over at Kendall. "Wait and see. That's the story of my life nowadays."

Kendall nodded, his smile gone. "We'd best get going, Gwen."

"Oh, sorry. I didn't mean to hold you up Kendall. By all means, let's go."

"Not a problem."

"Don't get lost, Ken." Luke's husky tone had a razor edge to it. "This isn't over, not by a long shot. I need that motor fixed today, and if I don't get it, *you'll* be the next one hurting."

Kendall winked at me but his words held the chill of the North Atlantic. "Just think about what I said. Olivia agrees with me. You would, too, if you weren't so pigheaded all the time. Open your eyes, Luke! You wanna get ahead, then get moving into the future. You're dumping money into a hole in the water. The Jane Anne's old enough to vote."

Luke unwound his arm from his wife's shoulders and rounded on the taller man. "Yeah? Old enough to vote, huh? Kendall Jones, you're a fine one to talk. Still living in your granddad's old place while it falls down around your ears."

"Hey, you got no right to throw all this on me. My house is *my* business not yours." He gave an injured sniff.

"Yeah, sure. You always do this. Dish it out, but you can't take it. Play the victim all you like. One day I'm gonna come over to that bait shack of yours and get my stuff. All of it. All those tools you've broken, burnt up, and lost. No more, Ken. You're not touching anything that's mine! You got that? I've had it! I need my boat. I need that part installed, and I need you to get off your backside, get over to my place and fix it like you promised. Then get out!"

Luke swung his arm back around Olivia's waist. "Come on." He swept the couple away from us without a backward glance, but Olivia, with the slightest turn of her head, looked at me. Or, more to the point, right through me, before she snuggled into her husband's side and slowed his deliberate angry strides.

I had no idea what was going on, but whatever it was, it had crawled onto my skin like a caterpillar and left me with the uncomfortable feeling I wasn't going to get rid of the itch.

Kendall shook his head. "Sorry about that." He scrubbed a calloused hand over his grizzled chin.

"I think I'm the one who should be apologizing to you."

"Naw. Luke just don't get it sometimes. Things get worse under pressure, and he's living with his own little pressure cooker these days." He grinned. "Smile. Tomorrow will be worse."

What did one say to that? I dredged up one of Father's favorite sayings. "Left to themselves, things tend to go from bad to worse."

He cranked back his head and let loose a bark of laughter, his angular Adam's apple dancing with the effort. "You got that right! Let's get you where you're going."

A familiar pickup cruised into the lot beside us and Stinson Scott, the younger, known as Scotty, leaned his head out the window. The sun glinted off his close-cropped copper hair and the sharp-eyed glare he leveled at me was cool as a fall breeze.

"You got the old man fixed up?" Kendall's comment broke through our eye contact.

"Yeah."

"He's a tough old bird."

Scotty nodded. "I can take her up, but thanks for stepping in."

"No problem, but I can't believe you never mentioned me."

"Gwen." Scotty gave me a brief nod, ignoring his cousin, as he vaulted out of the pickup.

I turned my attention to Kendall. "Thanks so much for your help. I hope I didn't get you in trouble."

"Naw, no problem. Glad to meet cha."

Scotty had my bags loaded in the back of his truck.

"Well, I hope I'll see you again."

Kendall nodded. "Yeah, bye." He ducked into his vehicle, and it started with a throaty rumble.

Scotty's hand on my back guided me to the passenger's seat. "Watch yourself. Kendall's always tinkering with engines. Gets carried away sometimes."

Kendall pulled out of the lot with a flash of a hand out the window, and roared down the road away from town. Presumably to Luke Faraday's house to mend a boat and some fences.

I was barely seated in the cab when my driver started the engine, and we were on the move. "You want to head right home or have lunch?"

"That depends."

Scotty slowed the truck to a crawl, turned to me and lifted one russet eyebrow.

"Do you need to go take care of your grandfather?"

"I'm the last person he wants hanging around."

"I don't believe that." They not only shared the same moniker, but a host of stubborn traits.

Scotty shrugged, shifted into third and picked up speed. "He got a fishhook caught in his cheek this morning. Wanted me to pull it out, but it was close to his eye so I took him to the clinic. Wasn't he ugly! But Sledge got him all squared away."

"It must've hurt."

"The air was blue for a few minutes, but trust me, he's fine now. And if *we're* smart, we'll keep our distance."

"What's this *we* thing?" I grinned. It was good to be back on the island and, regardless of my misgivings, I fit in just fine.

Scotty returned my smile. "Fair warning."

A few minutes later we pulled in at the faded sign of a clam in a sou'wester. *Barb's Lunch Box - Best Clam Roll in Coveside*. The trailer take-out was still summertime-busy this Friday before Labor Day weekend; all but one of the picnic tables in the rear was occupied.

Scotty was out and holding the door before I unclipped my seatbelt. "Order whatever you like. It's on me."

"Since you're chauffeuring me, I'd like to treat you."

"Not happening."

"This is the twenty-first century."

"So I've heard. You're still not paying for my lunch." His crow's feet accentuated the steel glint in his eye as we got in line.

I shook my head. "Stinson stubbornness?" Or was it a reminder of island ways rooted in centuries of closed community.

One eyebrow lifted and he smiled an easy smile … not one with antagonism oozing from it. I shook off the thought of Olivia, but the shadow of doubt must've crossed my face.

"Having second thoughts about chucking the mainland life?"

I'd missed his deliberate way of talking. "I'm only taking a year's leave of absence. It's not like I'm running away to join the circus."

"The old wing walker's rule, eh?" He nodded.

I shot him a puzzled look.

He grinned, yanked his well-worn coast guard cap out of his back pocket and pulled it over his gray-flecked, rust-colored hair.

He knew how to prolong the torture. I'd give him this one. "I'm not familiar with it."

"'Don't let go of something until you have ahold of something else.'" His blue eyes held a flicker of challenge.

He thinks I'm playing it safe. The thought rankled.

"Next!"

Scotty stepped up to the take-out window. At the shrill disapproving voice, I hung back but my escort beckoned me closer, and in the burn of his wing-walker comment, I took a stride up beside him to confront the frowning face behind the screen.

"Hey, Dot." Scotty smiled at his cousin.

"Scotty."

"Thought you were picking crabmeat this morning."

"Laverna needed a hand." Dot directed her scowl at me. "'Course I can use the extra money, what with Ron's place at our boatyard up in the air."

"He's still working at the Candle Island Yacht Company, isn't he?"

Her dark eyes flicked back to Scotty and ignored my

question. "What're you having?"

Hang the wing walker! Her son, Ron, was a fragile young man in an adult body, with a wife and a baby on the way. He was my friend, in spite of my rocky relationship with his mom. "Is Ron okay? I think a good lawyer could undo that draconian part of your husband's will."

What father disinherits his son for marrying into a rival family? What man leaves his million-dollar mansion to a fifty-year-old stranger? I didn't have the answers, but I was here to dig them up, even if it meant getting down and dirty.

Dot snorted and her hot gaze bored through me. "A lot *sh*e cares. She's got my house, might as well have put Ron and me out on the street. I gotta put food on my table somehow."

"I want to talk to you about the house."

Scotty's elbow gave me a gentle nudge in the ribs.

"I think I'll have the crabmeat roll, Dot," he said. "How about you, Gwen?"

I hated to take his hint, but he was right. Now wasn't the time. "Sounds good to me."

"Does that mean she wants the same thing?"

Oh good grief! Were we stuck in the middle school I'm-not-talking-to-her juvenile affectation, or what? "Yes, please." I kept my reply pleasant. Just barely.

"Just wanted to be sure." Dot didn't write down the order. "Can't trust a thing some people say."

Middle school it was. I was more than familiar with the mores and I wasn't playing along. "Look, Dot, let's get together whenever it's convenient for you and thrash this out." Not my best choice of words. "I'm going to be around."

"Oh, I've heard all about it. She's taking over for my daughter-in-law at the school. Just another way to harpoon my family."

"Forget about the harpoon. Might as well scuttle the ship," Scotty muttered loud enough for both of us to hear. I glanced at my companion but his lean face remained in profile as he shifted closer to the window. "Laurel will be fine, Dot. Gwen won't be taking anyone's job."

There was more than one way to buffalo myself into this stupid conversation. "I heard she went to the hospital to get checked out. I hope she and the baby are okay."

Both Scotty and his cousin glared at me. "Yeah, they hauled her off to the mainland first thing this morning with that niece of hers, Tasha, tagging along like a bad penny." She tossed her head at Gwen. "If old Doc Beckett was here, he would've told my daughter-in-law not to overdo and sent her home to rest. Sledge might've, too, if not for her niece's interference. Calls herself a nurse, but you couldn't tell it by me. Apple don't fall far from the tree." Dot's eyes narrowed to slits. "Just like her aunt, for my money. She'll throw her weight around at the hospital and do nothing but get my son on the hook for a bunch of expensive tests. No need of any of this."

Scotty laid a light hand on my tensed forearm, and I forced myself not to shake it off. Still mentally gasping from the bucket of ice-cold criticism thrown in my face, I tried once more to extend the olive branch, but I couldn't let the slur on my niece go unanswered. "I'm sure Tasha will take good care of both of them. Let me know when you'd like to come over and we'll talk."

"It'll be a cold day in May before I ever set foot in that mansion again as a visitor to my own home."

Laverna, owner of Barb's, nodded to me as she slipped the two crab rolls onto the counter beside Dot's elbow. A little dark-haired girl trailed in her wake as she turned back to the grill without a word. Dot shoved our order out the window at my companion and he passed her the money before I had time to reach for my stash. "I got this," Scotty said.

Dot glowered. "Got another man paying her way, I see. Some things never change. Watch yourself, Scotty."

"Dot." Scotty's voice was low but stern.

"Excuse me? You don't know me," I said.

"Maybe it's *you* who don't know any of *us*," Dot retorted.

Ha! No more "she," at least. I'd punched a hole through her dam of hateful defenses, and she'd finally unleashed her tirade directly at me.

"The island can kill you if you don't know your way around."

"I'll take that chance." I shook off the friendly restraining hand on my arm, and with it, my attempts at polite conversation. "You can play the injured party here, but I'd think you'd want to at least listen to what I have to say. The sooner we get this straightened out, the better for all of us."

Dot snorted. "Always talking out of both sides of your mouth, aren't cha? Scotty might buy it but, what with you moving the whole clan in up there, I've got my doubts."

"What?"

"If that's all, people are waiting."

Scotty's firm-but-gentle fingers clamped my elbow and steered me toward the pickup. "Let's go."

"But—"

"Live to fight another day, Gwen."

"But—"

"It's her poor-poor-pitiful-me phase. She'll get over it. Dot tends to blow hot and cold. Always has."

"I'm getting this inherited-mansion-mix-up off my back, if it kills me."

"Or me, most likely."

"You could talk to her. She's your cousin."

"And what am I going to say?"

"That I really *am* going to give her back her house."

"And what would you do then?"

"I don't know, but I'll figure it out when the time comes. Right about now, I'm considering joining the circus and becoming a wing walker."

"I believe that's barnstorming, not Barnum and Bailey."

"Then I'll be the first."

"Seems like an oxymoron to me."

"Ah, gotcha." I wanted to be mad but, if I was honest, this verbal sparring was one of the reasons I'd made the move to the island. "Perhaps I'll start out as a tightrope walker, without a net, and graduate to biplanes in the future."

Scotty nodded as he held the truck door open for me. "Sounds about right, but you could've warned me about the second career before we ordered lunch."

18

CHAPTER TWO

The crabmeat rolls sat on the bench seat between us as we made our way over the island back roads to Blind Man's Bluff. With the taste of Dot's appetizer of loathing-spleen-raked-over-the-hot-coals still on my tongue, I wasn't particularly hungry, so we'd opted to take our lunch up to the mansion. *Vance's place.* After Dot's rude comments, I refused to call it home.

But when Scotty slowed the vehicle on the last bend of the private dirt road, I couldn't stop the turn of my head as we passed the cape to our left, its weathered cedar shingles muted silver. I squinted against the glint of late summer sun on the glassed-in porch and the sparkle of water beyond. The cobble beach stretched wide at low tide, and a patch of pink and white phlox swayed breezily in the backyard.

This was the home of my dreams. Unfortunately, it was Vance Jones' widow's place. And while not everyone out here hated me, Dot hated me enough for them all.

I yearned to ask her if we could trade homes, but it was only a private fantasy … one I indulged in at least once a day. I wasn't proud of my greedy obsession, but a girl can dream. Despite what Vance Jones' last will and testament stated, I knew beyond a shadow of a doubt I didn't own the mansion I'd inherited. Dot did, so I had nothing to trade for this solitary cottage on Eyelash Beach.

The original Jones' family farm was like a fine woman

of old Yankee stock—strong and beautiful with age, and gracefully settled into her place in life. I took a last glance at the tiered rock garden, the landscape of wild goldenrod, frost flowers and perennials, before the dust from our tires obscured the view and we sped up the hill to my temporary abode.

The hood of the truck nosed over the steep grade and Scotty idled the engine down as soon as we topped the rise. The massive wall of brick and glass filled the entire view from the windshield and added a brick weight to my conflicted heart.

I'd contacted the lawyer who gave me the keys to this place, but Mr. Blevins counseled me to wait a year before making any big decisions about my inheritance. He was wrong. I couldn't wait another minute. I had to get rid of this place, even if I ended up homeless for the winter.

We pulled around the circular gravel drive and my eyes flicked over the formal evergreen landscape of cedar-mulched junipers, flat-top yews, and spiral dwarf Alberta spruce; perfectly manicured, incredibly unnatural, and hopelessly sterile. Not a weed or flower in sight. For the time being this was my lodging.

"You expecting anyone?"

I jerked my gaze to the frontispiece and there, lounging on the wide granite steps, his back against one of the white columns, was my nephew, Nathaniel. His grimy go-everywhere backpack lay propped on the ugly lion statue nearby. He sat enthroned on the stones in his cutoff jeans, battered sneakers, and black Blynn River White Water T-shirt as if he owned the place. My little gray-and-white cat was wrapped around his neck like a mink stole.

I shook my head. I must've made a noise in my throat, but I was unaware of doing so until Scotty's hand stilled on the door handle, and I felt his eyes on me. "One of yours?"

I met his steely gaze and nodded. "Tasha's twin brother, Nathaniel."

"He a nurse, too?"

I laughed.

"Didn't think so. You expecting him?"

"You never expect Nate. He just shows up. Actually, I thought he might be coming to Bookerton and staying in my old house for a while, but ... "

"He didn't show up."

I bounded out of the cab and Nathaniel leaped up. Balancing the cat on one shoulder, my nephew wrapped me in a sweet familiar bear hug. The outboard-motor-purr of the cat slipping sidesaddle on my cheek, and the faint whiff of gasoline and grease took me back to all those summer vacations when Nate and his sister stayed with me in Bookerton. That boy's hands were never clean. He was always tinkering on everything from my sump pump to that broken down dirt bike he bought when he was fourteen.

"You got a cat?" We broke the family clinch and the pet oozed down between us to the ground and wound around our ankles.

"He was a stray. Your sister named him Purry Mason."

Nathaniel rolled his eyes, scooped up the cat again and went nose to nose with the creature. Typical Nate. Not many men liked cats, but my nephew wasn't most men. "What did you ever do to deserve that?"

I glanced around at Scotty, his face unreadable beneath the shadowed bill of his cap, which was probably a good thing. He leaned one elbow on the hood of his truck taking it all in. "Some people call him PM, as in Post Meridian, Midnight, Twilight ... you get the drift."

Nate laughed, ending in a cough. "Post Meridian. I like that. Much more manly for a scrapper like you." He placed the cat at our feet and turned, perusing the three-and-a-half storey monstrosity pressing down on us and eclipsing the sun. "So, you're moving in for good?"

"No, just here for a while."

Nathaniel nodded and did a slow 360. "Nice locale,

definitely understated."

"You think so?" I laughed and he joined in; again the racking cough. The third member of our group remained silent.

"Tasha told me you'd come up in the world, but I didn't know you'd landed on the top of a mountain. Thought I'd better stop by and check it out. Locking your doors now to keep out the nephews and riffraff, huh?" He whistled through his teeth. "Security system with all the bells and whistles ... unbelievable! Looks like you won't be needing me to lend a hand with repairs on *this* baby."

With an aunt's eye I took in his sun-bleached longish hair curling around his ears, the summer tan on his sinewy golden-haired arms, and the raccoon-like shadows under those fried-marble blue eyes. "Are you alright?"

"Oh, yeah, just a little cough, a head cold from dumping in the Blynn River rapids one too many times."

"The whitewater rafting job?"

He raised his wrist, his forefinger flicking a paracord bracelet. "Not a total bust. When we had a group of teens, we did arts and crafts around the fire pit. I learned to make survival bracelets in the beautiful Blynn River Rafting Company colors of lively black and beige. But you would've smoked all of us."

"At survival?"

"At the arts and crafts." He grinned. "We ought to get Tasha here and spend the afternoon at Auntie Gwen's doing crafts, just like back in the day."

I laughed. It was just like Nate to tweak us off topic. "So, what happened to the job?"

"It got old faster than I thought it would."

I raised an eyebrow.

"Her ex-boyfriend came back." He grinned. "It got a little awkward. He took my job, which was his old job in the first place, so I did the gentlemanly thing and stepped aside."

"I thought this girl was 'just a friend.' "

"Oh, she was, but he got a bit territorial. No sense of humor." Nate shrugged. "I thought I might crash here for a couple weeks and see my sister. Besides, you and I haven't hung out in a while."

"Sounds good." I didn't like the sound of his cough or the husky gravel he couldn't quite clear from his throat. A little R&R and chicken soup wouldn't do any harm.

A clang startled me and I spun around. Scotty stood with his hand on the tailgate, one duffle over each shoulder. Since when did he need to open the tailgate to get out a little luggage?

"Let me give you a hand." Nate loped over to the truck just as my driver lowered one bag down on the driveway. Scotty nudged the duffle with his foot.

I quickly trotted up. "Scotty, this is my nephew, Nathaniel. Nate, this is my friend, Scotty. He looks after the place."

"You here to look after your aunt or vice versa?"

Tell us how you really feel.

Nate just grinned. "Nobody in their right mind looks after Gwen and lives to tell about it." He laughed.

Scotty glowered. "Whole clan moving in on you," he muttered.

"What?"

"Something Dot said."

I shook my head as her remembered comment sunk in. Dot had intimated I was moving the whole clan in … how had she known about Nathaniel?

"How did you get here?"

"I was in the store over by the ferry landing to pick up some cold medicine while I waited for the boat, and I ran into a dude at the counter complaining about his boat. Luke Faraday? His boat engine kept cutting out unless he gunned it full throttle. I offered to give him a hand. We monkeyed around with it, got it going fair enough to make the crossing, and he gave me a ride over. Providence and Gwen always go together, right?" He winked at me. "Obviously, I was meant to come."

"Obviously." Scotty's slow drawl drew my attention. "Looks to me less like providence and more like you've got a knack for sponging off folks."

I opened my mouth but he wasn't finished.

"A little old for that, aren't you?"

"Is he Uncle Neil's clone?" Nate's good-natured jibe kept my good humor intact. Scotty was ... well, Scotty. A bit of a German Shepherd, but would I want him to be a lap dog?

I hadn't seen it before, but under Scotty's retired Coast Guard exterior, there was a slight tip of the hat to my brother, Neil. Since Daddy died, as the eldest of four, Neil had become the self-appointed patriarch of the McPhail clan; most days a good thing. Once in a while he was a little heavy handed, particularly where Nathaniel was concerned. "Maybe."

Nate smiled. "No wonder we feel so at home. But no worries. I already lined up a job. Luke is shorthanded so I signed on to be his sternman, first mate, Gilligan, man Friday, you name it."

I was impressed. My companion, not so much. Scotty nodded. "The former 'Gilligan' ran off with a girl from the mainland. She and Wyatt were supposed to elope and go to Oregon, or join Green Peace, or work on an organic farm." He looked at me "You get the picture."

I did. And from the sarcasm dripping from every word, I knew Scotty thought Nate would wash out after one day. He didn't know my nephew, so I tried not to hold his low opinion against him. At least not yet. Nate might've been born a free spirit, but he'd been old enough to fight his own, and his sister's, battles from the get go, so if I was smart I'd remember that and stay out of both men's ways.

Nate nodded. "Worked out for me. I start tomorrow."

If Luke and Kendall got the boat fixed. The thought popped into my head unbidden. How odd to have run into

Nate's new boss this morning. Providential? I wasn't feeling it; more like weird. I shook off the shadowy emotion and chirped. "How about some lunch?" I ducked into the cab and pulled out the crabmeat rolls.

"Fine by me," Nate agreed.

Scotty led the way to the house, punching in the security code and holding the door open for us. "I hope you'll join us," I said as I brushed past him.

"Wouldn't miss it." The deep slow drawl belied the battle-ready shine in those vigilant blue eyes.

We divided up the sandwiches and I augmented the menu with all-dressed chips and boxed cookies. Not exactly a gourmet feed, but I'd been off island for a couple of weeks getting my mainland life in order. This trip I'd packed smart and brought enough of my stuff so I wouldn't be going back and forth on the ferry every other week. The only thing missing was my car.

"Sorry about not bringing my own wheels." The apology popped out, catching both me and Scotty by surprise. He glanced at me over the top of his glass as he took a final swig of raspberry iced tea. Our eyes held for only a moment, but his steady gaze might as well have been a billboard sign. I had no need of a car but, now that my nephew was here I couldn't expect Scotty to play Uber driver.

Nate laughed. "Waited too long to trade in that dinosaur, Gwen?"

"I think someone might've warned me a time or two to unload it." I shrugged. "It's developed a few issues so it's at the garage."

"You should've brought it over so I could take a look at it."

"I tried, but I couldn't get a tow truck to haul it onto the ferry."

"That bad, huh? What about Tash?"

"We've been sharing my car."

"I gotta have a talk with that sister of mine."

"Pot calling the kettle black," Scotty said, then skewered my nephew with a fatherly look. "So, meeting Luke at the boat tomorrow could be a problem."

I glanced back across the table at Scotty. It was a lot to ask, particularly since he didn't exactly take to Nate. But what better way for the men to get acquainted? Maybe? Probably not.

"I'll be by early." Scotty didn't sound happy about it.

Nate dusted some cookie crumbs off his shirt and nodded. "I'd appreciate it, but what about the wheels in the garage? I took a peek through the window while I was waiting. Nice Beemer. Did it come with the penthouse?"

Scotty's answer was as soft and smooth as car wax. "As a matter of fact, it does."

I shook my head. "No, that car belongs to Ron or Dot."

Nate turned those wide innocent blue eyes on me. "You haven't checked it out? Gwen, why not? You can't hurt a car by using it. It's not good for that thing to be getting dry rot sitting in a garage. It needs to be started and run every so often. You know, blow out the pipes."

I'd been on a few of his "blow out the pipes" sorties. A teenaged Nate learning to drive my stick shift had put the first strands of gray in my hair.

Scotty pushed his chair from the table, leaned back and crossed his arms. "And you volunteer?"

Nate shrugged. "Somebody's gotta do the dirty work. How long since it's been started?"

"I keep an eye on it," Scotty replied.

"So it'll start right up?"

"I should think." Scotty excused himself from the table and retrieved a set of keys hanging on the rack by the pantry door. "Only one way to find out." He dangled the BMW key ring from his thumb and forefinger.

It was like shaking catnip under PM's nose. Nate stood and grinned at me. "Want us to help clean up first, Gwen?"

"Thanks, but I'm all set."

"You could come with. We could all go for a spin. Check out the island," he offered.

"You go ahead. I'm going to do a little unpacking."

"Okay." He turned to Scotty. "After you."

Scotty closed his fist around the keys and raised an eyebrow. "I imagine we'll be back in a while."

"All in one piece, I hope. You might want to keep hold of the dashboard before you let go of the seat belt."

Scotty laughed. "I'll let you know how the view is from the wing."

Unaware of the biplane byplay, Nate simply went with the flow. "Can't wait. This way I can get the lay of the land before I head off tomorrow at 4:30." My nephew groaned. "Thought I'd put those hours behind me when I left the river."

"The river's nothing compared to the sea." Spoken like an old salt.

"Good deal."

I watched them traipse out into the garage, Nate's loose-jointed saunter following stiff-backed Scotty's quick stride. Nothing like a little road trip to bring out a developing bromance, or at least promote a little less hostility.

The car left a few moments later in a flash of sunlight bouncing off glossy ebony. I noticed Scotty was behind the wheel. Nate's arm waved from the passenger's side window.

I cleaned up the kitchen then unpacked my baking accouterments and recipe box. Seeing my colored cooking bowls stacked in the cupboard made it look and feel more like home. I was settling into my new life. I caught myself singing snatches of an '80's classic as I danced into the square of sunlight streaming in through the windows. *I could get used to it here.*

The truth wasn't shocking. It wasn't as if my heart hadn't already decided this is where I belonged. Well, not exactly *this. The mansion, her mansion.* Dot's angry accusations, echoing in my ears, stilled my song.

The island life I wanted. The albatross of the inherited mansion, I didn't—but could I get this whole mess straightened out and live happily ever after on Candle Island? Or was it my great white whale, always and ever just out of reach?

I shook off the depressing thought and made my way to the library. Who, or what, was there to stop me from setting things in motion today or, as Dot so politely put it, getting out the harpoon? I ran my fingers over the beautiful spines of first-edition books as I stepped past the shelves, warding off the temptation to stop and browse. I was on a mission.

I searched the drawers in the reading table and came up empty. Who in their right mind had empty drawers? Next, I searched the magnificent cherry desk on the far side of the room; nothing but a few pens, an ugly paperweight, and a couple of bookmarks from a charity donation. Didn't anybody write letters or use paper anymore? All I wanted was a little note card and an envelope. Would it be tacky to send Dot an invitation to lunch on one of her own cards?

I didn't have to worry. I fished around in the nearby cabinet and came up empty again. I was beginning to think the Jones family never used this room, or maybe Dot and Ron had taken the contents of the drawers when they moved down to the cottage. I liked to imagine that might be so, but the drawer corners were obscenely clean of dust and detritus.

I had a feeling from what I'd learned of my late benefactor, this room might've been more of a shrine to the great yacht builder of Candle Island than a family gathering place. As I let my gaze roam over the one-of-a-kind artwork, the marble fireplace, the beautiful wood, I glimpsed no stamp of Dot here; or maybe this frigid attempt at ambience was the cold sterile life they shared together when they lived here.

I refused to be dragged into the doldrums of the past and, instead, set my sights on Vance Jones' office. He ought to at least have some paper I could use. I climbed the stairs past the second-floor bedrooms and on up to what I called "the crow's nest." It was a man's room with its mahogany wainscoting, as richly appointed as the rest of the house save for the scarred desk and ancient easy chair. Vance's private retreat.

I barely glanced at his trophies of yacht races won, accolades, and framed awards. The far wall of glass beckoned with its unparalleled panorama of little islands dotting a pirate's-map-trail through the ocean waves back to the mainland. I gave the view a cursory glance before I sat down at the desk, as if I was getting too comfortable with my surroundings and took the spectacular view for granted.

I was anything but comfortable with this situation. I rifled through the drawers on the right side of the desk and found mostly Candle Island Yacht Company stuff, but not so much as a piece of official stationery or unused scrap paper. Nothing I saw interested me, but I should get Vance's son, Ron, in here to pick it up. It might be useful for him in trying to retain ownership of his father's business.

I tried the center drawer, but it wouldn't budge. Running my fingertip over the keyhole, I wondered if I could jimmy it open. I grabbed the whalebone-handled letter opener that looked more like a dagger than an office tool. I clenched it in my fist for a minute but set it down on the desktop and let common sense prevail. No need to destroy just yet. As much as I itched to get a look inside, the key must be hidden right under my nose.

I opened the left side drawer and hit partial pay dirt … not paper, but envelopes and a jumble of ordinary items— rubber bands, old, black-handled shears, sticky notes, postage stamps, pencils, pens, some thumb drives and CD's, but no key. I bent down to the lower drawer and ignored the gray spots floating in front of my eyes as I cut off my wind. I sucked in what I could of my muffin top and pulled open the last drawer. Might be time to get serious about some bona fide exercise. Obviously working in the garden didn't count. Without a car, that shouldn't be a problem.

The final drawer was filled with a mishmash of large mailing envelopes, some new, some used. The curled yellowed edges of an old newspaper poked out from about halfway down the stack. I pawed through the pile and pulled out a bunch of newspapers and magazines, all older copies, and, after a quick perusal, all contained articles on Vance and the boatyard.

I reached back down inside to get the rest of it and my fingers grazed a solid object at the bottom. I lifted out the remaining stack and set it on the floor. Some less-than-pristine paper with the Candle Island Yacht Company logo emerged and, gasping for breath, I dove deep, grabbed the paper and pulled out the prize underneath.

I tossed the letter material on the desk and leaned back in the chair, staring at the 4"x6" photo I held in my hands. Framed in handcrafted wood, the picture was as vintage as the barn boards making up the border. My fingers trembled as I clutched the wood. I'd recognize my father's handiwork anywhere. His craftsmanship—from Mama's corner hutch, to our barn-board-planked kitchen table, to the maple-stained frames on our high school graduation photos—had graced every room of our childhood home.

I blinked back the mist of the past and focused on the trio in the photo. I remembered that jumper I was wearing, a hand-me-down from my cousin, Jeannie; narrow wale corduroy in shades of blue, with little lavender flowers. I used to pat the soft material as if it were a security blanket. The faded colors were split where a splintered white line ran diagonally across the picture through the two men, a permanent crease where it had remained folded for a while.

I had the chipmunk cheeked smile of a four-year-old. The sun was in our eyes, and we were all squinting into the camera. I leaned against a young version of my father with his long sideburns, wavy brown hair without a streak of gray; his body strong, his large bony hand engulfing mine. I could almost feel his warm steady grip.

The thin wiry man standing to his left had features as sharp as an axe blade, his black hair slicked back from his forehead but 1970's rocker-long, touching his shoulders in the rear.

It was taken on our front steps when Mama had been in her paint-everything-yellow phase, one that lasted way too long in my opinion. The corner of the picture caught the leafy branch of the ash tree—back in the day my playground for a wooden swing, a ship's mast and, later, a multilevel treehouse.

I stared at the faded image, my mind filling in the colors, the scents, and the sounds of that long-ago moment. A different time. I didn't actually remember this instant, but obviously I was there. I suspected my oldest brother might've snapped the shot.

My parents weren't ones to waste time on photos. We had a small box or two chronicling camping and sightseeing trips, us kids in various scout and athletic uniforms, with beloved pets and grandparents, with teeth, without teeth, and in caps and gowns. That spanned the McPhail family life story.

But this photo must've been given to Vance Jones when he and my father worked together, buying old boats and restoring them. Why had such an arrogant hard-nosed businessman who, by all accounts had no love for anyone but himself, saved it for nearly five decades?

It probably got shoved in the drawer and forgotten, but I couldn't do the same. I set it on the desk and tried to focus on my original task of a cordial handwritten note. At least a written communiqué gave Dot the space to vent before we talked. I had the wherewithal to cut off any trace of Vance's stamp of ownership, and the result was a plain piece of squarish white paper. All that was left was for me to flower it up in black and white.

My eyes kept coming back to the photo, but I fought through the distraction and finally got down a sentence or two of what I hoped was a decent invite to meet with Dot Jones and call a truce. I warded off the restless temptation to go down and wander outside over the path along the cliffs of Blind Man's Bluff. After all, it was Labor Day weekend, and I deserved a little end-of-summer vacation time soaking in the sun and shore. I glanced longingly out the window but stayed put. If I got this right with Dot, maybe there'd be more Labor Days to spend relaxing on a little cobble beach down the hill.

I addressed and stamped the envelope and realized I had no official return address and, for the first time in my life, no mailbox. The silly thought left me a little dizzy as I made my way downstairs, letter and photo clasped in one hand. I was a woman cast adrift with the opportunity to paddle my way to a new horizon. Funny. I should've changed my address before I left town, but over the past few weeks I'd simply had my mail held at the Bookerton P.O. and picked it up when I was at my old house. And now?

Suddenly I wanted my own mailbox more than I'd wanted that blue three-speed bike for my tenth birthday. Both, in their own way, declared freedom—one for a fifth-grade girl finally old enough to ride over the back country roads to school (although only when accompanied by my older brother), the other the cutting of adult ties, as much a coming-of-age for a fifty-year-old woman setting out solo on the unexplored back roads of life.

I stepped across the marble chessboard floor at the foot of the staircase, nearly skipping. I detoured long enough to place the photo on the table and prop the letters on the kitchen counter before I bounced out of the house. Taking in the landscape with an eye for a mailbox placement, I then popped into the garage, grabbed Scotty's chainsaw,

and hiked around the back of the house searching the
nearby woods for a cedar tree to cut down for a post.

33

34

CHAPTER THREE

I was up early the next morning, stupidly excited about putting in my new mailbox, and concerned about my nephew. His constant barking cough had wakened me several times in the night, so I could only imagine how much sleep Nate got. Still, he was a grown man, and it would take more than a bad cold to keep him down.

Nevertheless, even a grown man could use a little TLC, so I was an early riser this Saturday morning making my one-hour cinnamon rolls, a recent internet find that had spiked my calorie intake and threatened to pad my thighs for years to come. That's why I'd made myself promise to bake them only when I had company. Nate's visit was the perfect excuse.

Baking was my sane time. I just needed to resist the temptation to sample my own wares, or at least limit myself to one bite, if only to make sure it was edible. As I measured, stirred and kneaded, I sang the song everyone my age sings on the Labor Day weekend. At intervals I let a pesky PM in and out several times before I slid the pan of rolls into the oven and made myself a hot cup of tea. Life was good. As the fragrance of fresh bread and hot cinnamon filled the air, I closed my eyes and thanked God for the blessings of being here and being alive.

When the fourth stair from the bottom creaked, I cocked my head at the comfort of familiar footsteps. A moment later my nephew sauntered through the swinging doors into the kitchen, face still creased from sleep and eyes heavy from lack of rest. He tilted his head back and inhaled. "Man, it's great to be home. Thanks, Gwen." He set his day pack on the floor.

"They'll be ready in a minute. There's coffee if you want it." I pointed to the modern contraption on the counter as I picked up a potholder and stepped over to the oven.

"What do you mean *if*?" Nate's voice was hoarse and raspy.

"You don't sound so good." I placed the cinnamon rolls on a trivet and quickly scooped out a few on a plate to cool enough so I could throw a little icing on the top.

"I'm fine. I got medicine if I need it." He took a sip of steaming coffee and gestured toward the backpack. "A few swigs of that nasty stuff and I'll be good as new."

I nodded. "Maybe ... but be careful today." I wanted to add *and come right home after, so you can rest,* but I bit my tongue. I'd vowed long ago not to be a nagging aunt, but Nate and his sister were my kids—if not by birth, than of the heart, so the resolution sometimes exacted a high emotional price.

I beckoned to an empty chair as I spread icing on the warm rolls. "Tasha called last night after you went to bed. She's staying on the mainland with a patient, but I imagine she'll be here when you get home."

"Can't wait."

I clattered the plate of rolls on the table between us and slipped into the seat opposite. We clasped hands and said grace. His hand might be calloused and his voice deep, but the old familiar words and touch took me back to their childhood. Sweet memories.

"Hey!" Nate came up for air after the first roll and picked up the photo I'd found yesterday. "Isn't that Grampa? And mini-you, right?"

I nodded. "I found it in a drawer upstairs. The man

standing beside your grandfather is the guy who gave me this house."

"No kidding? Makes more sense now."

"What do you mean?"

"I thought he was a total stranger."

"He is ... uh, was."

"But he knew you guys."

"A hundred years ago. He worked with your grandfather for a year or two restoring old boats, and then we never saw him again. I barely remember him."

Nate grinned and wolfed down another roll. "Obviously he remembered you."

"Yeah," I shook my head. "But it doesn't make sense. I was just a little kid, and forty-five years later he makes contact? After he dies, no less?"

Nate set the photo down and studied it as he slowly chewed another cinnamon bun and licked the frosting off his fingers. "Maybe he wouldn't have known how to fix boats and build his yacht company if he hadn't learned a thing or two from Grampa. He might owe all his success to his start with the McPhail family."

I gaped at him.

"What? I'm not just a ruggedly handsome face and a strong back, you know." He laughed and it morphed into a hacking cough.

"That's for sure. You favor your grandfather."

He cleared his throat and smiled. "I always thought I was the spitting image of you."

It was my turn to laugh. "Only the bad parts."

"What do you mean? You and I have no bad parts." He shoved his chair back from the table. "I'd better get moving, don't want to be late on my first day."

"I'll pack up some rolls so you can take them on the boat."

"If I don't scarf them down on the way to the dock." He picked up his empty plate and mug, turned toward the sink and barely nicked the corner of the framed photo with his dirty dish. Nate sloshed the last of the coffee on the table edge as he tried to juggle the dishes and catch the photo. He wasn't quick enough, and it tumbled to the floor, the glass tinkling when it smashed on the tile. He was on his knees next to the break in an instant. "I'm sorry."

I touched his shoulder. "It's okay. No harm done. Just leave it."

"No, I got it. You do the crime, you do the time." He gathered the shards of glass on his empty plate while I fixed a packet of the breakfast fare.

"What about lunch?" I held out a paper bag with two tuna sandwiches, an apple, snacks and dessert.

"Thanks, Gwen, you're the best." Nate set the broken pieces on the table and folded me in his strong arms. "Hey, you want to drop me off this morning so you can have some wheels?"

"No thanks. I plan to spend my day right here."

He released me and grinned. "Okay, but if you change your mind, I'll hide the keys for you."

"Shouldn't you lock it?"

He pulled a "Home Alone" face. That kid should've been an actor. "Who are you and what have you done with my locks-only-keep-out-honest-people aunt?"

I nodded. It was true enough with my own car, but this was Vance Jones' vehicle. Then again, at six feet under, I doubted he'd care about cars or locks at this point. "You're right. Besides, who could steal a BMW with the Candle Island Yacht logo on the door, on an island this size, and make a clean getaway?"

"Exactly. I'll be back." He grabbed the food and his day pack, and we walked to the door together as the early morning sky eroded the black to gray.

"Be careful."

"I will. Careful's my middle name ... just like you. Besides, it's only a three-hour cruise, right?" He grinned and ducked his head into the car. A moment later the engine pured and he pulled away.

I watched the red taillights disappear down the hill. I tried to picture Nate's breezy makeup working with Luke's dour demeanor. I lifted my eyes to the sky and watched the last stars wink out. Pale pinky-lavender rimmed the tree line. I shook my head and hoped for the best. Nate usually got along with everyone, so I shouldn't worry. Besides, I'd only met Luke Faraday for a few minutes. Granted, I wasn't impressed, but maybe he was having a bad day. Perhaps with his boat fixed he was a ray of sunshine.

I hiked over to the top of the cliff and watched the dawn steal across the water. It skipped up the sheer rock face and touched off the wakening birds' song and the stirrings of a breeze. I hugged my arms around me against the chill and finally hustled back along the trail, hobbling here and there as the roots and rocks jabbed into my bare feet.

As soon as I entered the kitchen, my eyes fastened on the shattered picture. The old frame had come apart on one side. I forced myself to sweep, vacuum for any tiny bits of glass, and wash the dishes before I sat at the table. I held the damaged photo in both hands. Daddy's frame could be fixed with some glue and well-placed clamps—I wasn't his daughter for nothing. But I'd need to get new plate glass cut and come up with a more rugged backing in order to salvage the picture.

I flipped it over and the warped rectangles of thin cardboard fell into my hands and revealed an index card filler. Mama's cramped penmanship leaped out at me as I gingerly plucked the 3x5 out with careful fingernails. The years dissolved when I read her old recipe for homemade peanut butter cookies. I knew it by heart. They'd been my brothers' favorite, a staple in the McPhail house cookie jar.

I guess Vance Jones must've gotten a taste for them, too, when he stayed at our place. I flipped the recipe card over and blinked back tears. One of Mama's old country blessings wavered in front of my eyes. I leaned over and grabbed one of the ubiquitous pairs of cheaters scattered around the house and one-handedly crammed them on the bridge of my nose. *"May God grant you always...A sunbeam to warm you, a moonbeam to charm you, a sheltering angel so nothing can harm you. Laughter to cheer you. Faithful friends near you. And whenever you pray, Heaven to hear you."*

I clutched the stiff card to my heart, stabbed with the piercing ache of missing Mama and Daddy. No matter how old I got, there would always be a couple of holes in my heart only they could fill. Obviously, Vance Jones had a soft spot in his heart as well, if he'd saved this little scrap of the past.

I intended to pry out the picture to stare once more at my father's former partner and my benefactor but, instead, I encountered folded sheets of paper. I opened them carefully, breath held, and was rewarded to find Daddy's strong black scrawl. My eyes devoured the missive. *Brother, You can take the credit, you can take the clients, you can even have the money, but what are you willing to give in exchange for your soul? Your self-respect? Our friendship? Your honor and integrity?*

It's not worth it to me. I know you don't believe that, but someday you will. I won't have any bad blood on my conscience, so now it's on yours. I was going to use the money for my kids, so if you want to salve that conscience, maybe you'll find it in your heart to put something away for my little girl's college fund.

Do what you will and, if that day comes when you wake up to find yourself in the far country eating pig swill, come back. I'll welcome you with open arms and we'll talk about the finer things. –Conner

With shaking hands I set my father's letter down and scanned the second sheet. It, too, was handwritten in Daddy's bold print, a brief list of materials, a sketch of an upscale boat with construction details penciled in, and a large numerical figure written at the bottom. My father's and

Vance Jones' signatures scrawled across the edge of the page along with two other names printed in my father's hand: Frederick Evangelos and Richard Arnold.

An old informal contract of sorts for one of the vintage yachts they renovated? Daddy's letter and the quick sketch of an original design said otherwise. I ran my fingertips over his name, seeking answers, but the only sound was the cat's claws zippering the screen on the kitchen window. I took off the glasses, hurried out onto the deck, and shooed him down from the railing. PM took his time and flicked an annoyed tail at me as he paraded into the house as if he owned the joint.

I ignored him, picked up the contents of the framed photo and wandered upstairs to my bedroom. I tucked my discovery in my Bible on the nightstand, the safest place I had. Slowly I got dressed, trying to process what I'd read. Both my parents obviously thought of Vance as family, but was the feeling returned? I squeezed my eyes shut and tried to remember something, anything, from that long-ago time, but my mind came up as blank as my classroom blackboard on Friday night. The only thought that popped was of myself at twelve years old trying to weasel my way out of a family function with the old "Do I have to go?" preteen whine. My ears echoed with my father's answer ingrained in me from years of hearing but not getting it: "You don't *have* to do anything." His message to Vance in so many words.

I shook off the brain tease before it grew into a mental obsession. Instead of driving myself crazy, I tucked away the info and went ahead with my day. I was out in an open bay of the garage, skinning the bark off my cedar post, when I was startled by the approach of a vehicle. The crunch of gravel under the tires as the pickup rolled close and stopped, brought a smile. "You're up early," I called to the driver.

Scotty swung out of the cab and nodded. "I was about to say the same thing. Gilligan made it off alright, I take it." He glanced at the risen sun. "Already hauling traps by now."

I followed his gaze and took in the cloudless blue sky … a nice day to be on the water, I hoped.

"Nice post. Where'd you get it?"

I grinned. "I cut it down out back by the cedar swamp."

He strolled around me, examining it with his eyes, hands in his pockets. "Nice job."

"Thanks. I might've borrowed your chainsaw."

"That hunk of junk comes with the place. Ron took the good one down to the cottage." He cupped his chin between a thumb and forefinger.

I was tempted to make him ask, but relented. I was grateful for the company and the diversion. What I'd discovered this morning stewed in my brain like mental acid reflux, no matter how much I tried to nullify the churning thoughts. Stick to the simple task at hand. "I'm putting in a mailbox."

He raised a copper brow, but his smile was a bit too wide for my liking. "Looks like it's getting permanent."

"Just temporarily permanent," I countered. "I might get some mail, so I want to be ready. Semper paratus, isn't it?" What I thought of as my clever comeback of the Coast Guard motto had no effect on his knowing grin.

"Vance had a post office box."

"Vance had a business in Coveside. I prefer not to have to leave home every day."

"Home?"

He wasn't going to let it go, so I tried to be the mature one and switched gears. "You know what I mean."

"I do. What about Dot?"

"Come to think of it, I've never noticed a mailbox down by the cottage. She must have a box in town."

"You know what I mean." How could putting up a mailbox turn into a major Act of Congress? All I wanted was my own private niche … *Admit it, already! Nothing says home like a mailbox with your name on it.*

He laughed at my scowl. "For what it's worth, I don't

think putting up a mailbox, or not putting one up, will make a difference in your standoff."

"But maybe it could. And thanks to you, now I can have that on my conscience as well." I thought about my nearest neighbor getting my invite to lunch, driving up, seeing my name on the mailbox and immediately squealing rubber and peeling out in a huff.

"Does that mean you don't want to get a mailbox?"

I shook my head. "Oh, I want a mailbox, but the question is, should I *have* a mailbox?"

"You're over-thinking it."

"Thanks to you!"

PM meandered by and twirled around Scotty's ankles before sharpening his claws on the end of my post. "The cat's all for it."

"You know the old saying, 'Every homeowner has a meow in it.'"

My companion groaned. "That's sick."

It was, but it clinched it for me. Since when was I so super sensitive? I wrinkled my nose. Maybe a post in the ground would at least get Dot talking. I ran my hand over PM's warm soft fur. "Do they sell mailboxes at Bernard's store?"

"No, but if you're not picky I know where we can get a used one. My grandfather has a bunch."

"Really? That's great! I'd like to check in on him."

"That's where I'm headed. Hop in."

"Just a second." I rushed inside and grabbed the leftover cinnamon rolls—one for Old Stin and one for his grandson. I popped back outside a moment later. Scotty waited at the door and activated the security system as I headed for his truck. "I was going to leave it open."

"I know you were." He was at my side before I reached the garage. He opened the truck door for me. "Not a good idea."

"Don't you trust your neighbors?"

"Some of them."

"That's awful!"

"That's reality. Come on."

"What about the post?"

"I'll help you set it when we get back. I'm not planning on staying at my grandfather's for too long."

I handed him a bagged roll as he settled into the driver's seat. "What's this?"

"A little coffee break without the coffee." Scotty unwrapped the roll and bit into it. He didn't say a word as he chewed, swallowed, started the engine and drove. We were almost to Old Stin's house when he finally spoke. "Did you make those for Gilligan this morning?"

"I did, and for the Skipper, too."

"You don't spoil the guy much."

I shrugged one shoulder as we pulled into the driveway. "I like to think of it as sharing the sweetness of life."

"It was sweet." He patted his lean belly. "I'd better watch myself around you. Glad you got one for my grandfather. He's gonna need some sweetening up."

Old Stin had the screen door open before I got out of the cab, his wild white mop of hair standing up like a rooster's tail, and that dear craggy face as fierce as an eagle's on the hunt. My gaze flicked to the butterfly stitch on his cheek. It gave him a slight pucker under his eye, a little like a buccaneer captain's leer that suited the old man. His glower said I'd best not mention it.

"You back for good?" he called as Scotty assisted me out of the truck.

"She's putting up a mailbox." Scotty ignored my jab to his ribs. "What? You don't think he's not going to put two and two together when I ask him for a mailbox out of his stash?"

My companion had a point.

Old Stin hooted. "I knew it! You can't deny that McMahan blood in your veins. Calls you back to the island every time. Take Young Stin, here. He was all up and down the country in the service, but now that he could go anywheres, where is he? Right back home." He gave me a stiff nod, the white shock of hair accentuating the sharp movement.

"Doesn't work for everybody. Look at Dad and Mom in North Carolina," Scotty drawled.

Old Stin glowered. "That boy of mine will come to his senses one of these days."

I hid a smile. Old Stin's "boy" had to be at least seventy-odd.

"Not likely."

I stepped into the friendly fire between the two Stins and held out a peace offering. "I brought you something."

"Why is it everyone thinks you need food when you get a little scrape?" In spite of his growl, the old man opened the baggie and took a bite of the cinnamon roll. "A mite sweet," he said between bites. "But since Young Stin didn't come over this mornin' like he said he would, it fills the hollow spot."

"It *is* morning and, in case you haven't noticed, I'm here," Scotty said.

"Yeah, just 'cause Gwen decided to come over, more'n likely."

"How are you feeling?" I ventured.

"Fit as a fiddle!" Old Stin flashed his saw-toothed grin as the last of the roll went down. "And, ya know, that sweet stuff's alright. You make it?"

"I did."

His blue eyes danced. "Didn't need to bribe an old codger to get what you want. Come on in and we'll set you right up with a mailbox." He gestured and I slipped past him into the past. His cozy home squatted next to the ledge and held an air of a life stamped with the blessings of everyday living. The worn vintage furniture, crocheted granny square afghan on the rocking chair, chalks of an old salt and his wife, and a "Jesus Never Fails" plaque on the living room walls took me back to a simpler time. Sun-softened wallpaper, green-striped with roses, and trim work painted apple green, spoke of a home built around two hearts in the truest sense of the word.

My eyes lit on a photo on the cobbler's bench—Old Stin in his Sunday best, complete with white carnation boutonnière on his lapel, his arm around a small woman with the beaming face of a sprite and the devil dancing in her eyes. Mrs. Stinson Weeks Scott, Scotty's grandmother. It occurred to me I didn't know her name.

Old Stin tugged on my arm. "They don't make nothin' to last more than a minute. Those modern plastic mailboxes?" He snorted. "Garbage! Gold-plated pieces of junk! They get one shot of ice or snow from the plow, and they shatter into a million pieces."

Shatter. His innocent diatribe brought to mind the flash of another photo lying shattered on the floor this morning. Why hadn't I shared the news with Scotty? Why didn't I say something about my discovery right now? These two men not only knew everyone on Candle Island, they knew the placement of each lobster trap and fishhook, all the secrets buried beneath the sod and beneath the waves. But I couldn't open my mouth. I told myself it wasn't a matter of trust in my new friends, it was a matter of ... what? I couldn't put a name to it; but, whatever it was, it kept my lips sewn shut.

"You got a post?" Old Stin's question drew me back from the dilemma that was quickly dissolving into niggling guilt.

"Gwen chainsawed down a nice bit of cedar yesterday," Scotty said.

"Why didn't you cut it down for her?"

"Didn't know she was set on putting up a mailbox."

"And why not?" Old Stin turned back to me. "You got the bark stripped off it? You don't and it'll rot."

"I'm working on it," I said.

Old Stin snorted. "Should've known you'd do it right." I smiled as the older man led the way to the cellar, stopping as he opened the door. "Mite steep down here, so watch your step."

"Why don't you let us go down and pick one out?" Scotty said.

"I guess I can get down in my own cellar. I go nearly every day." The older man glared over my head at his grandson.

"I know."

"I've got just the one for her."

"Lead on." Scotty leaned forward and flicked on the light switch before he stepped back.

I followed Old Stin down the steep stairway, grasping the railing tight when what I really wanted to do was grab ahold of the old man's arm or shirt back or belt and make sure he didn't take a header on the stairs.

We made it down without incident, but my heart skipped a step ahead of me all the way until Old Stin's feet hit the dirt-and-rock floor. "Right over here. It's a beauty." He ducked his head under the floor stringers, and I mimicked his movements as the ledge beneath our feet tapered up toward the cement-block cellar wall. He retrieved a blue mailbox from a cluster of three in various states of rust and dent. He dusted off his choice with his flannel shirt sleeve before he passed it to me. "Heft that. Got some real steel to 'er."

I took the galvanized steel offering. He flipped up the bright red flag and grinned. I nodded. "Very nice. I like the paint job."

"Used to go with an Uncle Sam I made. Remember that, Young Stin?"

"Yeah."

"The old gent held the box for years until some snot-nosed juvenile delinquent took a baseball bat to it. Did it in the dark of night, too, the coward! Don't know what this world's coming to. Folks stickin' their noses where it's none of their business, runnin' down this country…"

"Grampa, that was, what? Twenty-five, thirty years ago?"

"Yeah, and if I found out who did it, I'd still have their hide."

"I'll bet you would." I tried not to smile. "Thanks so much for this. It's just what I wanted and just what I need. I've had a mailbox all my life, and I don't know as I could survive without one."

"Gotta have somethin' that's gonna last up there for the rest of your life." He gave me a knowing wink as we hunched over and made our way back to the stairs.

"It's only temporary."

He snorted. "Nothin' says stayin' like a name on a mailbox." Like grandfather, like grandson.

"I'm not staying at Vance's place forever." We stood at the foot of the stairs. Old Stin leaned on the 2x4 railing and jabbed the air with his gnarled finger. "All this baloney of half here, half there, go, stay. All's I know, you can't be two places at once."

"Wingwalker," Scotty murmured.

His comment made mine a little more heated than necessary. "I'm only staying there until I get things straightened out with Dot."

"Mighty difficult woman. All that spite comes from the other side, mind you," Old Stin said. "Wife's family always was hot tempered when things didn't go their way. My Athleen was the exception. Sweet as Jersey cream." He grinned. "With just the right pinch of pepper when warranted. The rest of 'em were cocked and primed to fight ya on everything from the color of the sky to the salt pork in your chowder. Stubborn as all get-out. It's the Sullivan in 'em, if you ask me. Probably won't do you a bit of good to take her on, particularly while she's still got a full head of steam worked up from Vance's will."

"Thanks for the warning, but I'm gonna try."

Old Stin chuckled. "Wouldn't expect anything less."

"Hello? Anybody home?" A deep-though-decidedly-feminine voice drifted down from the floor above.

"A man can't get no peace some days, I swan. Go see who that is, Young Stin. Gettin' to be worse than Grand Central Station around here."

"It's Laverna, Grampa." Scotty made no move from his post on the other side of the stairs, but he leaned forward and directed his slightly raised voice toward the open door. "Down here, Laverna. We'll be right up."

"You should've gone up and told her that face to face. Would've been the polite thing to do," Old Stin retorted.

"You're absolutely right. After you." Scotty stretched out a palm and waited.

Old Stin huffed and stood his ground. I thought about running the gauntlet, but Scotty beat me to it. He gently tugged the mailbox from my grip. "Ladies first. I'll bring up the rear." His voice was pitched low, and I wasn't sure Old Stin heard it, but maybe that was the point. I certainly felt better knowing Scotty would be behind the old gentleman every step of the way.

I took the lead and emerged into the sunlight streaming through the kitchen windows. Laverna stood by the table, looking out to the sparkling water beyond. Her hair was screeched back into its usual severe ponytail, accentuating her hollowed cheeks and slightly hooked nose. She turned at my approach and nodded.

"Hi," I said.

"Mornin'."

Everyone knew Laverna Jordan and yet, looking at her hooded dark eyes and mouth as thin as a piece of fish line, I wondered if anyone knew her. Certainly, I hadn't been here long enough to claim the right of even casual acquaintance. By all accounts, she was a fixture at the lunch wagon, and having thoroughly sampled her menu, a very good cook and smart businesswoman, though spare with her words. I'd never seen a Mr. Jordan, but wasn't entrenched or stupid enough to ask such a personal question.

"I brought you some lobster stew and biscuits for lunch, Stinson. Just heat it up good."

"Laverna, you got no need to do that." Old Stin stepped into the room and stopped beside me. "But I do appreciate it." The old salt cast a baleful eye at the man flanking my other side. "Might starve if not for my friends and neighbors."

Scotty snorted. "Thanks." I wasn't sure if the monosyllable addressed his grandfather or their visitor.

"Sent some with Luke and your boy, too. He's a nice looking one. Favors you."

I was startled by her low tones and the appearance of a small smile. "Thanks." Surely a step above tuna sandwiches in a brown bag.

"Thought they'd be back early today," Scotty said.

Laverna shook her head. "Luke said he's going to the mainland and pick up some supplies. Didn't get everything he needed at Hanover Point yesterday."

I glanced up at my companion, the mailbox tucked under one arm, his attention totally focused on Laverna. "So, where's he headed?" He seemed more interested than I did, but I felt like an eavesdropper hanging on every word.

Laverna shook her head. "He didn't say exactly, but maybe Port Blackwall. He gets a lot of his gear over to that Crossjack Marine now."

"Heard it's not the same over there since Andersen's girl barged her way in and took the wheel." Old Stin elbowed his way in to the conversation. "The girl's alright, but they say that one she married wouldn't know a grapnel from a guppy."

"You couldn't tell by me. I never leave the island." Laverna bussed Old Stin's cheek. "Gotta get back to work before Dot has a hemorrhage. I left her there alone prepping for the lunch crowd. There's more of a mob here than on Fourth of July."

"Comin' out of the woodwork," Old Stin agreed.

"You take care and I'll be by to check on you." Old Stin followed her to the door, leaving us alone in the kitchen.

"Is she another one of your cousins?"

"No. Her folks were neighbors to my grandparents for years." Scotty gestured toward the living room. "Laverna's not the only one who needs to get moving. We have a mailbox to put up."

"What about Old Stin?"

"Go on." The old man stepped into the room and growled. "I'll stop by later on to make sure my grandson got the job done right."

CHAPTER FOUR

I sat on the deck in the late-afternoon sun. A chill from the stiffening breeze and the lengthening shadows crept up my bare arms, but I couldn't move. It had been a good day, my red, white, and blue mailbox a testament to that fact. The white-painted letters of my name dry and permanent. Thanks to Scotty, I'd even been able to get an unofficial, make that 'temporary,' box number from the Post Office, as well as a hearty-yet-gruff approval of the job from Old Stin.

I'd shared lunch with the Stins and now, hours later, I sat nursing a plastic tumbler of raspberry iced tea, ice melted, tea watery. Peace and quiet reigned except for the occasional gull's cry.

I gazed at the backyard from my lounge chair but barely controlled the urge to jump out of my skin. *Nate should've been back by now.* The thought skipped through my mind like a broken record. Regardless of the trip to Port Blackwall or Crossjack Marine or Timbuktu, he should be back here safe and sound.

Despite the posture of my body, every muscle tensed as I strained to hear the crunch of tires in the driveway. I'd come back here to stop my glancing out the window every few seconds. Even my usual go-to coping mechanism of baking like a crazy person while awaiting bad news hadn't worked for me this time. The kitchen counter was strewn with recipes but no culinary results. I couldn't settle because

I feared for the worst. *And who says it's going to be bad news?* Yet the downward tug was relentless, like a cold coming on, the stiffness in every muscle, the scratchy throat …

I couldn't deny the sluggish beat of my heart and the dread sitting like a snowball, a cold indigestible lump, in my stomach. I tried to pin the phantom despondency on Tasha's call.

My niece had phoned from the hospital an hour or so ago with the news Laurel had miscarried. She'd put a tearful Ron on the line. Both Laurel and Ron were understandably heartbroken but, physically, Laurel was okay and there was no indication she wouldn't carry to full term the next time. Thankful news in the middle of the shock of expectations shattered.

I tried to focus on *my* expectations, what this might mean for me employment-wise, but I honestly didn't care. I grieved for the young couple. Losing their first baby was a tough way to start a family and a life together. In their case, I hoped it would strengthen their fierce bond.

For my part in this, if I wasn't needed to sub during Laurel's maternity leave, I knew I could find something to keep me busy. I had no intention of going back to Bookerton and Brier Elementary with heart in hand, begging for my old job back.

The phone rang and my whole body spasmed out of my melancholy into a sitting position. The tumbler toppled off the arm of the deck chair onto the planking, tea splattering my sandals. I grabbed for the phone on the nearby table and answered on the first ring.

"Hey, Gwen, got your message." My brother, Neil's, resonant, calm voice—just what I needed. "What's up?"

I took a deep breath so I wouldn't come off sounding like a mother hen with her head cut off. "Well, Nathaniel got a job as sternman on a lobster boat out here on the island."

"Hope he's sticking with it."

"It's his first day and he's not back yet."

"Well, when he shows up tell him to keep at it for more than a week this time, and you can quote me on that."

"I will." *When he shows up.* My brother didn't know anymore than I did, but I clung to the solid prognostication of his words and tried to build on it. *He's coming back.* He might be at the dock right now, unloading their catch, maybe talking and hanging out with the other guys.

"You didn't call just to tell me Nathaniel's there. Something's up."

My eldest brother and I were miles apart in temperament, but we shared a similar intuitive streak Mama had referred to as her sixth sense.

"Yesterday I found a photo of Daddy and me when I was about four years old, taken with Uncle Jonesy, the guy who left me this albatross. We're standing in front of our old house and I'm thinking you might've been the photographer."

"Probably true, but I can't say I remember it. Thankfully, my Francis & Freelan Stanley photo obsession didn't last long."

"Behind the photo was a paper with the sketch of a classy boat. It had a few rough schematics drawn in, and an estimate of materials and cost. It was handwritten by Daddy and had both his and Vance Jones' signature on it. Our father had also written down the names Frederick Evangelos and Richard Arnold, two boat-building clients, I think. Does any of it sound familiar?" I tried not to rush the telling and betray my agitation.

Dead silence. I could picture Neil's broad brow furrowed like a contour-plowed field funneling down to the bridge of his nose. He'd frown and push up his glasses and rub his right temple as if he could dislodge an answer.

During the wait, I hustled inside, ignoring the stick of my sandal soles on the tile, and hurried up the stairs to my room, phone pressed to my ear.

"Not ringing any bells, sorry. Maybe it was one of the old sailing yachts they fixed up."

"Maybe, but I think it was a new one, perhaps an original design. It looks like a quick rough draft, drawn as a ballpark idea for the client. There was a letter hidden in there, too, written by Daddy to Vance, I believe. Just a second." I sat on the edge of the bed, flipped open the cover of my Bible and pulled the letter from its hiding place. "You ready?"

"Fire."

I read the missive, hearing not my voice but my father's kind, stern tones. When I finished, my brother whistled through the slight gap between his front teeth, an affectation he'd had for as long as I can remember.

"Hey, Gwennie, way to bury the lead. Sounds like Vance's conscience finally came knocking."

"But why now, after all these years?"

"Hard to say. Probably he's the only one who knows the answer to that question, and he obviously won't be sharing that information. But I'd say he ripped Dad off and stole his boat design."

"That's what I thought, too, but are we reading more into it? Maybe Vance just wanted to take the business in a different direction so he and Daddy parted ways. I thought Daddy took the fulltime job at the shipyard because it was better money, more secure employment."

"Not sure of all the why's and wherefores."

"Do you remember Daddy and Vance arguing?"

Neil laughed. "Dad never argued with anyone, but I *do* know Vance left in a hurry. He was there one day, eating supper with us, and the next afternoon he was gunning his pickup out the driveway when we got off the school bus. Now that I think of it, we waved and I'm pretty sure, he didn't. And Mama and Dad talked a lot that night, but they kept their voices down and always stopped when any of us kids came into the room to bug them for a glass of water and the usual bedtime stuff.

"Once I asked where Uncle Jonesy had gone, and they said he went home. Period. End of discussion. Not much help, but I was ... what? Twelve or so at the time, and pretty self-absorbed with all things baseball."

I tried to remember something, anything, but it was a total blank. Neil may have been caught up in Little League, but I was totally clueless, growing up in a home where I was privileged to remain innocent and secure, shielded from adult drama. In my childhood cocoon, I never suspected any bad things happened in our family.

"What are you going to do?"

That's what I loved and hated about Neil. He could boss all of us around like George Patton, but after dumping all his unasked-for advice on my siblings and me, he always left the big decision up to the individual. "I'm not sure. I think I'm just going to sit on it for the time being."

"Understood." He laughed. "But I can't picture you actually able to do that."

"Thanks a lot for the vote of confidence."

"Don't play Miss Innocent, you know what I mean. You're already thinking about how you can shake a few trees and turn over some of those island rocks out there. You can't help it. It's the Durrell/McPhail curse. We've got it from both sides. We just gotta know the rest of the story."

He was right, but I wasn't about to say so.

"Anybody home?" Scotty's voice piped up the stairs.

I put my hand over the phone. "I'm up here, be right down!" I tucked the papers away, left the bedroom and started for the staircase.

"Hey, I've got to go, someone's here. Thanks, Neil."

"Okay, keep in touch and let me know what's going on. And Gwen ..." He purposely paused long enough to force a response.

"Yeah?"

"Promise me you won't let Nathaniel take advantage of you."

"Never."

"Always. I'll let you go. Have a good night."

" 'Night." I pushed the disconnect and hurried down the stairs.

Scotty stood on the marble tile, staring up at me with his cap in his hand.

"What's up?" I asked.

"The Jane Anne hasn't come in yet."

"Jane Anne?" The name sparked a dim response buried too far in my cluttered brain to retrieve.

"Luke's boat."

I nodded, unable to speak through my clenched jaw. It was what I'd expected. *Please God* was the only thought that spiraled around in my head. I was unaware I'd grabbed his arm until his rough, calloused hand clasped mine.

"Hey, it's not necessarily bad news. They could've had engine trouble, maybe put in on one of the smaller islands while they try to patch her up."

"Maybe, but wouldn't they have sent out a distress call or shot up a flare or something?"

"Not necessarily. Luke is a DIY guy."

And so is Nate. I tried to picture them in the lowering light, heads bent, tinkering on the motor, thinking that just one more tweak would fix it good enough to make it back, but with each moment, each wave pushed them farther off course, farther away from a safe harbor. "Isn't there some way you can track them, like GPS or something?"

"We're looking into it now."

"Who's *we*?"

"A bunch of us are going to take our boats out and look around. They were at CrossJack Marine and left Port Blackwall about twelve-thirty."

"Twelve-thirty?" I choked and glanced at my watch. Five-forty-seven. The sun would set by six, and then...?

"We'll do our best to track them down." Scotty squeezed my hand. "Try to relax."

"Yeah, right. What about the Coast Guard?"

"I put in a call to a buddy there. Olivia doesn't want to get them involved."

"Whyever not?!"

"Says Luke will have her head if we panic and call out the troops when there's no need."

I shook my head.

"She's probably right. Luke's a belt-and-suspenders guy. He won't do anything risky out there. And if anyone can pilot a boat home, it's Luke Faraday."

"Wait a minute." I shrugged off his words and rushed to the kitchen, picked up the phone and dialed Nate's number. "The caller cannot be found." I strangled the phone in a death grip at the emotionless voice in my ear. I forced myself to end the call.

"Olivia already tried to get in touch with Luke." Scotty stood close, looking over my shoulder, both of us staring at the useless device in my hand. "She got his voice mail. They could just be in a dead zone."

"Bad choice of words."

"You know what I mean. The cell companies want you to believe there's nowhere they can't service. Out here it's at best fifty-fifty."

"Yeah." When did we get so dependent on technology to solve all our heartaches and mental pains? There were better ways to solve problems and I turned and looked at one of them. "I'm coming with you."

"Absolutely not."

"If you didn't want me to come, why are you here?"

I tossed the phone onto the table and darted about, putting on a jacket and hat, grabbing a day pack and throwing in food and water, until Scotty clamped a gentle hand on my arm. "You're not coming."

I shook off his touch and crammed Nate's sweatshirt in the front compartment of the pack. "Try and stop me."

He turned me to face him, planting both his large work-worn hands on my shoulders. "I'm taking Kendall. He's worked with Luke off and on. He knows the Jane Anne inside and out. He knows the route Luke usually takes. He can help fix the engine *when* we find them."

I took in a deep shuddering breath. "Look, I can be a help, another set of eyes at the very least." I stepped back and picked up a pair of binoculars from the shelf. "I'm not going to go all hysterical on you, if that's what you're worried about."

Scotty had the audacity to hold up his palms and grin. "Furthest thing from my mind, Gwen. But you're not going."

We stood in the kitchen glaring at each other, any shred of humor gone. "Wing walker," I muttered. It made no sense, but it popped out.

He nodded, breaking eye contact. "You keep hold of the shore and I'll take hold of the sea and God'll set it right in the end. Come on."

I grabbed the pack and raced ahead of him to the truck. We drove in silence to the town pier. "You know you're still not coming with me, right?" He parked behind a jeep in the growing line of vehicles on the side of the road.

I nodded. I'd hoped he'd change his mind, but my heart knew better. I looked past the small crowd gathered and saw Scotty's boat, Semper Paratus, waiting with Kendall at the wheel. "Go on," I managed.

"Never give up hope in the face of a miracle." He slammed the door and was off, striding through the knot of neighbors and friends to the waiting vessel.

I sat in the truck until his boat cleared the harbor. When I finally got out, it hit me. Scotty always opened the door for me, a courtesy that had been lost under the onslaught of vanishing manners. He hadn't done that today. He was a man on a mission.

As the last of daylight faded, I bowed my head and prayed for that miracle. The petition only lasted for a breath. I couldn't sit here doing nothing. I hopped out of the truck with all my useless paraphernalia, binoculars slung around my neck as if I could see through the unknown in the gathering darkness.

"Gwen."

I only made it a few steps onto the pier before I was assaulted by Olivia's tremulous hail. She stood under a light, dabbing at her eyes, a small dark-haired girl clinging to her. The child's huge blue eyes were dry, but her narrow face was a porcelain mask of what certainly looked like anger to me. *Luke's devoted granddaughter?*

Olivia shook off the small clutching hands and glided toward me. "Honestly, Jacey. Calm down!" Olivia's smeared mascara and borderline hysteria screamed she needed to heed her own advice. "You came."

I nodded, looking first into the darting eyes of a worried wife, then into the solemn, questioning eyes of a child. I knelt down and forced a smile. "You must be Jacey. Your grandfather told me how smart and brave you are and that you're going to kindergarten this year, is that right?"

She nodded.

"I thought so. I'm Miss Mac. I might be helping Miss Laurel with your class this year, so I hope we'll be friends."

To my surprise she stuck out her hand and I engulfed the cold little stick-fingers in mine and gave them a gentle squeeze. I'd been prepared to struggle with winning over Luke's granddaughter, but she was nothing like I'd imagined. Olivia's *tsk-tsk* rained down on our heads. Maybe I shouldn't give myself too much credit. At this moment I was doubtless the lesser of two evils.

"I don't know what you've heard," Olivia said, and Jacey slipped her hand from mine and retreated a step, once again hanging onto Olivia's sleeve. The women spared the child a quick scowl and returned her attention to me as I slowly rose from my scooch.

"Nothing, only that they aren't in and no one can reach them."

Olivia twisted her hands in an elegant-but-endless movement like she was trying to catch the air and shape it. Me … I fisted mine. We all cope one way or another. "It's not like my darling Luke to make me worry. We always talk during the day. Always! He calls to tell me he loves me."

Fortunately, I was too concerned with the problem at hand to have any gag reflex over her syrupy emotions. "So, you talked with him?"

"Yes, I did. As I said, we always talk. We can't bear to be apart. But the last time he called me was when they were leaving Blackwall."

"Did he say where they were headed?"

"Home. He did say your nephew was sick and not much help." Olivia shook her head. "Makes me wonder if my Luke had taken Kendall or Jeff with him today..." She chewed on her bottom lip, her narrowed gaze accusing. "He wouldn't be in this predicament."

"And what predicament is that?" Nothing like someone dissing family to kick out the worries and kickstart the lioness gene. I should probably thank her for that. Maybe later

"Well, I'm just saying..."

"Yes?"

She laid a black-clawed hand on my forearm, her array of rings an obscene sparkle in the artificial light. "No one here would've been seasick, particularly on a day like this. I'm not suggesting anything every one of us here hasn't thought ... including yourself, if you're honest." She gave an academy-award-winning mewling moan and grimaced as she gestured toward the knot of neighbors standing vigil. "You can hear it in their whispers. This is Nathaniel's first day on a boat. I mean, he's charming and devil may care and attractive, but that doesn't do any good. When things get tough, his type cuts and runs. That's what has me so upset. My darling Luke, alone out there."

His type? "Nate never cuts and runs."

"Maybe not, but you couldn't prove it by me. He has no experience whatsoever, wouldn't you agree?"

I compressed my lips so tightly they must've been turning blue. I was aware of the murmur of other voices farther out on the pier. So far, they kept their distance, and I wondered if it was me, or Olivia, or both of us "from-aways" that held us apart. Personally, I would much rather be at the end of the dock, straining my eyes to see over the dark waves, but the woman in front of me held us all hostage.

"If Nathaniel had been a more experienced sternman, maybe Luke wouldn't be out there stranded who-knows-where." Olivia's voice rose as hysteria crept in once more. Olivia was an odd one—a genteel emotional wreck one moment; the next, a steel magnolia slashing her manicured finger, sticking it to you.

It didn't sit well. "Did Luke say seasick? It doesn't sound like Nate." My nephew might have a longer odd job résumé than Santa's bad-boy list, but it included crewing on a schooner one summer. He didn't get seasick. My thought was Luke had only been referring to Nate's bad cold.

"Luke didn't have to. He and I have that special bond, a silent connection. I call it lover's language."

I'll just bet you do. My gag reflex was back and working overtime.

"Jacey, Honey, stop your fussing." She swatted at the young girl, but Jacey sidestepped, and I saw the fat lower lips, the pout-sprout, on both their faces. "I called Luke's daughter to come get Jacey. No answer. Typical Erica."

I bit my lip to stop the spewing of worry-fueled accusations. It wasn't Olivia's fault she was a less-than-sympathetic woman; or that her husband's old boat with a finicky motor rode the waves out there somewhere just beyond my sight. It never paid to trade insults, especially at a time like this.

"I just don't know what I'll do if—" Olivia broke down in a sob. "I told him not to go out in the boat. It's had one problem after another. Kendall even warned him to get rid of it, but my Luke is so sentimental." She lunged forward and oozed into my arms.

I stiffened in surprise before compassion kicked in and I rubbed her back, like you would a small child, and murmured reassurances I wanted to believe, too.

My mind flashed back to yesterday when I got off the ferry and stepped into their argument. It was all about a boat? At least that's what Olivia wanted me to believe, but I hadn't dreamed up the undertones of a darker element, Not just anger, but bitter hatred between the two men, particularly on Luke's part. Kendall was just trying to keep the peace; or was he just better at masking his true emotions?

Why such thoughts tripped across the uneven contours of my brain at this inappropriate moment left me disgusted at myself. I should be focused on a missing boat and lost fishermen, on a weeping wife in my arms, not on trivial suspicions.

I felt small hands clutch the waistband of my jeans and looked down into Jacey's upturned pinched face. Should she even be down here on the dock, with Olivia such a weepy seesawing emotional wreck?

"Hey, Gwen!" I looked up into the pleasant, tanned face of Sledge Knox. Even at his most serious, Angus "Sledge" Knox, MD., the island's hometown-son-turned-doctor exuded a calming, solid, joyful presence.

I opened my mouth to reply but wasn't quick enough. Olivia unlatched her hold on me and, quick as a magnet, stuck fast onto the doctor's rugged arm. "Oh, doctor. I don't know what I'll do!"

Sledge patted her shoulder but his eyes never left mine. "Wait and pray, Olivia. It's all we can do for now, and we'll be ready to help when they come in."

"When?" Her voice hushed. "I wish I could believe that."

Sledge shook his head. "It takes more energy to believe

the worst than it does to believe in the good. Besides, I've known Luke all my life. He knows these waters better than most, and he knows how to handle the Jane Anne." He gave a small sad smile. "I remember going out on her when Luke would take my brother and me fishing with his daughter, Erica. We were all total pains in the neck. I'd trust him with my life."

Sledge tucked the distraught wife under his sturdy arm. Olivia launched into another onslaught of tears, although her emotional angst was much quieter this time around.

Me? I took comfort from the solemn hazel eyes that met mine over Olivia's bowed head. They never left mine; his shining gaze as unwavering as the Candle Island ledges. Sledge didn't know Nathaniel, but he knew Tasha. As doctor and nurse, they worked together at the island clinic and Sledge and my niece were on the fast track to becoming something more than friends.

Insistent hands tugged on my sleeve. Jacey still held onto me; not surprising, considering the basket case alternative. Before I could crouch down to her level, she pulled me away from Olivia and Sledge. I let myself be towed toward the shadow of the nearby building. *Poor little bug.*

"Can I see your binoculars?"

I smiled. No need to get a swelled head. The girl wanted my stuff, not me. I took them from around my neck, knelt next to her and handed her the glasses. "I'm afraid they won't work after dark."

She ignored my soft words and held them up to her eyes, their big lenses covering up her pug nose and small elfin face. Jacey turned in a slow circle before she lowered the field glasses and thrust them back at me. "They don't work. They're s'posed to be green so you can see in the dark. Kendall has some like that. He stole 'em from Grampie."

"Ah, sorry. I don't have the see-in-the-dark kind." We stayed like that, side by side in silence, until the little girl heaved a huge sigh, too big for one so young.

I wanted to put my arm around her and comfort her, but I refused to spout false hope and promise things I had no power to deliver. "You know, Jacey, my nephew Nathaniel is out there with Grampie. It's a big ocean, but God knows where your grandfather and Nate are."

Jacey nodded, leaned close and whispered in my ear. "I know, too."

"You do?"

"Yeah, 'cept Moo won't listen."

"Moo?"

"Moo. Mean Old Olivia." With each word, her delicate forefinger tapped her open palm as if counting out the acronym. "Olivia hates it when I call her that."

I bet.

"But Kendall made it up for me." Her small white teeth flashed in the dim light before the pout returned. "She's so mean! She never listens to me, and she tries to get Grampie not to listen to me neither."

I didn't care about mean old Olivia; only this child and the skinny hope of a lead on the two missing men.

"Where is he? Where is Grampie"

"It's our secret." She whispered and I leaned in closer. "He's on our special island. Grampie said he'd take me there for a picnic before school started. It's where we always go without Olivia. She hates the island."

I caught my breath. Hadn't Scotty said if Luke had boat trouble they might've put in on a small island? I took a moment to slow my thoughts and my words. No need to go all Olivia on Jacey and spook the child. "And where is your island?"

Her little chin came up and, even in the shadows, I recognized that spit-in-your-eye look all too well. "I can't tell you."

Of course, you can't! More to the point, you won't, you stubborn little cuss! "I understand. It's your special secret, but what if Grampie needs help? What if his boat is broken down and he needs Kendall to come and fix it? Maybe you could tell Kendall."

Jacey shook her head, her ponytail whipping against the sleeve of my jacket. She even wrinkled her snub nose in Olivia-like distain. "Nope, we don't like Kendall anymore."

Great! "Oh, but doesn't he still help your grandfather fix up his boat?"

"Nope, he isn't allowed to touch Grampie's and my boat, or come over, and I'm not allowed to talk to him, ever again."

Huh! "Maybe you could tell someone else where Grampie is, like Scotty. He can keep a secret, and he could take his boat over to the island and help Grampie get home tonight."

"Nope."

Strike three! Jacey had the kindergarten vocabulary down pat. I'd been up against this three-and-a-half-foot wall of childish defiance for decades and, if I was truthful, I knew exactly where the attitude came from. I still had a smidgen of that child-spite inside, although I tried to keep it well hidden behind my adult façade.

I had no doubt I'd find a detour around her five-year-old-stubborn roadblock, but I chafed at the time factor. I didn't have the luxury of days to become friends with this little girl and win her trust. I had only hours, maybe minutes.

"Gwen." I flicked my eyes up at the deep throaty tones.

Jacey pushed off from me and wrapped her thin arms around Laverna Jordan's waist. "Mimi!"

"How's my Jacey Jane-bug?" Laverna smoothed the child's bangs back from her forehead with a work-worn-but-tender hand. The girl was still for a moment before she burrowed her face into the robust stalwart sanctuary of someone she obviously trusted.

"Came when I heard. Doesn't mean they're not both safe somewheres. Just missin'. Scotty'll find 'em."

"Jacey Jane Faraday! You come over here, right this minute!"

The child gave no indication she heard Olivia's strident command, but Laverna's arm tightened around the little girl and hugged her closer.

"I said *now*, little missy!" Olivia strode over to us, back straight as a corseted Scarlett O'Hara, the tilt of her nose just as queenly and entitled. She grabbed Jacey's arm and pulled her away from the other woman. Laverna had the good grace to let go and step back. Jacey wailed.

"See what you've done? Poor little darling was upset enough over Luke, without you coming here to cause trouble," Olivia raged.

"I only came to help."

Olivia pointed at the writhing child. "You want to help, Laverna? Go home. This isn't your business. Stay away from me and my family."

Olivia muckled onto Jacey's sweatshirt and tried to drag her down the pier, but the kid planted her heels in the planks and leaned back with all her skinny sinew. In a surprise move, Olivia picked the child up, clamped her arms around her and strode away, steel-magnolia style with an angry twitch to her hips.

"It's a free country," Laverna muttered as she brushed past me and stalked toward the parking lot.

A murmur from the crowd stole my attention as the wave of bodies gravitated like low tide toward the end of the dock. "They got one of 'em!"

I ran through the pools of light to the dark ocean beyond.

CHAPTER FIVE

I wormed my way through the press of people. Sledge was at the dock edge before Scotty's boat drew alongside. Another man, a stranger to me, caught the line from Kendall and pulled them in. Scotty cut the engine as Sledge jumped aboard. My eyes strained to see the body wrapped in a blanket, huddled on the floor by the wheelhouse, but the doctor's sturdy bulk blocked any more than a glimpse.

I swallowed hard and sent up a wordless prayer before I stepped forward. Scotty's rough hand was there, outstretched to grasp mine and pull me onto the deck.

"Nate's wet and shaky, but he seems okay." Scotty's voice close to my ear was pitched below the rising chatter of the crowd. "Sledge'll have a look-see, probably take him to the mainland to get checked out."

I nodded, blinking away the blur of tears. Scotty guided me over to Nate, my nephew's dark lips obscene in the ugly dishwater-gray face. I grasped his frigid trembling hand in mine. "Some first day, huh, Gwennie?" he croaked. The childish nickname tore at my already ragged heart. I stroked his cheek and hair as if he were still six years old and recovering from the flu. His skin seemed clammy but hot to my touch. Sledge did his thing, leaning over, listening, palpating, touching here and there. I barely noticed. My eyes never left my nephew's face.

"Let's get him into dry clothes and get him out of here."

I helped Sledge pull off the wet things, not easy even as a two-person task.

My nephew's attempts were more hindrance than help. "Sorry for the stink," Nate rasped. The smell of vomit and diarrhea filled my senses but the feel of my boy's chilled solid flesh under my busy hands was all that consumed me. The doctor produced his own stash of fleece pants, long underwear, and a dry blanket. I ripped off my backpack and together we wrapped him in the hoodie. Sledge then produced some of those cheap thermal heat packs and put them inside Nate's shirt and pants, neck, armpits, and groin.

"See if you can get some of this hot broth into him and I'll see about getting him to the mainland." Sledge clasped my hand in a strong grip. "He checked out okay so you can relax a little, but keep praying, Gwen. He's dehydrated, cold. Pre-hypothermic, and we need to rule out possible pneumonia, but he's young and strong. He's not in imminent danger from what I can see, so probably just as quick to take the boat ride to the hospital as call out the helicopter, unless you have any objections."

I shook my head. "No, you know what you're doing. Thanks."

"If you're okay with riding over with him, I'll stick around for when they bring in Luke."

"Yeah."

"Keep him warm and out of the wind. I'll call the hospital and Tasha and tell them you're coming."

"You up for a walk, Man?" Scotty reappeared at my side. Nate nodded. He and Sledge helped my nephew stand and Nate staggered in red-toed bare feet as they ushered him off one boat and onto another docked nearby, engine running.

I followed a step behind, hands fluttering as useless as road-ditch garbage in a windstorm. As soon as Nate was seated on the floor of the small cabin in a nest of blankets, Scotty drew me aside. "Tinker and Old Stin'll get you to the hospital. I've gotta go see if we can piece together what Nate told us and find Luke."

I squeezed his hand. I'd had my miracle and I prayed there was a second one with Luke, Olivia, and Jacey's names on it. "Go on."

He nodded and both he and Sledge hopped ashore just before helping hands shoved us off into the moonless night. I looked back at a small human island of candle and cell-phone lights holding forth hope for one more man to come home safe.

I settled myself on the planking next to Nate, vaguely aware of the two men talking. Old Stin growled about a buoy. Tinker put in a syllable occasionally, but I didn't pay much attention. I didn't even marvel at the readiness of this boat or the appearance of Scotty's grandfather coming to the rescue. Later I'd take it all in, but for now I had one arm around my nephew as he gagged down a little of the broth.

"I can't, Gwen," he protested. "Any more and I'll hurl."

"But—"

"I'm fine."

"How many times have I heard that lie before?"

"This time it's true." He sagged against me and closed his eyes.

The trek across the waves jumbled in my mind in a kaleidoscope of stars and running lights reflected on the water, the murmur and hiss of the sea at our passage, the rattle of Nate's uneasy breathing, Old Stin's rumbling reassurances, and my heart flip-flopping between relief and fear.

When we finally docked on the mainland, an ambulance was waiting. They whisked Nate away. Old Stin, stiff as a post, his white hair punk-pink in the flashing lights, grabbed hold of my elbow and rasped in my ear. "Want me to stay with ya?"

I shook my head. "Thank you, but no. We'll be fine."

"Figured as much, but you call me if you need

anything."

I nodded, unable to speak.

"We'd best be gettin' back, then." He squeezed my arm. "We'll let you know..."

"Thanks," I whispered, and hugged his bony form close.

His sinewy arm came around and patted my back. "It'll be alright. You go on, now, and tend out to your boy."

I stepped away and followed Tasha to the borrowed car. I glanced back once and saw him standing where I'd left him, straight and proud as an ancient warrior, watching and waiting until we drove out of sight.

I don't know if it was having a niece who's a nurse, or if it was simply a slow night at the ED, but every prayer I'd ever prayed was answered in that hospital. Their competent and compassionate care was the best I'd ever experienced. *How often does that happen? Only in fiction.*

They got Nate hooked up. I watched the numbers on the monitor, steady and strong as Sledge predicted, while they started an iv and tucked my nephew in heated blankets. The doctor breezed in, listened to his heart and lungs, did a quick poke-and-prod exam and promised to return after they took an x-ray.

Only when they took Nathaniel away to radiology did Tasha and I have time to talk. "What happened? Sledge told me Nate went overboard but he was fine. No danger of information dump with *that* guy." Tasha sat next to me in the ubiquitous plastic chairs. She reached for my hand, eyes sparkling with unshed tears as she glared at me demanding answers. She wasn't a McPhail for nothing.

"He went off lobstering this morning with Luke Faraday, and the boat never came back. They're still searching for Luke, but they found your brother on a navigational buoy or something." I closed my eyes, trying to recall fragments of Old Stin and Tinker's conversation on the trip over. "I'm not sure of the whole story."

"Natey will fill us in with all the gory details, I'm sure."

His sister's grip on my hand tightened. After a while her low voice trembled in the cool, antiseptic room. "What if he never came back?"

I wasn't going there. "But he did."

"Yeah, I know. We're blessed, but I've been praying for Luke and his family."

"Me, too. Do you know him?"

Tasha shrugged. "A little. I know his wife, Olivia, better. I met her at the Coveside Coffee and Coiffure one day when I had my hair trimmed. She was having her hair and nails done so we had time to chat. She knows Nate."

"What?" *Olivia and Nate?* It made no sense, but my brain was so waterlogged with stress nothing much was floating to the top for processing.

Again, my niece shrugged. "Who *doesn't* know Nate?"

"Good point." I'd remember to ask my nephew about it later. There were more important issues. We were in a hospital for one! "What about Luke?"

"Luke might be the strong silent type. Not sure. I got that impression when he came in to the clinic with his granddaughter a couple of weeks ago. A minor boo-boo, but he was all business. He seemed nice, though, and he obviously thinks the world of Jacey."

"Yeah, he does. Let's hope and pray for the best for all of them."

They wheeled Nate back into the room and helped him into bed.

"The doctor will be in shortly," a passing nurse promised as she stuck her head in the door.

"Hey, Bro!" Tasha released my hand and took her sibling's. "What did you get yourself into this time?"

Nate groaned. His face was still whiter than a bleach bottle, but he favored us with a tired smile. "Remember that time when I visited you in that little apartment you had off campus? I ate the leftover Chinese from your fridge?"

Tasha shook her head.

"It was toxic."

"Oh, yeah." She gave her brother a gentle slap on the arm. "How could I forget? You camped out in my bathroom all night."

"Yeah, thanks to you."

"Those egg rolls weren't even mine. It belonged to my roommate, Jessica, and I told you not to touch it. That stuff had been in there at least three weeks."

"It wasn't egg rolls, it was left over pu pu platter, crab rangoons, and fried rice."

The familial banter slipped around my aching body like a comfy security blanket. *It's going to be okay.* I breathed in the realization, ignoring the tremble that spread from that indrawn breath to my legs and arms. I fisted my hands to hide the shake.

"Hey, it didn't smell funky, and it didn't have any mold on it. It was good going down but deadly once it hit bottom." Nate shook his head. "Today was like that. One minute I'm good, the next I was sicker than a dog, puking my brains out. It hit me super fast and explosive, if you get my meaning."

"Oh, we get it, alright." Tasha wrinkled her nose.

His words suddenly sunk in. *The tuna fish!* It couldn't have been the cinnamon rolls, we'd both had those for breakfast, and I was fine. "It must've been my sandwiches. I thought it was all fresh but..." I patted his knee under the hospital-issue blanket.

"I don't know. I don't think so, so don't beat yourself up, Gwen. I had some other stuff, too." Nate's brow wrinkled. The putty face was leaching out its ill and his natural color was seeping back in so he looked much more human. "They were having some kind of Pirate Labor Day Weekend street fair thing, so while I was waiting for Luke to get what he needed at CrossJack Marine, I sampled a bunch of stuff."

"Like what, exactly?" I wanted to believe I hadn't poisoned my own flesh-and-blood, but I wasn't convinced.

"Only a turkey taco and some wrinkles, onion rings, and a piece of peanut butter fudge."

Tasha gently swatted his arm again. "No wonder you were sick."

"Hey, I was hungry. We didn't have lunch until we shoved off and started back to home port."

"I thought you said you ate the tuna."

"I did, after we got underway. I ate one and gave one to Luke because he insisted I have some of his chicken soup. Actually, Olivia had insisted. She made a ton extra so he could share her special homemade soup with me. It was salty as all get-out, but Luke loved it. He was scarfing it down. I ate a little to be polite, then deep-sixed the rest over the side while he was talking on the radio."

"And then you got sick?"

"No, I was still hungry."

"Glutton!" Tasha teased.

"Hey, you try getting up at four in the morning and putting in a whole day's work before lunch."

"Sounds like you're talking about a typical twelve-hour shift at the hospital."

"Yeah, yeah, I know. Nobody works harder than nurses."

I cut through their sibling banter, tuna fish the only thing on my mind. "So what else did you eat?" I had to agree with Tasha. Even under the hospital blankets, my nephew's inert body exuded athletic fitness. Where did he put it all?

"One of Luke's friends gave him some wicked good lobster stew, so I had some of that to get rid of the chicken soup aftertaste. Olivia's stuff was nasty."

"Then you got sick?"

"Oh, yeah. *Big* time. I was hurling over the side when I heard Luke's phone ringing. Finally, when he didn't answer it, I tried to make it back to the pilothouse to check on him. He was slumped over the wheel but he must've put the boat in neutral before he passed out, or maybe the engine had quit." He shook his head. "I'm not sure. I don't think there was any engine noise. Someone was talking on the radio, but it was garbled. Then the phone stopped ringing, probably went to voice mail. By that time, I was back at the rail, heaving my guts out."

The doctor stepped in and gave us the news. "You've got pneumonia. You've had this for over a week, you say?"

Nate grunted in agreement.

"We'll give you some meds, should take care of it. In the meantime, we're going to keep you overnight for observation. They'll get you cleaned up and admitted. A hot shower ought to make you feel much better."

The MD studied the numbers for a moment before he felt Nate's neck and throat. "We'll keep up the IV, make sure you get rehydrated. You still feeling nauseous?"

"A little queasy, but mostly just weak. The cramps are gone, so I'm a happy camper."

"That flu can pack a nasty punch," the doctor said.

"Could it have been a case of food poisoning?" *Get over the tuna fish issue!*

The doctor turned to me, his voice calm, showing no irritation or surprise. "I suppose it's not out of the question."

"Do you have any other cases from the pirate festival?"

He grinned. "Not yet, but the night's still young. And I'm not saying you're right, but it could be a possibility. Food poisoning happens more often than people think." He ran a hand through his dark hair. "Course, if we really knew all the bugs, trash, and bacteria we eat, particularly when we eat out, we'd give it up and all starve."

"Thanks for that visual," Nate joked.

I smiled, glad my boy was back, safe and almost sound.

"But our bodies are resilient." The man nodded. "Yours will bounce back, Nate, but you'll need to take it easy for a few days."

"I'll see he follows medical advice," Tasha said.

"It isn't often you get your own private nurse."

Nate groaned.

The doctor chuckled. "I wouldn't mess with Nurse McPhail. But, like I said, we'll keep an eye on you overnight and in the morning you'll likely be going home."

"Sounds good." We all spoke as one.

"Nice to meet you all." He exchanged a few more pleasantries, shook hands with Tasha and me, and left.

We went to the snack bar while they got my nephew settled in his room although, after all that talk of food, I didn't go for the tuna and I only picked at my packaged salad.

"You okay?" Tasha asked.

"Yeah, just afterward jitters. And I've been thinking about Luke Faraday."

"I'll give Sledge a call and see what I can find out."

We cleared our trays and walked outside. The air off the ocean had turned raw, but the bite felt good on my skin after the claustrophobic disinfectant hospital atmosphere. I walked over to the small garden area and left Tasha standing under the lamp while I wandered down the cobbled path into the shadows. My foot caught against a trailing arm of juniper and the pungent scent filled my senses as I rubbed my temples, trying to make sense of the last hours. Maybe that was it—none of it made sense. It was an accident. One was safe and the other . . .

"Auntie!" I pivoted, caught Tasha's beckoning gesture and quickly joined her in the pond of artificial light. She put the cell phone on speaker without any preamble. "Gwen's here."

"You made it okay?" Sledge's baritone was calm and steady as a fluke anchor.

"Yes, thank you. How's Luke?"

"Still missing. They've got the Coast Guard involved now. Scotty and Kendall just came in a few minutes ago. He wants to talk to Nate, if he's up to it."

"Sure." We both answered at once.

"I'll call you back when we get to my brother's room."

"Sounds good. I'll get Scotty up to speed. He's around here somewhere, probably eating. The Pier opened its doors and a bunch of the restaurants brought in food. Can't say it helps ease the tension, but it gives people something to do with their mouths besides speculate. Catch you in a few. Bye."

Tasha shook her head but I caught the slow smile as she slipped the phone in her handbag. "Like I said, the guy isn't one to waste words on the phone."

"As long as he says what needs to be said, that's all that matters."

"Oh yeah." Again, the smile. Tasha looped her elbow in mine, and we strode to the hospital entrance and straight to Nate's room, two women on a mission.

He was sitting up, sipping ginger ale and, typical Nate, chatting up a cute blond-haired CNA. Although she was doing most of the talking, Nate was holding his own. It would take more than a near drowning, pneumonia, and food poisoning to slow that boy down. "This is Marissa," he said.

"Thank you for taking care of him," I said.

I was surprised and pleased when Marissa simply smiled and said, "I'll leave you to visit. If you need anything, just push the call button."

"I will," Nate replied, but his eyes focused on mine. When the last sneaker squeaked on the floor as Marissa left the room, he put the soda on the tray. "What's up?"

"Still looking for Luke."

Tasha punched in Sledge's number and handed me the phone before she mouthed. "I'll be back in a minute." She followed the CNA out into the hall and disappeared. I suspected she was on her way to the nurse's station to get the official lowdown on her brother.

"Hey, I got Scotty and Kendall here," Sledge answered without preamble.

"Nate's here." I clicked the phone on speaker and leaned

over my nephew.

"How you doing?" Scotty asked.

"Never better." His voice might be scratchy but his face was all business. "You find the boat ... anything?"

"Not yet. Coast Guard's been called in and they're searching the area where we pulled you out. We'll go out again, but you can help us."

"Whatcha need?"

"How'd you end up on the whistle buoy?"

"I don't know. It sounds stupid, but I've been trying to figure it out. One minute I was puking over the side, the next I was overboard, trying to swim and puke at the same time. I don't know if we caught a wave, and I pitched over? It was almost like something maybe slid across the deck, but it hit me high and took me out so I lost my balance. I can't be sure."

"Okay. Were you at the buoy, or did you float around and swim for it?"

"We were fairly close to it, but when I came up for air, I wanted to go for the boat. I was thrashing around, trying to get my bearings, and the boat had already drifted off a little. I swam to the buoy because I was throwing up and I grabbed hold of the nearest thing. I hollered for Luke, but the engine started, and I swear the boat drove away, but that can't be right." He shook his head. "I know I wasn't in good shape, so I probably was hallucinating or something."

I didn't think so, but I held my tongue. I wasn't there.

"Which way was the Jane Anne headed?" Scotty's questions kept coming like friendly fire, at least I think it was friendly. If I didn't know him, I might've taken offense.

"Toward Hackett's Island, I think." Nate rubbed the golden stubble on his chin. "Luke had been arguing on the radio with some dude a while before. He asked where we were and that's the last thing I remember Luke saying ... I think. I don't know for sure. It's fuzzy." He balled the blanket in his fists. "By the time I pulled myself up on the buoy, the boat was gone. That's why I think maybe I must've flaked out for a while. Luke couldn't have driven off. He looked in bad shape, and if he came to, he would've heard me."

"You say you heard the engine start up. Did it quit?"

Nate's brow furrowed. "I'm trying to think. I got sick and after I puked my guts out, I don't remember the engine running. When I went into the wheelhouse and found Luke passed out, the boat was already drifting. But I didn't pay attention to the boat. I thought maybe he was having a heart attack, but he had a strong pulse. I remember checking on that before I went back to the rail."

My nephew closed his eyes and took a deep breath. "I thought I heard an engine, but not the Jane Anne's. Smaller, and it had a knock in it, but that doesn't make sense either. If another boat was there, I would've seen it." He shook his head, his voice filled with disgust. "I was going back to send a call-out on the radio when I fell overboard. I left Luke on a disabled boat."

"Maybe," Scotty said. "We'll know better when daylight comes. Hang tight and I'll keep you informed."

Talk about a guy who wasn't one to waste words. Maybe it was a Candle Island man-thing. "Wait!"

I clicked the phone off speaker and hurried into the hall. I glanced in both directions like a fugitive before I rushed to the ladies' room, not particularly caring what any bystander might think of the crazy woman staring at her phone.

"Okay," I said trying not to sound breathless as I locked the stall door.

"Okay, what?"

"Okay, what's next?"

"Hang tight and I'll keep you informed."

"I got that the first time. What's going on out there?"

"We're doing what we can."

"And?"

"And nothing, so far. Daylight may help. Can't hurt."

His terse voice went hoarse, and the silence reeked of frustration. It penetrated my defenses and left my hopes flat. "You ought to get some rest."

"Yeah. I'll check in with you tomorrow. Gotta go."

"Okay. Be careful." His answer was a click and a buzz. I slowly made my way back to Nate's room.

Tasha was seated beside the bed. "We should go and let him sleep."

I nodded. I gave him a gentle hug and, cheek-to-whiskered-cheek, I whispered the old childhood rhyme in his ear. "Good night. Sleep tight. Don't let the bedbugs bite, and I'll see you in the morning light."

"Come back early, I want to get out of here so I can help with the search."

"Go to sleep," Tasha said. "Or you won't be going anywhere."

"Couldn't have said it better myself." I mustered what little bravado I had left. "Good night, Nathaniel. Sweet dreams."

"Night. Remember ... bright and early," he called after us as we went out the door.

Early? In his dreams. Considering the ubiquitous snafus of hospital discharge!

There was no such thing as sweet dreams that night, just an unending torrent of faces and what-ifs. And I imagined I was better off tonight than most, in my rented motel room with my niece snoring in the next bed. My family was safe.

I thought of Nate clinging to a buoy, surrounded by nothing but waves and darkness; of the island pier crowded with family and friends clinging to hope; of little Jacey, her earnest eyes and her small clinging hands. She and Olivia were as mismatched as little Avery Brooks' fashion sense with his highwater purple striped pants, neon socks, plaid shirts, and that peagreen polka-dotted hat he insisted on wearing, even when my other kindergarten students made fun of it—though never when I was in hearing distance.

Avery was now in eighth grade and the master of the droopy drawers jd-look of the baggy falling-off jeans, wide expanse of boxer shorts, and always a black T-shirt. Maybe an improvement. Probably not.

This wasn't the time to be dredging up haunting boorish tales of kindergarten past. Jacey was kindergarten present and, in all my experience with five- and six-year-olds, her insistence that Luke was on an island held a ring of truth to it. Of course, both of us wanted to believe it was so and he was safe, but as one o'clock tortoise-ticked to two, I became more convinced I needed to get back to the island and talk to the little girl, *if* I could get Olivia out of our hair for two seconds. For someone who disliked children, she wasn't one to take her eyes off Luke's granddaughter.

I closed my eyes, rolled on one shoulder, bunched up my borrowed pillow and settled back into the scent of foreign laundry detergent.

Olivia was holding onto what was hers, I supposed. Laverna, on the other hand, was a surprise, but not really. Jacey must've been the little girl I'd glimpsed trailing Laverna at Barb's take-out the other day. And I'd seen firsthand how kind she was to Old Stin. Still waters. Good neighbors. She'd called our Nate a nice-looking boy, so she couldn't be all bad.

Instead of focusing on the unknown I went with the known—planning down to the least detail what needed to happen before I got back to the island. After three hours of sorting thoughts like dirty laundry and trying to keep my mind off buoy rescues and sinking boats, it came down to simply one thing—get Nate settled at my Bookerton place with Tasha. Hopefully the twins wanted to hang out, and sister would look after brother for a while. And brother wouldn't be too much of a pain. And I could get back on the ferry to the island as soon as possible.

I took an early morning shower to pass the time and tiptoed outside with Tasha's cell phone as the sky lightened over the King Neptune Motel parking lot. I took one quick glance at the dawn tinged clouds on the horizon and hit Sledge's number. He answered on the first ring.

"How's it going out there?" I asked.

"Nothing yet. We're having a prayer vigil on the town pier in the morning."

I swallowed hard, trying to dislodge the fear and worry. "It *is* morning."

"Huh."

"Is Scotty out?" If anyone could find them, he could. No pressure there, but it was the one thought that kept me going through the night.

"No, he and a bunch of the guys are putting their heads together to map out what boat goes where so they can cover as much territory as possible. They'll be heading out any minute."

"Any chance I can talk to him before he leaves?"

"Don't see why not. I'll call you back in a few. Hey, how's Tash and Nate doing?"

"Tasha's sleeping in the motel, and I hope Nate's doing the same in the hospital, but when we left last night everything looked good."

"Good to hear. Okay, bye."

I walked back and forth on the slab of tar like a plane taxiing for take-off, but after ten minutes I was getting nowhere.

Tasha popped out of our room just as the phone rang. I gave her a smile but clamped her phone firmly to my ear. "Hello."

"Morning." Scotty's slow voice growled with no sleep and frustration.

No time for chitchat; he wouldn't appreciate it anyhow. "I think you ought to talk with Jacey before you go out."

"Luke's granddaughter?"

I pictured him taking off his cap and rubbing his forehead. "Yeah, last night she told me she knew where her grandfather was. She said they have a special island they go to sometimes and he promised to take her there.”

“Look, Gwen, we’re not grasping at straws yet.”

“It’s not a straw. She was so determined, and you said if they had engine trouble, and it sounds like they did, they might pull in to one of the smaller islands.”

“And what is this kid, four?”

“She’s five.” I tried not to sound defensive, didn’t quite pull it off. “I just thought if you could get her to tell you which island it is, you could check it out.”

“You don’t know what island?”

“Well, no, not exactly.”

“Okay, well, I’ll keep that in mind. Our best bet is to do a grid search where the Jane Anne was last sighted and, according to Nate, that was at the whistle buoy. How’s he doing?”

“We haven’t been to the hospital yet this morning, but when we left last night he was much better. They gave him antibiotics for his pneumonia.”

“Sounds promising. So, you’ll stay put over there for a while, I take it.”

The conversation had taken a jog in the there’s-something-he’s-not-telling-me direction. “No. I’m planning on coming back today.”

“No need. Sledge’ll keep you informed. You probably want to stay with your nephew.”

“He’s got Tasha.”

“And you.”

“She’s a nurse. Maybe we’ll all come back over if he’s up for the ferry ride. Nate wants to help. He feels responsible.”

“The best way he can help is to stay put on the mainland and get his feet back under him. You, too.”

“I’ve got my feet under me.”

“Yeah, I guessed that. Just do me a favor and stay there for a few days until ... He sucked in a deep breath that made him seem like he was right here. "Look, I've gotta go. Give my best to Tasha and Nate and—"

"Wait!" Was he trying to force me to be a wing walker, holding on here with nothing to reach out to there?

"I was gonna say, I might've been a little harsh on him the other day. He swam to the buoy while he was sicker than a dog, pulled himself up and had the sense to slip the line through his belt loops and tie himself to it. Smart. Knows his knots, too. Should've known it runs in the family. Gotta go. And Gwen ... try not to worry. Bye."

I punched off the phone wishing I could punch a certain someone as I handed it over to my helicoptering niece. "No word on Luke or the boat?"

I shook my head, instantly ashamed of my petty attitude. "Not yet."

"Was that Scotty?"

Who else! "Yeah. I think everybody who has a boat is going out this morning." I checked my watch. Still too soon to even think of getting to the hospital. "How about I treat you to breakfast, and we strategize, if we can find an early-open diner?"

"Sounds like a plan. Did you talk to Sledge?"

"Only for a minute. You might want to call him later and get the scoop." There was more than one way to pry open a clam.

"I take it Scotty wasn't talking."

I smiled and Tasha grinned. "Between the two of us and the two of them, we'll see if we can piece together the rest of the story."

CHAPTER SIX

Add to the usual rigmarole of hospital discharge, the fact of the holiday weekend and the pirate celebration influx of partying wounded. As we waited, I was pleased to see my nephew acting bright, despite the raccoon circles under his solemn blue eyes. Yesterday's buoy escapade had taken a lot out of him, whether he was willing to admit it or not. And, for Nate, it was the typical not.

Although I didn't agree with Scotty about my returning to the island, I was totally onboard with Nate staying put in Bookerton. Now I just had to bring both the twins around to my way of thinking. I'd been outmaneuvering them since the day they were born, so how hard could it be? I had a feeling they might say the same thing about pulling the wool over their aunt's eyes, so it'd be interesting to see what transpired. I was confident.

While Nate finally got dressed in Sledge's laundered fleece and sweats, Tasha and I stepped out and she was already on her phone before I could voice my less-than-subtle prompt. And, like me, this time she didn't put it on speaker but went to the corner of the waiting area and conversed in low tones.

I looked out the window, staring at nothing. I tried to mentally focus on the garden. A few of the leaves on the shrubs were blushing scarlet for the coming season, but the flash of beauty didn't instill calm or kill the urge to pace. But with Sledge on the other end of the line, I didn't have long to mentally fidget anyway.

Tasha marched toward me, a frown marring her usually sunny features.

"Did they find Luke?" *or his body,* my overactive imagination added before I could stop it.

"No, no news yet, but..."

She drew out the word as if she were ten years old again, stretching out her bubble gum and snapping it.

"What?" It came out sharper than I intended, which only deepened her scowl.

"They're saying things about Natey."

"Huh? Who?"

"Doesn't matter. It's the island."

"What's that supposed to mean?"

She shrugged and chewed her fingernail, an old-time habit she never resorted to except in high-stress situations.

"What're you talking about?"

"They're saying Nate took the job with Luke because he wanted to start things up again with Olivia?"

"What?"

"It gets worse. The word is, Luke found out and they had a knock-down drag-out on the boat. Nate attacked Luke. Luke cracked hit his head on the rail and went overboard and drowned. Nate panicked, scuttled the boat, and tied himself to the buoy so he'd look like the victim."

I shook my head. "That's stupid." I make a big deal about my students using the "s" word, but there was no other word for this situation except maybe idiotic, moronic, soap-opera fiction.

"Yeah, tell me about it."

So, this was why Scotty was anxious to cut me off! "Let's get your brother out of here so I can get back to the island and set things straight."

"You mean so *we* can get back to the island."

I put gentle hands on my niece's rigid shoulders. "Relax,

Tasha. Nobody with half a brain would believe any of that trash." *Would they?*

"Maybe not, but I'm going to find the person who started the rumor about my brother."

Unless I get there first. "I want that, too, but I was hoping you'd stay in Bookerton with Nate for a few days to make sure he does what he's supposed to and gets plenty of rest."

"But—"

"I don't trust him on his own."

"Well, neither do I, but—"

"Look, we don't have to tell all we know, here. Let's get your brother settled at my place then we can work out the details. One thing's for sure, Nathaniel doesn't need to know any of this."

"Yeah, that's why Sledge let me in on it. Didn't want Nate out there." She shook her head and wrapped her arms around me in a quick hug. "Who'd say those things? The Coffee and Coiffure isn't even open today, and none of those girls are that mean."

"Sometimes when people are stressed out, afraid of bad news, they create their own backfire story to keep their minds off what they fear the most." *Where did that come from?*

"Huh! I never thought of it that way."

Neither had I until I made it up two seconds ago. It had a nice ring to it, but whether it held a grain of truth any more than the nasty trash talk about my nephew, remained to be seen.

"Best case scenario, I go back to the island after we get you both ensconced in the cottage and find out what's really going on. Hopefully, whatever it is, will've blown over by the time your brother's well enough to come back to Candle Island, and he's none the wiser."

"Oh, he'll know eventually. He's Nate. But my brother can take whatever they throw at him, and so can I." She took a step back and thrust out her chin. The only things missing were the doubled-up fists of childhood.

The twins always had each other's backs, even when they were squabbling between themselves. They'd take on the common enemy and then let loose on each other.

This time, I needed to be the one who had both their backs, and I needed to do it on the down low. "I know." I patted her arm. "But don't you think both of you have enough to deal with right now? Yesterday was a huge shock."

Tasha nodded and her chin wobbled as she took her turn staring out the window. "You're probably right, but I'm only staying out of it for a few days."

"Fair enough. Let's go get your brother."

On the forty-minute drive to Bookerton in Tasha's borrowed car, I tried to get my mind off the island drama and trauma, but it was moth-to-the-flame time and I decided to fly a little closer and worry about singed wings later.

"So, Nate, I was talking with Olivia while we were on the pier waiting for news and I got the impression she knew you. Was she at the boat to send you off that early in the morning?" Too pointed? Too bad. It wasn't like I had the luxury of a journey of 1,000 miles on this one. I needed info, and I needed it yesterday.

I leaned slightly forward from my place in the backseat behind Tasha. Since Nate had the front passenger seat fully reclined, we were nearly nose to nose when he opened his eyes.

"Yeah, she was there. I guess she does that sometimes. Likes to see Luke off." He didn't sound all that interested or pleased with my conversation but, as his eyelids lowered once more, I kept at it.

"She doesn't seem like an early riser."

Nate's eyes opened and he held my gaze, fully alert now. He indulged in a husky laugh that turned into a cough. "Now see what you've done? Don't make me laugh."

"What's so funny?" Tasha asked.

"Gwen. She's going to pester me 'til I get better."

"Just like old times," his sister said.

"I learned it from you guys." I jumped in, but I was already in with both feet anyway, no sense in pretending with these two. We knew each other too well.

He grinned. "What do you want to know?"

"Everything." This from Tasha.

"Okay, the Olivia I knew was a night owl."

Not exactly the information I wanted to hear, but obviously they did know each other. I wasn't sure if this was good news or bad, but there was only one way to find out ... go further down the rabbit hole.

"What are the chances you'd know the wife of the guy you met by chance at the ferry landing, and who just happened to give you a job?"

Nate smiled. "I know, right? Providence, Gwen? Six degrees of separation. Small world. You name it."

"That's so totally normal in your world. So how *do* you know her? And don't tell me she's Olivia-not-my-girlfriend old girlfriend!" Obviously, Tasha wasn't feeling the need to pull any punches on the invalid.

Nate fell into another rasping laugh. "You guys are killing me!"

"And you're killing me, Bro! What's the deal with you and Olivia Faraday?" Tasha demanded.

I let them have at it. All I had to do was listen and maybe referee. They needed to be on speaking terms before I left them alone to spend the next few days together at my house.

"She was Olivia Jackson back in the day, said she was a great-great-great-something-or-other relative of Stonewall Jackson, a long-lost daughter of the Confederacy, if you can believe it."

"Really." I wasn't seeing it. I wanted to say so much more, but Tasha did it for me.

"You trying to tell us you met her at a Civil War reenactment?"

Nate threw his head back and howled. When he finally caught his breath he said, "Hey, I'm sick. You're supposed to be taking it easy on me."

"Yeah?"

"Okay, I worked with Olivia, and we dated for a while."

"Worked with her?"

"Define 'a while.' " We spoke over each other but it didn't matter. Nate was into one of his tales and would meander around whatever facts he chose to reveal or keep hidden. I'd pick up the breadcrumbs he tossed my way.

"At the Bear Bonz-A-Petit Bar and Grill. Remember that, Gwen?"

I groaned. "That snobby Boston watering hole?" I'd been down there once after a doctor's appointment, spent the night in the city and visited my nephew. I didn't remember Olivia but, at the time, I wasn't looking.

"We preferred to call it trendy, but yeah. I got some great tips there."

"And Olivia? Isn't she a little *old* for you?" Tasha. Bless her heart for reading my mind.

Nate shrugged. "What's a few years, give or take?"

More like a decade, I'd wager; but I had to hand it to her, Olivia looked great. Although up close, I could see she gilded the lily to pull it off.

We rode along in silence over the dyke, the salt water blending with the fresh of Blynn River, the marsh grasses beginning to yellow, the greens and grays of the water swirling as the tide came in.

"So, what happened?" Tasha asked.

"We never were really serious. At least I wasn't. Turns out we both liked to have some fun, but she wasn't interested in poking her nose outside, especially in cold weather, and she hated ice hockey. She watched me play once and it was torture for both of us. She hated all sports, actually. Her idea of fun was to go out to eat, go to the movies, parties, or whatever. The old champagne-on-a-beer-budget type. Me being the perpetual beer-budget guy, I think she would've dumped me soon. But first of the year, I left the Bear Bonz for that gig on the cruise line out of Florida and we never saw each other again." He hunched one shoulder. "Until yesterday. She hasn't changed much."

What was that supposed to mean? He closed his eyes as if the conversation was over. Maybe he was just worn out. I sympathized, but he'd have all day to lounge in bed at the Bookerton cottage and get over it. I eased up just a little. "Scotty said you tied yourself to the buoy." Did he? Or was someone else there to do it for him? Had he passed out like Luke? Had his guilty conscience been filling in the blanks in his memory?

During my sleepless night I'd tried to connect the dots, but there were too many gaps in the account. It seemed to me the something missing might be *someone*. Was there someone else on that boat, or had Luke revived and taken off without Nate? If that were true, where was the Jane Anne now?

His eyes flapped open. "Yeah. Who knew that little arts and crafts survival bracelet actually worked?"

I glanced down at his bare wrist. A red scrape adorned the side of his forearm. Why hadn't I noticed that yesterday? What else was I missing?

"You mean you took it apart?"

"It wasn't easy. It was soaked. I was soaked. I used my teeth before they started chattering, but even then, I thought I'd pull out my front ones before I got those knots out." He sighed. "I didn't want to take the chance I'd pass out like Luke and fall overboard." He closed his eyes and kept them shut, I suspected to avoid my scrutiny. "And I got rescued. Any news on Luke?"

I squeezed his shoulder. "Not yet, but they're all searching."

Guilt washed over me like a seventh wave. It was time

to back off to safer topics and let my nephew rest and heal. I checked into capable-aunt-mode as we turned in the familiar driveway between the sturdy old lilacs. We got Nate settled on my couch and I took a run downtown to restock the fridge. I admit I skulked around the grocery store, trying not to run into anyone who'd ask too many questions.

When I drove past the garage, my car was still in the broken-down zone. What did I expect on a holiday weekend?

I left town and headed down the lane. I breezed into the cottage, put the groceries on the kitchen table, and made it clear I was leaving. "You ought to call your mom and dad."

Nate groaned. "Dad's on a cruise with Penny, I think."

"Yeah, and Mom and Greg are doing some kind of half-marathon or iron woman and man competition or something." If anything, Tasha sounded even less enthused at the idea of connecting with either parent.

"Call them."

"We will," Tasha promised.

I hugged both of them tight and took with me the hurt in Nate's eyes and the fury in Tasha's.

I called my friend Pearl to take me to the ferry landing. On the drive she regaled me with the usual Brier Elementary scuttlebutt. School hadn't even officially started yet, and it promised to be another year of petty politics and manufactured intrigue. I supposed I made halfway intelligible remarks, but what Lois Boyle was doing, rearranging and putting her stamp on my former kindergarten class, didn't interest me in the least.

I spent the ferry ride over to Candle Island squinting across the sun-flashed waves, searching for the slightest movement, the smallest bit of spindrift. Nothing except shags and gulls, porpoise and seals, boats off in the distance, and the small islands and buoys.

I wasn't sure which buoy was Nate's, or even if we were anywhere near it. I didn't know the location of Hackett's Island, but it brought to mind Jacey and her island. Perhaps they were one and the same. Finding out would be my first order of business as soon as my feet touched the island ledges. The second nipped at the heels of my conscience—finding out who started the smear campaign on Nathaniel.

When the ferry docked, I hurried off and walked to the town pier. Summer-Pastor John Hersey was speaking to a larger crowd than yesterday. I slipped toward the back of the gathering just as they collectively bowed their heads. As he prayed for the lost and the searchers, my mind and furtive glance wandered.

Some visiting tourists stood reverently nearby. Others gawked. Most were intent on their holiday fun, bursting out of the nearby restaurant, chattering and laughing, ignorant of the local disaster. Through half-closed eyes I scanned the crowd and noticed Olivia and a squirming Jacey up beside the pastor. How could I get the child alone for a few seconds with Olivia's death grip on her arm?

I echoed the corporate "Amen" with a silent apology for my wandering thoughts and sidestepped through the crowd toward the pastor. I ignored a few sympathetic looks and glared down a few accusing stares. I shook John Hersey's hand. "Thank you for being here."

He offered a grim smile. "Gwen. Nowhere else I'd rather be, and no better place to be than at the throne of Heaven with our needs."

"Oh yes." Olivia curled her hands onto John's arm and leaned against him, setting Jacey free for the moment.

"Olivia, would you like me to take Jacey for a walk so you can have a moment with the pastor? That is, if both you and Jacey are okay with it." It came out rushed, as if I had ulterior motives. *As if?* Who was I fooling?

Olivia gently blotted her tears and sniffed. Whatever she had on for eye makeup must be industrial strength. Even in her distress, no streaks, no runs, no errors, no panda eyes. She looked like a million bucks.

"Oh *could* you?" she asked in a wobbling wail. "You be

good, little Missy!" She shot the young girl a narrow-eyed glower. There was still steel in the magnolia.

"What do you think, Jacey? Want to take a walk and get an ice cream? We won't go very far so you can stay in sight of Olivia."

She nodded, but the drop-dead look she shot me wasn't encouraging. I held out my hand and Jacey left me hanging long enough for me to take the hint—she wasn't happy with me; as if her dark scowl hadn't already said it for her. At last, she reluctantly slipped her cold little hand in mine. I held it gently but firmly and we walked off the dock and over to the small white-and-teal trailer parked by the side of the road. Pop's Not so Famous Ice Cream lived up, or down, to its name; but located just beyond the ferry landing, it got plenty of summer business.

"Pop" Clyde Seeger had an ongoing dispute with some in Coveside who claimed his seasonal business blocked traffic and delayed ferry loading and unloading, but since the ferry was just now pulling away from shore, all was well.

"What would you like?" I asked.

Jacey turned those stormy eyes on me. "Can I have whatever I want?"

"Sure." I wasn't above bribery.

"I want a hot fudge sundae with peanut butter cup ice cream and a cherry on top."

I nodded to the gawky teen manning the window. "Make that two," I said, then mouthed "and make them small." He nodded and smiled.

"Where did you go?" Jacey demanded, startling me out of my whirling thoughts of how to thaw her frozen heart enough for her to throw a little trust my way before the ice cream melted.

"I went to the hospital with my nephew."

"Oh."

"Have you been here since last night?"

Jacey shook her head. "Moo made me go home and go

to bed."

"Who stayed with you?"

She shot me a thundercloud look. *Wrong question.* Maybe Olivia had gone home with her, but I doubted the drama queen could stay out of the spotlight of this unfolding trauma for a moment. It wasn't a charitable thought, especially at a time like this. I pushed it from my mind and focused on my little charge.

The ice cream came, and I was given the chance to back peddle as I paid for our sundaes. We sat at a nearby table with the skeletal remains of an umbrella sprouted overhead. The wind slapped the few annoying shreds of faded yellow canvas directly above me. I waited while Jacey played with her whipped cream and cherry, finally popping it into her mouth.

I took a different tack, I hoped. "Did anyone go out to your secret island and look for your Grampie yet?"

She shook her head and stabbed her plastic spoon into the frozen treat. "No. If they did, they would've already found him."

"Good point." I let the import of her words sink into her own stubborn little brain while I indulged my sweet tooth. It might not be the best hot fudge sundae, but I never met ice cream I couldn't eat.

Who did I know that could get the name out of Jacey? The rumor of Nate's treachery had no doubt made the rounds. From some of the cold shoulders and dirty looks in the crowd, not a single likely candidate came to mind.

Pondering our situation, I looked down the main road while we ate in silence. Apart from her missing grandfather, Jacey didn't appear to have a wide circle of friends here, either, except for perhaps Luke's ex-best-friend Kendall, and Olivia's persona non grata, Laverna Jordan.

I wasn't sure what was going on between the two men, or the two women, but with Olivia's blond hair in view against the sparkling-water backdrop, I didn't dare risk taking Jacey up to Barb's on the off chance of speaking with Laverna. That left Laurel Shaunessy Jones as the likely choice; Jacey's favorite teacher. She and Ron had come back from the hospital late yesterday but, with the search on, I hadn't given them a second thought.

I should go visit the young couple, but it was hardly appropriate to kidnap Jacey and bring her along when they were dealing with the emotional miscarriage.

"How's the ice cream?"

"Good. Thanks. Moo always makes me get a cone."

"Cones are good, too."

"I hate cones so I have a scoop in a bowl."

"Smart. I used to hate cones, too, but one day I tried some of my dad's sugar cone and I liked it. I don't know how that happened."

She stared right through me; on purpose, I suspected. "I don't have a dad. He died."

Way to stumble into all the conversational mine fields at once. "That's too bad. My dad is gone, too."

"But you're old." Jacey looked me over as if to verify the obvious.

Touché. "Yes ... yes I am. But—" *you still have your grampie*. I bit my lip to stop the cruel half-truth from escaping.

"I don't care about my dad." The little girl shrugged her delicate shoulders. "'Cause I've got Grampie."

I nodded. *I hope so*. He'd already been missing for too long to hold out such unbridled hope. It had been twenty-four hours since anyone had spoken to the Jane Anne. If it seemed a lifetime to me, how much more to Olivia and Jacey? I had to try. "Too bad we don't know where to look to find him."

"I do. I could find him, but he's hiding."

"Hiding?"

"From Moo, I think. They had a fight." She stirred the remaining half-inch of ice cream into a light brown soup.

"He's waiting for me to come to the island so we can take the boat and get away."

"How are you going to get there?"

Jacey chewed a stray piece of hair that had escaped from her ponytail. I let her chew on the possibilities for a minute. "Well maybe I could row across Devane's Rip in the old dory."

"Jacey, you little Jane-bug, what are you up to?"

Providence? I'll say! Laverna Jordan marched toward us, lugging a sack of onions on her hip. Jacey jumped up from her seat and threw her arms around her. "Mimi!"

I nodded to the woman as the child buried her face into Laverna's waist. She set down the onions and her dark eyes met mine. "Thought you'd be over to the hospital."

Talk about minefields. As the proprietor of Barb's, Laverna knew everything that went on, especially all the island gossip. "I was, but my nephew got released this morning."

"How's he doing?" She stroked the girl's hair.

"He's got pneumonia, but he's going to be okay. Thanks for asking."

She nodded. " 'Bout time we got us some good news around here." She tossed her chin toward the changing human mosaic on the town wharf. "Don't listen to some of them. Been there with my own boy. They got nothin' better to do than run their mouths about anything and everything."

"Thank you."

"Thanks for looking out for my granddaughter. Did you say thank you to Gwen for the ice cream?"

Jacey wiggled around until she was facing me as she leaned against her grandmother. Laverna's Rosie-the riveter arm rested around the girl's neck and shoulders. Why hadn't I seen it before? The hair color, the set of the chin? And speaking of stubborn jaws, I set mine. Now or never.

I never hold with telling tales out of school, but when lives are at stake, I make an exception. "Jacey tells me she knows where to find her grandfather." The tattle earned me a frosty blue glare and a pout from the little one.

"That so?" Laverna didn't spare me so much as a glance. She looked down at her granddaughter and chucked her under the chin until the girl craned her neck back and looked up. "What do you know?"

"I ain't telling."

"Jacey Jane Faraday, that ain't no way to talk and you know it. None of this sass. You tell me right now." She spun the child around and went down on one knee so they were nose to nose.

"He's on our island waiting for me."

Laverna pulled her into a crushing hug and looked up at me, chin resting on Jacey's head. "Ahhh." She rapidly blinked her eyes but a tear escaped and slid across her hollowed cheek. She shrugged and wiped it on her shoulder. "Not this time, Jane-bug."

"But he promised," came the petulant whine.

"I know he did. You know what? You haven't brought me one of your angel rocks today, have you?"

Jacey stepped back and shook her head, her ponytail dancing.

"Think you could find one right down there?" Laverna pointed to the small span of rocky shore beyond the ferry landing.

Jacey nodded.

"Okay, you go on and look, but stay where I can see you."

"I will."

Laverna pulled the girl close and whispered in her ear. Jacey nodded and smiled before she turned and ran for the rocky stretch, feet and hair flying. Laverna shook her head.

I wished this carefree moment would never come to an end for the little girl, but I knew, as did the woman who rose to her feet and eased into the seat across from me, that darker times were coming. "Kids always remind us of sunshine," I murmured.

Laverna's rough hand gripped mine in a human vise. "I need to ask you a favor."

I stared into solemn dark eyes—hers narrow; mine, no doubt, big as hubcaps. "Me?"

"Just hold on until I have my say."

"Okay."

She pointed her chin toward the shore where her granddaughter bent to pick up a treasure, totally absorbed in her search. "I ain't got much time, so here it is. Will you help me get my granddaughter back if Luke doesn't come home?"

Of all the things she might have said ... "Why me? I mean, we don't really know each other."

"That's why. And another thing, you don't sugarcoat it."

I shook my head, trying to dislodge the confusion from my brain.

"I know more about you than you think. Been working with Dot the past few weeks."

I groaned. "It seems like that would be all the more reason not to involve me."

"Nope. I know Dot. Feel like I know you. Olivia don't want Jacey. I *do*, and she needs me." She dropped the load of common sense like the sack of onions.

I nodded. "Yeah, she will."

"I don't know what's coming, but I need to be ready. That little girl's all I have."

A million questions flashed in my brain like a fourth-of-July sparkler. Where was her son? What about Jacey's mom? Where did I fit in? I bit my lip to barricade them in a safe place. "Okay." I let the one word slip out. I couldn't keep it in, even if it was a promise that promised unknown heartache.

She waved. Jacey waved back and started toward us. *Talk fast!* "Jacey always talks to me about Luke being on that island."

Laverna shook her head. "She's not one to carry on

about things, but I imagine she's just trying to cope with Luke's disappearance the best way she knows how, same as all of us. Wishful thinking."

"Do you think there's any truth to it? She's seems awfully determined, and she's convinced me."

Laverna gave my fingers a painful squeeze before she let go and sat back. "Thank you. Whatever happens, thank you."

I was losing traction and time. "Do you know where she's talking about?"

"Sure, everybody knows her 'secret island.' "

Not me!

"It's Stub Island. Been in the Faraday family forever, but with his Uncle Tyner passing a year ago spring, it became Luke's lock, stock, and castle. Luke built Jacey her own little camp out there a year or so ago."

So much for secrets, but what if no one looked because they assumed someone looked? "Maybe someone should check it out. Is it off Faraday's Mistake?"

Laverna shook her head while I mentally shook mine. You'd think the Faradays would live in the cove that bore their name, but no, that'd be too easy.

"No, straight across Devane's Rip over by Luke's house. Somebody would've checked it out already. 'Sides, if Luke was there, he could yell across the channel."

Now who was indulging in wishful thinking? If Luke was there, he might not be in any shape to move, let alone yell.

She dashed a tear from her cheek. I'd gone as far as I could go on that one. "Do you know who spread the rumor about Olivia and my nephew?" I blurted.

"I got my suspicions."

The girl exploded into our conversation and slammed her little fist on the tabletop. She opened her dirty fingers to reveal three small rocks. The first she picked up and gave to her grandmother. Laverna examined it carefully, traced the small white stripe at the top with her forefinger and smiled. "One of the best ever."

"Here." Jacey plunked a similar rock in my hand.

"It's beautiful. Thank you."

"It's an angel rock. See the halo? Mimi and I always find them. Sometimes we put glitter on the halo and draw eyes and smiles. Angels always smile or sing."

"That's true. I see the angel." I mimicked Laverna's fingertip-gesture and traced the white halo strip around my rock. "I'll put it in my kitchen window so I can see it every day."

"One for me, too." Jacey held hers up to be admired.

"Jacey!"

Laverna and I jumped at the stern caw that came from the pier. Jacey's little body stiffened. She stuffed the rock into her jeans' pocket before she slid onto the seat and leaned against her grandmother's side.

"I've got to get back to the wagon."

"Take me with you," Jacey pleaded.

"Not today. You be a big girl for just a little bit longer and stay with Olivia."

"But Mimi..."

"Suck it up, Buttercup. You mind what I say and I'll have a talk with her and see if you and I can't go over to the mainland and do some last-minute school shopping."

"She'll say no. Moo already bought me some stuff for school."

"Don't hurt none to ask. You might need to pick out a few things by yourself."

"Just you and me?"

"Just you and me."

"Promise?"

"Promise." With a quick hug, Laverna rose and hefted the onions in one smooth motion. She was striding off down the road by the time Olivia came huffing up to join us.

"That woman! She's got no right to be sniffing around

here."

Jacey scowled and glared at me.

"She was buying onions for the wagon. Probably would've passed right by but I stopped her to say hi."

"And why would you do a thing like that?"

"She's been kind to my family and friends."

"Your family?"

"Yeah, Nathaniel."

"Nathaniel? I don't believe she even knows him!"

But you do!

"Six degrees of separation, small world, you name it," *And you ought to know!* My nephew's cavalier words became my own.

"Typical. And how is Nate?"

"He's going to be okay."

"Well, that's good for you."

"Yes, it is, and I'm very grateful for everyone's prayers and support. I understand you know my nephew."

"Just in passing. Come along, Missy."

"I don't want to go back to the pier."

"We're not. Come along." Olivia grabbed Jacey's hand, but with the other hand the little girl's spider fingers clutched my wrist in a brief embrace. "Don't forget your rock."

"I won't," I assured her, and was rewarded with a little smile before the pair went off, their squabbling, like the gulls' bickering cries, trailing behind them.

CHAPTER SEVEN

I watched them make their way to the parking lot before I wiped up the dribbles on the table and threw away our trash. I tucked my angel rock in my pocket, my thumb and forefinger rubbing its wave-and-sand-polished surface. Childhood innocence of ice cream, and beach rocks worn by the storms of life ... It didn't seem fair, but the small weight in my pocket was a token to that childhood, and a hard reminder we all had a charge to safeguard the little ones God brought into our lives.

And now this wisp of a girl was in the charge of a vain, selfish, woefully immature woman. And what was I to do about it? Help Laverna get custody of this little waif *if* Luke never came back? How in the world?

It was too big for me to contemplate at the moment. Luke wasn't permanently out of the picture yet, and I'd do well to remember that and not write him off. I gazed out at the silver bright ocean, praying once again for that miracle before I sauntered toward the lot, in no hurry to get there before Olivia's vehicle pulled out and sped away.

I tried to make sense of any of it as I slipped into Vance Jones' BMW and felt under the seat. My questing fingers connected with the keys and brought a smile. Family connections. Maybe that was the answer to all of it— Laverna yearning for her granddaughter and asking a near stranger for help; Olivia's possessiveness of a child she clearly didn't like, but her husband adored; my need to guard a little child from the coming hurt, and protect a nephew from the present hurt of foolish words when he was more than able to fight his own battles … and probably with less temper and more grace than I; and Jacey, sad accusing eyes haunting me, hoping, waiting for her grandfather to come and take her away to their secret place.

I started the car and it hummed with suppressed energy when I slowly bumped up onto the road. I crept past a cluster of tourists and bikes splayed over half the road as they pointed up at the widow's walk sitting high as a crow's nest atop of one of Coveside's old Captain's mansions.

I barely acknowledged the beauty of the intricate architecture, gingerbread trim, and tall narrow windows, as I nosed toward the far side of the island, intent on looking at the charts on the wall of Vance's home office. If Stub Island was in shouting distance of the shore, what was to prevent me from taking a little sightseeing trip this Sunday afternoon?

The closer I got to Blind Man's Bluff, the more the idea grew roots and sprouted Jack-in-the-beanstalk style. I couldn't just sit around; I'd go crazy. I needed to do something, and nothing else came to mind except maybe setting up my soapbox down at the town pier and decrying the slander on my family name. Definitely not in good taste, considering all the folks there waiting and praying for Luke's safe return.

I sent up a prayer of my own as I turned onto the private lane. Dust kicked up behind my wheels, a tribute to the dry August we'd had. I slowed as I passed by Dot's cape, and spotted her son, Ron's, fire-engine-red pickup in the drive. I fought the urge to pull into the yard. Instead, I gunned the engine and sped up the steep hill to the mausoleum. My mind had kicked into high gear as well. Dot was working at Barb's with Laverna. Laurel and Ron were there alone. What better time to visit?

I parked the car in the garage; arriving on foot would be safer. No sense dumping gasoline on the fire by flaunting her late husband's car, if Dot should return home while I was still there. I had no doubt she was aware of us using it so it probably didn't matter, but I'd walk anyway. Wouldn't hurt to pretend I was getting fit.

I hurried into the house and did the StairMaster® tribute up to Vance's office. Heart pounding, head swimming, I studied the chart on the wall while I puffed like a freshly landed trout, a chubby one. This fitness just might kill me. My finger traced the small outline of Stub Island, just a stone's throw from shore on the chart but located nearly the length of the island from Blind Man's Bluff. Still, it wouldn't hurt to take a look.

I headed back down to the library and grabbed a prayer shawl I'd just finished knitting, soft as kitten fur in pastel shades of yellow, lavender, pink, and turquoise. Before I could question my motives, I strode out the door and down the hill as if training for a marathon.

I marched past the outcropping of ledge and the little clearing of goldenrod and black-eyed Susans, without my usual rest to admire their beauty. *No time for reflection, it could derail my whole mojo.* A few minutes later, I arrived at the old Jones' family place. I caught my breath and knocked on the door.

Ron poked his head out, turtle-like, his light brown hair sticking up like a dandelion, his eyelids only half opened. "Is this a bad time?" I whispered.

A wide smile broke out on his broad face as he wiped the sleep from his eyes and drew me into a not-so-gentle bear hug. "I knew you'd come."

"I don't want to intrude. I just wanted to see how you and Laurel are doing."

He released me and his lips settled into a grim line, his eyes shadowed by sadness. "Okay, I guess. She's sleeping a lot, but that's good, right?" He spread his palms in the air. "I mean, when she's awake she gets crying and there's nothing I can do."

"Just being there for each other will help you through it. Here." I passed him the shawl, and, to my surprise, he rubbed it against his cheek, the softness catching on his unshaven jaw. "It's a prayer shawl. Maybe when Laurel's wrapped up in it, it'll bring a little comfort to know she's held close and warm in our hearts and prayers."

He crushed me in his muscular arms once again and sniffed into my hair. Ron Jones, only son of one of the most powerful men of the island, was a sensitive-soul-and-mind in a man's powerful body. That touch of neediness for reassurance didn't help him in establishing his place in life, or in his late father's yacht-building business.

"Thanks, Gwen. I wish..." He sighed and stepped back, looked me squarely in the eye and, though his eyes were moist, I saw a hardness that hadn't been there. He suddenly flicked his glance up and looked past my shoulder to the world beyond.

"What is it, Ron? I want to help, if I can."

His eyes swung back to mine and the steel I'd glimpsed was gone, his gray gaze as soft and changeable as island fog on the water. "I wish Mum could be more like you."

Oh no. Dot Jones and me, alike? Don't go there! This was a relationship minefield I'd be wise not to venture into, but when was I ever that smart? *Tiptoe.* "She loves you and just wants to keep you safe."

"I know." The square beefy hands sketched the air as he grabbed for the right words. "But she's been kinda hard on Laurel, especially after losing the baby."

"Maybe you need to think about getting your own place." *Not my business!*

"That's what Laurel says, but it'd kill Mum if I just moved out and left her alone."

I nodded. Unhealthy as all get-out, but if it wasn't for me they'd be living up the hill. The idea popped into my brain like Edison's exploding test light bulbs. If the three of them moved back to Vance Jones' mansion, they could easily set up separate living quarters and needn't even see each other for days in a house that size.

The thought was so loud and big it threatened to gush out of my mouth like water from a fire hose, but any hint, any word before I got things straightened out with the attorney and with Dot, would only fuel her blazing suspicion and hate, not extinguish it. "Maybe if we all keep our eyes and ears open, a solution will present itself." *Lame.*

"You think so?"

Oh yeah. "I do. I've already got some ideas."

"Like what?"

Sometimes Ron reminded me of my kindergarten students—all curiosity with no guile; not a liability when you're five, but a danger at thirty-five. "They're only half-hatched. Too soon for me to even put them into words."

He grinned. "You always make things better."

I shook my head. "Not always, and you *know* that's true."

He shrugged one shoulder. "Mum will come around eventually."

I couldn't muster up any realistic reply to that fantasy. I had a feeling Dot might "eventually" progress from open hostility to veiled hatred, but it had all the earmarks of grinding ahead at glacial speed.

"Did you just come from the wharf?"

I nodded.

"Any news?"

"Nothing yet."

Ron balled up one fist and tapped it in his open palm. "I wanted to do my part, you know, look for Luke. Dad would've been out there first thing, probably found him, too. He was good at leading the men. They all looked up to him." His fist opened and he scratched one ear then smoothed his thinning hair. "But I can't go now. I can't leave Laurel like this."

I put my hand on his forearm to still his agitated antics. "It's alright. I'm sure everyone understands."

He shook his head. "I don't care if they understand or not. I'm not Dad, and everybody knows it so they don't expect much, but I thought I'd take one of my boats. I know it probably sounds like a Mickey Mouse idea. A plastic boat in a bathtub, that's what Dad would say about it, but I thought I could sail along the shore of the island, maybe see something, maybe find Luke or his body. The others are all out on the water searching, but things wash in with the tide all the time." He clasped my hand. "It'd be a small thing, and nobody'd know unless I found something but *I'd* know. You know what I mean?"

I nodded and sent a gentle squeeze back to his meaty calloused hand.

"I have to do something. The Jones' family has always helped out when there's trouble, and I'm the head of the Jones family now."

He was trying to step up. Good for him, but his words jabbed into my brain. *...it'd be a small thing, and nobody'd know unless I found something* "I could do it. It might be a small thing, as you said, but if you show me how to operate your boat I'd like to try to help, too."

Ron's eyes widened and stared.

"It's not that far-fetched of an idea," I said. "We'd be partners and we'd keep it to ourselves."

"Unless we found something."

"Unless we found something." *Or someone.* I didn't really want to think too long and hard about that possibility or I'd talk myself out of this harebrained scheme.

His eyes narrowed to slits and I could see the resemblance to his mother. I could almost hear the synapses firing like torpedoes as the man in front of me waded into the idea. "Yeah but..."

It wouldn't do for either one of us to give this too much scrutiny. "You've showed me your boats before, and I know how to sail. I grew up sailing with my brothers in a boat my dad built." Had I given it too hard a sell?

"Why would you want to go out?"

"In case you haven't heard, they're blaming my nephew for the whole thing."

"Yeah, I heard. Mum's all over it." He flung his arm toward the wall as if shoving the gossip away. "But I don't believe it. I'd never believe it. I'll bet he's just like you and Tasha."

I could've kissed the boy. Such unadulterated loyalty was priceless, and just what I needed to bolster my fluctuating courage. Of course, I wouldn't be surprised if Ron's mother was the one behind the nasty tale, but I was never one to visit the sins of the parents on the child. "Thank you, Ron."

"I mean it."

"I know you do. So, what do you say we do a little search on our own?"

"I don't know."

I retreated off the granite doorstep and tilted my neck back to the serene azure dome overhead. "It's a perfectly calm day, what could go wrong?"

"You'll stay in sight of the land?"

"Of course."

"Okay, we could give it a try. You got your cell phone?"

I pulled it out of my pocket and smiled. "I'll call if I find anything."

"Okay." Ron glanced over his shoulder and cocked his head, but the house was silent. He slipped out and gently latched the door shut behind him.

"I can get myself off."

"No, I'll help. It'll only take a few minutes."

He was right about that. He loped to the small wharf at the edge of Eyelash Beach, and I hurried to keep pace. Ron's hands were quick and sure as he got the sail up and the tiller in place. "My fiberglass one with the new design is at the boatyard, so you're stuck with the old wooden Pequod. It's slower, but she's earned her stripes. Laurel and I go out hand lining in her and sometimes escape to one of the little islands."

"She's perfect." I meant it. Bright yellow with white trim, it harkened back to the days of peapods and dories, but it was a slicker combination of both with good sturdy lines, oars, sail, tiller and keel. What else did I need?

"Yeah, I love this design. If Les Bigelow would just get off my back and give me a chance! Let me have one small space at the boatyard to set up shop, I could fill that place with apprentice boat builders like that." He snapped his fingers. "It wouldn't interfere with the big yacht orders. In fact, it'd bring in lots of small business and local interest in the long run, but he won't even give it half a listen. Just like my father. Mum always called them peas in a pod."

Leave it to Ron to bring up the Candle Island Yacht Company at a time like this. His father, my dad, the old letter I'd found. It jumped to the head of the line of thoughts in my head. "Has Les Bigelow worked for your dad for a long time?"

"Since before I was born. He isn't exactly a partner in the business, but he helped Dad get started and has been at CIYC ever since."

Maybe Les wasn't the only one who helped Vance Jones get his start, maybe Connor McPhail was a part of it, too. When we found the Jane Anne and Luke, and got Nate out of the woods, then I'd have to find a way to talk to Les Bigelow or Dot Jones or both. A tall order, but not doable today. Ron must've picked up on my vibes. He shook off his business pitch and gave me a sheepish grin. "Sorry. Laurel says I get crazy when I talk about my boats. I'd better get back to the house. I don't want her to wake up all alone. I need to be there."

"Yes, you do. I'm sorry to keep you so long."

"Are you kidding me? With Old Doc Beckett off for cancer treatments, I don't know who to talk to about some of this stuff. Thanks, Gwen." He tossed me a lifejacket from the small shed on the shore and watched like an old mother hen while I put it on and fastened it. "Are you sure you'll be okay?"

"I'll be fine." I stepped into the boat and had to grab the side to keep my balance. "I got this."

"I'll cast you off." He untied her and gave the Pequod a hefty push away from the wharf.

Legs unsteady, I crashed down on the seat and hoped it looked like I knew what I was doing as I grabbed at the oars, shoved them in the oarlocks and started rowing out to sea. "Thanks!" I called.

He stood on the shore, hand raised, and shouted something about the sail.

"Okay!" I figured that ought to cover the answer to any comment or question. When I cleared the nearby ledges, I boated the oars and concentrated on catching the gentle breeze that came off the cliffs of Blind Man's Bluff behind me. The sail flapped and slapped me as I fussed with the line and groveled over to the tiller. It had been a while since I'd been in a small sailboat ... close to twenty years?

It didn't pay to do the math at times like this. Factor in the small omission that I'd only sailed on lakes, never on the ocean; I shook my head as the sail fluttered before finally catching the breeze. Boat sailing? Like riding a bike ... I hoped.

The breeze took me at a good clip, but I found myself heading out to sea. I glanced back at the wharf but there was no sight of Ron. Eyelash Beach was already partially hidden by the rock outcropping, now behind me as well.

I tried to relax and get used to the feel of the boat under my hands. Except for the knowledge I needed to tack toward land immediately, I thought things were going well. The water had more of a chop to it as I cleared the small point and left the Jones' cottage in my wake. No worries, I could always let down the sail and row to shore.

I glanced over my shoulder at the rock ledges rising sharply along this stretch of shoreline. I brought the boat around until the sail went slack. I tried to ignore the tug and slap of the canvas as the Pequod bobbed in the wavelets and I formulated a plan. In spite of my fantasy of going to Stub Island, that wasn't an option today. It was pure stupidity. I had no business and no skills to take this small craft that far from homeport.

Ron had the right idea. If I just cruised along the shoreline for a short while, searching for Luke's cooler or anything from the Jane Anne, *please don't let it be a body,* that was the best I could hope for in offering a small token of help. Although "cruised" wasn't exactly the right word. It was more like slopping sideways and being pushed away from shore.

The breeze tangled my hair against my cheek, obscuring my view of the cove on my left. Might be best to get rid of the sail now and row to the cobble beach to get my bearings. The breeze was picking up and every moment I delayed was going to hurt me in the end. I was far enough out right now to test my rowing skills.

I quickly undid Ron's tie-off and dropped the sail with a clumsy bonk, fending off the boom and heavy canvas attack with a stiff arm. I gathered it up and gave it a messy wrap before clacking the oars in the oarlocks and striking out for the beach.

I pulled with a will, a niggling fear lending frantic iron to my back and arms. This was one of the stupidest things I'd done in a while. I'd be okay, but I'd pay for it tomorrow. I could already feel the quiver in my shoulder blades but I didn't stop. With each stroke I felt the Pequod slice through the water as I leaned forward and pulled back once more with all my force. I drew in a calmer breath as the boat cleared the ledges on my left and I hit a lee from the wind. The beach was ahead of me, close enough so I could ease up and coast for a moment. Although now that I was here, I was rethinking my decision as I tipped back my head and surveyed the rock cliffs hedging the pocket cove. I wasn't going to be able to walk along the shore to get out of here, and rowing or sailing back wasn't likely to happen either.

Smart move! Now they'd be searching for two instead of one. I took one more pull with the oars and let the boat drift as I punched in Ron's number on my cell. Nothing! Reception on the island could be sketchy and it didn't take a rocket scientist to know my rocky surroundings weren't helping.

I heard a horn behind me and turned. A familiar white boat pulled into view at the mouth of the cove. Relief mingled with self-disgust. No way did I want to be rescued, especially by the Semper Paratus, but fools and beggars and all that.

Before I could turn the Pequod around, Scotty was barking orders. He lowered a small Zodiac and was behind me in a matter of minutes. "Beach the boat," he commanded as he idled past me to the shore.

I nodded and rowed hard until the keel ground on the rolling rocks. Scotty's waiting hands hauled the Pequod higher, grabbed the rope and tied it to a dwarfed gnarled spruce that grew out of a fissure at the foot of the rocky cliff.

As I stepped out on shore, he took my hand and guided me to the Zodiac. Without a word he shoved off and ferried us out to his boat.

The efficient ex-coast guardsman got us both on board with no fuss, but a boatload of guilt and shame off-loaded with me. I waited until we were underway before I ventured into the chilly silence. "Thank you."

He gave a curt nod, neck as stiff as a woodpecker, his eyes on the waters ahead of us.

"I'm sorry." Why was I talking in "One fish, two fish" sentences? Because I was an idiot and we both knew it. At least he had the good sense not to call me on it, but I wished he would. "Say it! I deserve it."

Finally, he looked over at me, his blue eyes narrowed to slits. "Davy Jones' Locker! Do you know how close you came to being another Luke Faraday?"

"You found him?"

"No! Look out there." He jabbed his finger off across the waves. "Nothing. Nothing to stop you from drifting away into oblivion. Nothing to save you. Nothing to drink. Nothing to eat. A slow death if you're lucky."

I gripped his arm. "Hey! I know. I get it already. You can rake me over the coals later. Shouldn't you get back to the search?"

He gave me one last glower before he thankfully turned his gaze back to the helm. "I'm not taking you on the search."

"I get that, too." Guilt had bubbled over into defensive anger. I wasn't proud of any of it, but sometimes I had to let the blooming idiocy run rampant and get it out of my system. Hopefully soon. "Just drop me off and I'll walk back."

He shook his head. "You saw how that worked out. Wait'll I get my hands on Ron."

I glanced down at his white knuckles clenched around the wheel. "It wasn't Ron's fault."

"It's his boat and you didn't steal it."

"I might have. I might have been going to Stub Island to check it out because a certain guy wouldn't go there."

He cut the throttle and turned to face me. "If a man speaks in the middle of the ocean and there's no woman to hear him, he's still wrong, eh? Not this time. You're not gonna put this on you and me. He had no business getting you out here in his little teacup."

"It's my fault."

"And don't think I don't know it, but Ron never should've let you go wherever in blazes you were going. And where exactly was that?" He raised one rusty brow and it disappeared under his cap.

Might as well confess and flounder my way out of my freefall into the quicksand of self-loathing. "He wanted to live up to his father's..." I cleared my throat, trying to dislodge the tremor of sanctimonious excuse I heard in my too-fast ramble. "His family's legacy and help in the search for Luke. He was going to take out the Pequod and just search the shore for any trace of the Jane Anne, but he couldn't leave Laurel alone."

Scotty shook his head. "And he called you to take a look for him?"

"Not exactly." Confession might be good for the soul, but keeping it as vague as possible might be better for my flattened self-esteem.

"I get the picture, but I'm going to pin his ears back when we get in." I opened my mouth, and he closed me down. "Don't say it. He's a grown man, he doesn't need you to look after him. He's already got Dot, and that's more than enough ball-and-chain for any guy."

He took off his cap and ran a hand through his graying auburn buzz cut. I blinked and took in his usually-clean-shaven grizzled jaw. The haggard beard, the shadows under those sharp eyes, popped my anger like a needle to a balloon. It didn't occur to me until much later that I didn't look a whole lot better. But at that moment, all I knew was I'd sunk to a new low. "Look, I *am* sorry, but this isn't the time or place. You can ream me out six ways to Sunday when this is over. I deserve it. For now, just dump me off wherever. I deserve that, too. And do what you've got to do."

I looked at the sky. Mackerel clouds had floated up from the horizon, creeping toward the afternoon sun ball. The breeze continued to strengthen; a storm was likely coming and that upped the need to find Luke now. "I'll take you back to the pier. Can't do anything right now. I'm waiting on Kendall."

I glanced around the tidy craft. "Where is he?"

"MIA. Typical Kendall. He's supposed to be getting one of his jury-rigged contraptions that he says will help locate the Jane Anne, but I can't locate him."

"It sounds promising." In the undertow of his growl my voice was chirpy, my comment superficial and annoying as a bleach bottle floating on the tide.

"If it's true, why didn't he think of it sooner?"

I decided to treat that as rhetorical.

The boat maneuvered closer to the coastline. Scotty thrust a pair of binoculars into my hands, and I scanned the shore. My shoulders burned and my eyes smarted by the time we neared the end of the island, and I'd only been at it for a short while. My heart ached for everyone. What if they never found Luke or the boat? "What if Luke doesn't want to be found?" I blurted.

"And why would you think that?"

Olivia! I turned to him and shrugged. "I don't know. Maybe he made sure Nate was safe on the buoy before he took off."

Scotty shook his head. "Nope."

"Nate thought he heard the boat engine start. Don't you think it's strange there's no trace of the Jane Anne?"

"Here we go again. What is it with you thinking everyone's cutting out of their life and assuming a new identity?" He gave me a grim smile, more like a grimace. "Look, this is what we know. Nate wasn't sure of anything that happened. Your nephew was in rough shape."

"I know, but—"

"The North Atlantic is strange and unforgiving. Sometimes you can't believe what you see and there's no reasonable explanation for anything, but that doesn't make what goes on out here out of the realm of reality." He sighed and pointed. "There's Stub Island." He pulled out from the shore and bypassed the boiling channel of water that ran between the larger Candle Island and the smaller oblong one. Instead of scanning the rocky shore of Stub, I gazed back across Devane's Rip. I spotted the roof of what might be Luke and Olivia's place poking up through the spruce trees.

Laverna's words jumped to my mind, *"If Luke was there, he could yell across the channel."* And so he could. None of it made any sense, but I wasn't inclined to blame it on the unpredictable waters lapping against the shore. There was too much weirdness in Nate's experience to give the ocean all the blame.

"What are we doing here?" I didn't feel any triumph at finally getting my wish. In fact, a whirlpool of guilt sucked at my spirit. Scotty had been on air-sea rescue for decades. I was a stranger to this place and had no business assuming I knew anything.

The answer was slow and held a hint of sarcasm. "Leaving no stone unturned. Check the rocks."

I scowled at him before I lifted the glasses to my eyes. "I don't appreciate you humoring me." Or me being the butt of some perverse joke.

I glanced over and he pretended to look over my head and scrutinize Jacey's island. I held my tongue in the silence and outwaited him. "See anything?"

"No." I wanted to strangle him with the cord from the binoculars, but I'd already proved my brainless side in spades today. No point in more airing any further gaps in the gray matter.

My eyes roved back from the shoreline. Nothing but rocks and evergreens. I focused my search into the trees looking for Jacey's camp. "No need for the silent treatment. I was coming by here anyhow to see if Kendall's over to Luke's."

A snatch of light blue flickered in a patch of shade. "Wait!" It came out in a squawk. "What was Luke wearing?"

"Blue shirt, why?" Scotty idled down the engine.

"It's probably just a toy or something. Laverna told me Jacey has a little camp out here."

He nodded but circled the boat around and beckoned for

the glasses. "Where?"

I finally zeroed in on the swatch of color and glimpsed yellow as well. My grip froze on the frame, and I swallowed hard. "Right here."

He stooped over and I relinquished my vigil, but I was still tethered to him by the cord around my neck.

He was silent for too long. We stood, arm brushing arm, and I could barely breathe. Finally, he grunted, handed me the binoculars and took the wheel. The boat surged forward, and his profile was set in stone.

"Well?"

"Unknown, but it bears checking out. Luke's got a buoy over on the other side of Stub. We'll tie up and take the Zodiac over."

CHAPTER EIGHT

I clenched my jaw, my fists, and any other body part that had enough muscles to manage the stress. Scotty suggested I stay on the boat, but he was all action and didn't have the time or inclination to enforce his request. Besides, I'd asked for this, hadn't I?

Moments later, he beached the Zodiac on a natural-sloping flat rock, helped me out and pulled it up from the rising tide before he looked at me. "If you're set on coming, stay behind me and do what I say."

"Understood," I croaked.

Scotty's long stride made staying behind him a given. We marched along a narrow trail, the exposed spruce roots threaded across the beaten soil and ledge like varicose veins. The air smelled of sun-warmed needles and mossy earth, acrid and tinged with the sting of the running tidewater.

I caught a glimpse of what must be Jacey's camp ahead of us ... a good-sized shack, its shingles weathered gray, a small window, and a faded Jolly Roger flag hanging off to one side of the pink door.

Scotty pivoted sharply to his left and put a hand behind him to still my progress. His fingers barely grazed my arm before he was off. "Stay here." He ducked under a spruce limb and hustled down a rocky slope toward the shoreline, out of sight.

I purposely tore my eyes from my companion's

vanishing back and took a step toward the small shelter. Now that I was here, my brash plans torched and incinerated under the cruel stubborn heat of life's short wick. I bowed my head and stared at the sun-dappled yellow lichen settled timelessly on the rock beneath my sneakers.

I should pray or do something, but I couldn't think, couldn't move, could only wait; my mind circling the drain. I inhaled such shallow breaths I nearly suffocated, yet I feared disturbing the tranquility of the scene. Paralyzed—the sough of the breeze above me, the murmur of waves surrounding me, and the clear bright call of a nearby chickadee only enhanced the moment of being separate from time as the world spun under my feet.

My mind dimly registered the tread of his boots, the clack of a rock spun loose, and I forced myself to slowly turn as my companion emerged from the trees. I opened my mouth but no coherent sound emerged.

Scotty shook his head, his face grim, and put his hand on my arm. "Let's go." This time he directed me ahead of him as we traversed the path to the beached Zodiac.

Neither of us spoke until we were back aboard the larger vessel and Scotty pulled out his cell phone.

"Did he drown?" I had to ask.

"No." The answer, though spoken in a normal tone, hit my ears as a shout in response to my whisper. His weathered tan couldn't hide the sagging defeat and pallor that marked his weary features. "I've got to make some calls ... call in the boats and call out the troops."

I nodded and left him in the wheelhouse alone. I trudged to the stern and studied the shoreline—a rugged wharf, a small strip of mowed grass, and the gravel road curving out of sight behind a large grouping of cedar trees. Beyond those trees was a home with a little girl and a wife, their hearts and lives about to be shattered.

I leaned my elbows on the rail, hunched over, and stared at the water below, my murky image distorted in the passing floatilla of seaweed and spindrift. The engine started and thrummed beneath my feet. I turned robotically and walked back to the man standing at the helm. "You okay?" he asked.

I nodded, but it wasn't true. What if that had been Nathaniel? I was so euphoric my nephew was safe in my home in Bookerton—that clamoring thought drowned out all others. Today was an island community's sorrow for one of their own. I shared in that, but it wasn't a deathblow to my heart. What kind of person reacts that way to a life cut short? A fluish mishmash of guilt and relief churned inside me and I was sickened by my shallow response to the tragedy.

"You sure?" Scotty wasn't helping. His warm hand on my arm only served to flay my already-bruised-and-bloodied conscience.

I shook my head. He put his arm around me and drew me against his side. I felt like a wimp. I *was* a wimp and a horrible person.

"I called Ron and let him know where he could find his teacup."

"Oh." I'd forgotten all about that episode. *Get it together, Gwen!* "Thanks."

"And you'll be happy to know I didn't call him on the carpet ... yet. Thought I'd slap him upside the head in person." His arm tightened but I couldn't look at him.

I nodded and stared out at the narrow strand of Sandy Beach as Scotty piloted the craft around the butt end of Candle Island.

"Gwen?"

I shook my head and shifted away from his comforting shelter. His arm fell away, and both his hands rode easy on the wheel. I stared at those strong, calloused hands for a moment. Scotty would always do the right thing; never a drop of doubt. Me?

"I'm a hypocrite." My initial blurt fast deteriorated into a mumble. "I feel so sad for Jacey and Olivia, but I'm so grateful our Nate is safe."

"Nothing wrong with that."

I swatted his arm. "Yes, there is. I'm lower than snake spit."

He flashed me a grim smile. "Snake spit, huh? That's a new low for me. I hate to break it to you, but it sounds about normal to me. Survivor guilt. We all get the 'there but for the grace of God go I' sentiment, but it always comes with a 'thank God I'm not going there today' chaser." He quickly sobered and his eyes fastened on mine. It was an uncomfortable challenging stare but I couldn't break the pull. "False tears won't bring him back. It'd be more hypocritical to carry on about someone you never knew. You never even met Luke."

I glanced down at the deck, at his feet and mine standing braced, steady and safe, and took in a deep breath. His words trickled into my fogged brain whether I wanted them to or not. "Yeah, I did. I met him at the ferry landing just the other day when Kendall came to pick me up."

"What? For all of two seconds?"

"Possibly three or four." Normalcy wrapped its comforting tentacles around us, one word at a time, pulling me back to ordinary life. I hated and admired the man at my side for what he was doing to me.

"So why try to drum up fake grief? You're not the type." Scotty scratched his jaw and his piercing blue glare narrowed. "I've seen more death than I care to remember, but you can't take to heart everyone else's tragedy and take them all home to bed with you. It'll kill you in the long run. All I know is, be compassionate to those who are suffering, and do your best to help get them through it. But there's nothing perverse with being grateful to be alive. There's nothing wrong with you, Gwen McPhail."

His words had built up slow, but now his gruff conclusion struck me like a hammer, and I was the nail head. I couldn't admit he was right. My guilty conscience wouldn't allow it, at least not yet. His efforts did find their mark and pummeled me none-too-gently out of my emotional doldrums. My thoughts were already slogging through self-reproach to pursue unanswered questions. "How did he die?"

It was his turn to shift his gaze and look out to sea. "Looks like he slipped on the rocks and hit his head."

"On dry land?"

"Yeah. His body hadn't been in the water, far as I could tell, but I couldn't disturb anything. I felt for a pulse and that was it."

I closed my eyes at the unbidden image of Scotty bending over Luke's body, but I couldn't go there yet … if ever. I opened my eyes to the dimming sky and shattered the image.

"We've got to wait for the Maine State Police Crime Scene Investigations unit to come and do their thing."

Better to focus forward than back. I made the mental leap. "But how did Luke end up there? I mean, where's the Jane Anne? And why didn't he just holler across Devane's Rip and come home?"

"Whoa, hold it!" He rubbed the furrows in his forehead with the heel of his hand. "Glad to see you've recovered your gift for gab. I was worried there for a couple seconds."

"Hey, it's your fault! You shouldn't have done such a bang-up job of talking me out of my guilty conscience."

"I'll remember that in the future."

I ignored his droll comment. "But it *is* odd. Doesn't it make you wonder?"

"No. If *we're* smart, *we'll* let CSI handle it from here. The Coast Guard's on their way to secure the scene until the investigators arrive, so our part's over and done with. No one's allowed to go over there."

"And you're driving this point home because..."

"Because I know you."

"You *think* you know me. Didn't you just say we should do our part to help out?"

"I meant send them a sympathy card, bake a casserole,

let Olivia cry on your shoulder."

"I got the first two covered. She's got people a lot closer than me to do the crying-on-the-shoulder bit, but there's got to be more to this whole thing than meets the eye. And don't tell me it's the mysteries of the North Atlantic. I don't believe an albatross picked up Luke from the bridge of the Jane Anne and dropped him on his head on Stub Island. Nate was second guessing himself before we found Luke, and he's right. Something strange went on out there."

I covered my face with my hands in an effort to school my thought. When I came up for air, Scotty had that infuriatingly patient look on his face, the one I used when I talked with a wayward student. "I'm not sure how Nate's going to take it. I owe it to him to find out the truth."

"This is exactly what I'm saying. There are professional 'truth finders' on the way. Leave it alone."

"They'll ask you questions."

"Maybe, but only about finding the body. This is their get. We're completely out of it."

Our arrival at the wharf tabled our discussion, but the heavy burden of telling Nate and Tasha loomed large on my horizon. Better to hear it from me than get the news of Luke's death secondhand, but I needed to do it in the privacy of my own space. Not here.

As soon as we tied up, a Coastguard guy approached and gave me a hand out of the boat before he leaned back in and shook Scotty's hand. "I'll see you later," I said.

"Wait, Gwen. I'll take you home," Scotty said.

Kendall stood down the dock talking with Old Stin. "That's okay. You're busy. I'll see if I can hitch a ride."

"Gwen." Scotty's voice was half-captain's reprimand, half-compassionate friend.

"No, I'm good. I'll catch up with you later."

As if on cue, Scotty's grandfather turned toward me and beckoned me over. His shock of white hair rose like a fright wig in the wind. "That grandson of mine knows his onions.

Who would've thought Luke was within spittin' distance of his house? Don't make a lick a sense."

Amen to that!

"Right peculiar if you ask me." Kendall shook his head.

Obviously, I'm not the only one to question the circumstances, Mr. Scott!

Kendall's lank hair clung to his skull, and he strangled his cap in his hands. Like Scotty, he was unshaven, sallow cheeked and hollow eyed. "I've got to go down there and deliver the news."

"Maybe you should have someone go with you," I said.

Kendall shook his head again, tears rolling down his sunken cheeks. "Me and Luke were always there for each other. Like brothers. No way I won't be there for his family." He left without another word.

And I was fussing over telling Nate and Tasha. I didn't envy him. Didn't envy anyone here today.

Old Stin and I watched him go, bowed over, his gait unsteady. "Hittin' him hard. Hits all of us when somethin' like this happens. No guarantee when you go out that you'll be comin' back in."

I nodded. "Would you mind taking me home?"

"Be my pleasure." In a gesture so like his grandson, Old Stin placed a hand at the small of my back and guided us to his truck.

We made the journey with barely a word. I popped my seatbelt before he pulled to a stop in front of the mansion. The old gentleman turned to me, his hawkish face freezing my fingers on the door handle. "I 'magine you'll be calling that boy of yours."

I nodded.

"Ain't his fault." Old Stin's thin lips disappeared into a scowl.

I nodded again, blinking back tears. His tanned age-spotted hand slid over and covered mine in a rough grip. "I've heard all that flannel-mouthed cock-and-bull baloney.

Been a while since I've defended a Lady's honor and family name, but I still know how. Don't you worry none about that claptrap. It ain't so, and Young Stin and me'll set the record straight and get it all squared away." His snarl and bark was there in every word.

"Thank you," I whispered, and wrapped my arms around this dear man, in spite of the impediments of steering wheel and gear shift.

He patted me on the back. "Go on with you, now."

He wasn't one for tears or compliments, so I sucked up both. I pulled back and managed a trembling smile. *What had I done to deserve such a loyal champion?* "Thanks for the ride."

"Anytime, and you mind what I said."

"Yeah." I opened the door, and he verbally gave me one more pat on the back.

"Don't know if Young Stin'll be tied up for a spell, but I'll be around if you need me."

He'd better quit or I'd lose it. I had all I could do to look at that sweet craggy face and not turn into a blathering idiot. "I know, and I'm right here if you need me."

That produced the familiar saw-toothed grin. "I know. Bye, now."

I stood in the driveway long after the truck disappeared down the hill. PM sashayed up, tail high, and wound around my ankles doing his usual annoying-cat-best to trip me up *if* I ever got moving.

I told myself I was conjuring up the right words but excuses didn't cut it, and stalling only increased the likelihood Tasha and Nate would hear about Luke's death from someone else. Yet if *I* was struggling with survivor guilt, it was bound to be a hundred times worse for Nathaniel. I forced my steps inside, the small gray cat shadowing every stride. I sat in the rocker in the library with the purring pet on my lap and dialed. Tasha answered on the first ring.

"I've got news."

"I heard. Sledge called."

God bless Dr. Sledge Knox. Who said everyone on the island hated my guts! "How did your brother take it?"

"I haven't told him yet. You want to do it?" Her voice trailed up in a hopeful plea.

'Want' was a far stretch but ... "Yeah, okay, how's he doing?"

"Okay. He's been sleeping most of the day, which is normal and good. But I'm so used to him bugging me every minute … it creeps me out a little when I look in on him and he's just lying there."

"Well, it makes me feel better to have you staying there with him."

"Me, too. And Sledge said Luke was found on an island way off from the buoy where they picked up Natey, so that ought to kill the rumor mill."

I thought of Old Stin's gruff promise. "Yeah, I'm sure it will."

"Good, because as much as it pains me to admit it, you were right, Auntie. We both need to stay right here for now. Sledge says they'll manage the clinic without me for a few days."

"Sounds good."

"Hey, I've got Natey right here."

Before I could catch a breath, my nephew's voice came on hoarse and urgent. "They found Luke?"

"His body."

He grunted. "Did he drown or have a heart attack?"

"Neither. Scotty found him on an island far away from where they rescued you." A paraphrase of Tasha's words tumbled out in a rush. "Looks like he tripped and hit his head on a rock on dry land."

"What?"

"I know. It doesn't make any sense. And there's still no sign of the Jane Anne."

I could picture my nephew scratching his head and pursing his lips to one side as he pondered the situation. "Huh! So maybe I *did* hear the boat engine start and take off without me."

"Looks like it."

"Luke wouldn't have done that. Something must've happened."

I'm right there with you, kiddo! It was just like Nate to stick up for Luke, a man he'd only known for a couple of days. Now that the bad news had been delivered, my nerves hit bottom and left my arms and legs heavy but no longer shaky. "There'll be an investigation."

"I'm sure. If I need to be out there, I can come," he said.

"If anyone asks, I'll point them in your direction, but I think you're set for now. Just concentrate on getting well. I'll keep you updated."

"Thanks, Gwen. You're the best."

As I hung up the phone, his familiar words brought back the moment at breakfast less than forty-eight hours ago. Time had rolled over us in a tidal wave, then sucked back into the guzzling sea and left us high and shivering and stunned. Nate's leave-taking yesterday flooded my mind. He'd folded me in his strong arms and promised *I'll be back.*

Had Luke made Olivia and Jacey the same promise?

Regardless of Scotty's logic, guilt crab-walked its way back into the recesses of my heart. I pushed the indignant cat off my lap and hurried to the kitchen. If I sat still, I'd go crazy.

I barged into the kitchen and started rattling the bowls and measuring cups. I'd make something for Olivia, but I wasn't sure what. Jacey was easier. I started with Mama's peanut butter cookie recipe and added some mini milk chocolate chips, knowing it wouldn't stop the sadness but might bring a tiny bit of comfort.

Comfort food. My mind sorted and discarded multiple offerings from mac-and-cheese to lasagna—the staples of bereavement visits and sympathy cooking. Instead, I finally settled on homemade Anadama bread, something they could have alongside the comfort casseroles.

Evening stole over the house, first quiet with spiderweb wisps of fog. After a while I could hear the muffled dripping onto the deck as the moisture collected and slithered off the roof.

The house smelled of freshly baked bread and cookies, but I had no appetite. I fed the cat, left the culinary attempts to cool, and trudged up the stairway to my bedroom. My mind was heavy, nearly as dead in the water as it had been earlier when Scotty found Luke's body. As sluggish as I was, I couldn't settle into a book or a mindless spider solitaire game, or even television, the chewing gum of the brain.

Instead, I sat on the edge of the bed and took out the papers that bore Daddy's strong hand. So much had happened in a few hours; it seemed like weeks since I'd slipped them into this safe place and left my mind to ponder my next move. Maybe this was exactly the type of diversion I needed tonight.

I felt around in the nightstand drawer for some cheaters but came up empty. I'd worn them on my head downstairs last night, but had no urge to go in search of the missing spectacles. I held the missive at arm's length, knowing they weren't long enough, but it didn't matter. I knew what was there. It wasn't like I hadn't been thinking about it.

Talking with Ron today had prodded me to get some concrete thoughts going. So far, Ron had been a trooper under the edicts of his father's strangling will, but he was beginning to chafe under the constant agitation. In spite of what Scotty thought, Ron Jones could use a hand up to get him out from under everyone's thumb, especially his well-meaning over-protective mother, as well as boatyard manager, Les Bigelow, who might as well own the Candle Island Yacht Company, for all his dictator tactics.

I had no doubt Vance Jones' crony would do his best to

box Ron out of his inheritance, just as some said I'd ripped off Ron and Dot by inheriting the mansion on Blind Man's Bluff.

If today taught me nothing, I was well aware life could change mid-heartbeat. And I'd rather figure out the next change before I got blindsided. I stared at the boat schematics until the lines blurred. It was easier to admire the grace and innovation of my father's sketches than dwell on the letter he'd written to my benefactor.

"You okay?"

I jumped a mile when Scotty simultaneously knocked and popped his head in the open doorway. The papers in my hands flew up and drifted to the floor as I stifled a yelp.

"Sorry. I rang the bell and knocked downstairs, but I got nothing. Grampa mentioned you might be a little down so I thought I'd just do a quick check on my way home."

His "way home" was in the opposite direction.

Scotty bent and quickly retrieved the papers. I wasn't so quick at thought retrieval until I saw his sharp eyes glance at the missives.

I wasn't ready to go public. Not yet … maybe never. I shot to my feet and, none too ladylike, snatched them out of his loose grip.

Scotty whistled through his teeth. "Been keeping secrets?" He tilted his head as if digesting the entire contents of my private life.

"It's not what you think." I primly folded the pages and put them in the drawer of my nightstand, pretending to ignore his gaze.

"And you know what I think? Looks like a can of worms to me."

And you're the one who always accuses me of sticking my nose in . . .

"No, it's not like that." What were the chances he'd drop it before I spilled my guts?

"If you say so." He pulled on his ear. "'Course if our

roles were reversed, you might be pressing me for more info, and I'd likely give a little."

"That'd be the day."

He flashed his irritating boyish grin. "Could it be you're hanging onto the past and you're not ready to let go and make the leap of faith into the future?"

A wing-walker jab? Seriously? After all that had happened today? He was probably trying to get me out of my head and, with my ill temper on a slow simmer, he'd succeeded admirably. "You get one question. Shoot."

"Conner McPhail is...?"

"Was my father." The queen should speak so haughtily.

"Ahhh." Scotty turned and strode out the door. "Didn't intend to disturb you. Just wanted to make sure—"

"You could still get under my skin." I trod behind him, nearly stepping on his heels.

He stopped and I prided myself in pulling up short, a paper-width away from his broad back. He turned his face millimeters from mine and sober as stone. "I was about to say, make sure you survived the day."

"If that were totally true, I'd say thanks." I'm sure it had started out that way. Old Stin's promise dumped a bucketful of soothing friendship on my ire. Whose fault was it that I'd been so engrossed in my private thoughts it had taken an atomic bomb to rouse me?

"What's your grandmother's name?" My not-so-subtle change of subject was rewarded with both russet brows tweaking up to his hairline.

"Why?"

"I just thought I ought to know."

"Seems more like a little quid pro quo going on." He threw the comment over his shoulder as he led the way down the grand staircase.

"Have you had any supper?" I asked when we hit the marble chessboard main floor.

He shrugged one shoulder and inhaled. "Smells good. I

might be persuaded, but don't go to any trouble."

"I might be persuaded if you were to answer my question."

"Father or mother's side?"

"Father's."

"Athleen Faye Sullivan Scott."

"Ahhh." I sashayed by into the kitchen, but as soon as I pushed my way through the doors I deflated. I hadn't been here long enough to have much of any good leftovers in the fridge. "I've got some beef stew I made yesterday ..." *when Nathaniel didn't show up.* "...and some homemade anadama ..."

"Like I said, don't go to any trouble on my account."

I turned at the muffled tone and caught him stealing a cookie. "You'll ruin your supper." My mother's words jumped out and I laughed.

He smiled. "I was just testing them." He picked up another and sobered. "For Luke's family?"

"Yeah, the cookies are for Jacey and the bread is for both of them."

CHAPTER NINE

The next morning, I fiddled around the house for as long as I could bear being cooped up inside, cleaning nooks and crannies no one would ever see, dusting blinds—things I only do when I'm avoiding. The house was tomb-quiet, and the weight of the silent dirge crushed my usual urge to sing as I worked.

My patience with my procrastination finally wore thin enough to face up to the task ahead of me. I threw on a nice pink blouse, grabbed my offerings for the Faraday family and headed off toward Devane's Rip. I slowed the car as I drove past the clinic and onto the down slope of Fossett Road. Too soon I came to the dirt driveway leading off to the right, the blue sign unmistakable: Jane Anne Lane pvt.

As I crept down the narrow track through the sun-filtered olive shadows of spruce and fir, I couldn't stop the thought of Olivia, her scarlet lips swollen in a permanent pout. How she must hate this: Luke's boat and the private road to their home all named after his first wife—the equivalent of rural sainthood. Not literally, but close enough.

Jane Anne Faraday ... one woman never to be forgotten in the minds and hearts of the islanders. Certainly made it difficult for anyone breathing to compete with, or replace, such a beloved memory, especially when cancer struck so cruelly and death came too soon. And now Luke, too, was gone and, with him, perhaps, all that was Jane Anne. Except for the stubborn heart of one little girl.

I pulled into a clearing and parked next to Olivia's blue sedan. The house was a two-story saltbox, its clapboards painted smartly white with royal blue trim and matching blue door. To the right of the spacious lawn, on an outcrop of ledge, sat a small stack of lobster traps and buoys mimicking the colors of the house. It was a nice place, well kept landscape, but I noted the trimmed grass with no flowers or lawn art in the yard.

Olivia's pristine painted nails flashed through my mind. I shook off the catty thought and gazed at a gambrel garage overshadowing the side lawn. It was nearly as large as the house. I thought I recognized the pickup parked in the shade of the building. Someone must've brought Luke's truck back from the Coveside lot; one of so many tiny devastating details that can overwhelm the broken heart.

I took a fortifying breath and opened the car door to be met with an assault of frenzied barking. A little yapper dog tore out the house door and raced toward me. Not a man's dog, yet I could picture Luke holding the pipsqueak in his beefy arms, and both of them trailing Olivia around an exclusive clothing store, captives in the wake of her perfume.

The ankle biter's puppy-cut coat was almost blue-white, and I was amazed he/she was allowed outside to get dirt on those feet. The dog jumped up and wiped its paws on my pant leg, so my worries about dirt were quickly transferred.

"Magnolia!"

At the tenor male call, I glanced to the doorstep. Kendall Jones stood there in white undershirt, old jeans, and white socks. He held up a hand in greeting and called to the pet again. "Maggie, get back here!"

I ducked my head into the backseat as Maggie's moist nose snuffled up my calf.

"Go home," I muttered under my breath, but I'd obviously acquired a new best friend as Magnolia cavorted on and between my feet with each dance step we took toward the house.

Kendall finally hot-footed out in his sock feet over the marble-chip walkway and scooped up the dog, but even as he tucked her under one arm, she wiggled, yipped and whined.

"Hold on a sec." He pivoted and none-too-gently thrust her into the house, closed the door, and turned back to me.

"I just stopped by to offer my condolences. How's Jacey doing?"

Kendall shook his head. "Inconsolable. She's holed up in her room. Barely made a peep this morning. Must be cried out. Olivia's a wreck."

"I imagine."

"That's why I'm here." He shrugged. "I don't know what to do, but somebody ought to be around, you know, and look out for them."

Who's he trying to convince? Himself or me? "Yes." I passed him the bag of cookies and bread. "Here. It's not much, but I figured you'd be overloaded with casseroles."

"You'd think, but no one's been by 'cept you." He shook his head and gazed over my shoulder to the quiet yard.

"I'm sure they'll come. Probably everyone's still in shock."

"Doubt it's that way. Olivia never did get on with the folks here. All I know is, if things were reversed and Luke was left it'd be a different story. Folks oughtta get their butts out here and show a little respect for Luke. He lived here all his life."

"Kendall." Olivia shuffled out the door, eyes red-rimmed, the dog hugged to her breast like a heart-attack pillow.

Kendall clamped his lips shut and his eyes held mine begging me for ... what? Help? My silence? I wasn't sure, but even if I'd gotten the visual message, I was uncertain at this moment what to say. The usual platitudes echoed harshly in my brain, almost like a stream of profanity.

"Magnolia woke me." Olivia's voice trembled until her eyes focused. She shot me a glare frigid enough to flash freeze any traces of grief from her ice-princess face. Her breathless whimper escalated to full-blown indignation with a shrill side of wounded sarcasm. "How *dare* you? I would think you'd be the last person to show your face around here. Your nephew will get what's coming to him. If it takes 'til my dying breath, I'll see to it!"

Magnolia's growl added bite to her threat.

Olivia put her claws around Kendall's wrist and choked out a sob before she whispered in his ear. He nodded, placed my food offering on the step, patted her arm and escorted her and her dog back into the house. If I had any doubts about their exchange, the drop-dead look she cast in my direction made it abundantly clear. That worry about conjuring up the appropriate thing to say got yanked right off the table like a barbeque-stained tablecloth.

Kendall's tall lanky form broke our eye contact as he slipped back outdoors. By the time he traversed the steps to the walkway, Olivia had disappeared. "I'll just keep your goodies outside for now 'til things cool off in there."

"They're pretty icy already, if you ask me." If I'd known the dip in temperature at Devane's Rip, I would've worn a winter coat.

Kendall flashed his toothless smile. "You got that, huh?"

"Pretty hard to miss it."

"She'll come around."

"I'm sorry I upset her."

"You didn't. She can't help it. She's out of her head with grief, but don't worry about it." He rubbed his temples then leaned his forehead against his long fingertips.

"What did she mean about my nephew?"

His hand flopped down at his side and Kendall sighed. "Like I said, it's the grief talking."

We weren't going to tap dance around the conversation all day, at least I wasn't. I shook my head. "There was something more than grief talking. She blames Nate. Why is that?"

"She's heart broken, Gwen. She doesn't know what she's saying. She's even let loose on me more than a few times. I don't take it personal."

"That's big of you."

"If I did, I'd never be talking to nobody around here. Everybody says things they don't mean. I've had more than my share of their trash talk tossed in my face. Everybody's got some sort of flea biting them, and every once in a while they gotta scratch and blame it on someone. They get bitten, they bite back." He shrugged. "Like I said, you can't take it personal."

I tried not to take his refusal to respond to my question personally, but my patience had been paper thin when I came. Now, with all this talk of fleas, I was itching for some straight answers. "True."

He rubbed his eyes, and I took in the hollowed cheeks and deep grooves around his mouth. I needed to remember Kendall wasn't the enemy here. He was hurting just as much as Olivia … maybe more. He stretched his neck back in a crane-like movement. "You need some rest," I said.

"No, I'm good. I can rest when I'm dead." He choked on the last word. "Luke used to say that to me all the time. 'You can rest when you're dead,' he'd rant. Funny how things work out, huh? I could kick off and nobody'd miss me, but Luke had it all." He scratched his unshaven jaw. "That's why I'm not leaving them here alone. Olivia couldn't manage Jacey, not in the state she's in."

Was he referring to the state of woman, or child?

"Them two are like oil paint and water, right from the get-go. Never gonna stick to each other. That's why I've got to stick around. Luke would do anything for his girls, and now that's on me. I don't care about the talk. I gotta be here for him. He was my best friend."

Wasn't it oil and water? They might be oil paint and water, but resentment and grief stuck well to each other, and I didn't want them sticking to an innocent five-year-old and tarring her fragile soul. Jacey deserved better than to ... how had Kendall put it? *Have all Olivia's trash talk tossed in her face.* My promise to Laverna stuck in my conscience like a burdock.

Probably not the time, but it wasn't a time for much of anything else. There was nothing I could say to make him feel better, and there might never be a more convenient time for the truth. If Nate was still under a shadow of suspicion, the sooner we got to the truth the better; and I would think that would be so for Kendall, and for Jacey and Olivia, too. "Jacey led me to believe you and Luke had a falling out."

I don't know what I expected, but his hoarse laugh knocked me off-balance. "Happens once a year or so, regular as clockwork. I used to think it was me, the curse of Murphy's law on everything I touched, but it wasn't me." He stared at me with those light eyes, made more intense by the sooty sagging flesh underneath, his angular face sober as the leader of a temperance march. "Luke could be like that. All of a sudden, he'd blow up and I'd just stand clear until the wind direction changed. It always did."

Okay, so now I not only had Nathaniel, Laverna, and Jacey on my conscience, but Kendall as well; but I pressed forward, hoping for some sort of resolution to bring closure for us all. "Until now," I said softly.

Kendall buried his face in his palms and snorted in a deep shuddering breath. He looked up, his eyes wet. "I keep expecting him to come out of the garage there and give me what-for. Never again, eh?"

I shook my head. I knew the feeling of turning when the door opened and expecting the loved one to stroll in and shatter the nightmare of death with light and life, but it never happens. You don't get over the loss; you just learn to accommodate the hole in your heart after the fallen leaves of days and weeks and years pile up and soften the ragged emotions a little.

In my book of grief, it helped to figure out what comes next. Of course, that might not be true in Kendall's case, but the words tumbled out low and scratchy before I exerted the sense to stop them. "What do you think happened? I mean, you and Scotty and a fleet of boats searched everywhere, and no sign of the Jane Anne. Not even an oil slick floating on the water. And Luke right across the Rip within shouting distance. It doesn't make sense."

Kendall scowled. "No, it don't. And him getting cut with that bait knife don't make no sense either."

My ears perked up. "What bait knife?"

"He had a bait knife stuck in his shoulder like he'd been stabbed. That's what's got Olivia all worked up. She says it's Nate's knife, at least the one he would've been using that day on the Jane Anne."

So, Nate wasn't in the clear. And all this time Scotty knew it! *We're completely out of it.* His words taunted, banging around the confines of my skull, leaving my brain black and blue. *We're not out of it! Not by a long shot.* Sympathy for Kendall warred with outrage, and the rage threw a knockout punch. I swallowed hard and kept my voice even, although I heard the traces of a defensive shrill in it. "I thought he fell and hit his head."

"Might've done. I've heard a million different tales, none of 'em probably has a whisker of truth to it."

Maybe not, but I knew what version of the truth Olivia believed. Kendall, bless him, stood in no man's land. Scotty, on the other hand, was standing neck-deep in hot water.

"Well, I'd better get going. Give Jacey a hug for me."

"I'll try, but she's not speaking to anyone right now."

"Maybe she should be with Laverna."

Kendall snorted and a spray of saliva shot out of the toothless gap and hit the white marble stones around my feet.

"Never happen. This morning Laverna give me some corn chowder to bring down. Its Jacey's favorite. Soon's Olivia found out who sent it, she slung it out the backdoor right in front of Jacey. Terrible waste, pure and simple. Jacey ran to her room and locked the door. End of story."

"Well, she can't stay in there forever."

"No worries. I imagine Erica will be over tomorrow and take her off island. It's probably for the best. Olivia needs time, and so does Jacey. Time apart will do them both good."

Amen to that. I could only hope Erica was ready to cope with the loss of her dad *and* the demands of a five-year-old daughter. "I made Jacey some cookies." I nodded toward the bag sitting on the step.

"I'll see she gets 'em. Like I said, I'm here for the long haul."

"Thanks, Kendall. If I can help in any way, give me a call."

"Nice to hear someone say that but, between you and me, until Olivia gets a handle on this, I think it's gonna be just her and me for a while. It's all she can handle."

"Understood, but just the same. If you or Jacey need me, give a call."

"Gottcha. Bye, and thanks Gwen." He retreated and hefted the food bag in a farewell gesture.

I walked back to the car and, as I opened the door, a movement in the upstairs window caught my eye. I looked back at the house and the upstairs curtain twitched. Jacey's pinched pitiful face hovered in the glass. I raised a hand, and she placed her palm on the pane for a brief moment before the curtain swung back into place and she was gone.

My heart broke for the little-girl-lost, and I prayed her mother would come and take her away from here to someplace safe where she'd be happy again and loved.

I slowly opened the car door. The need to honor my promise to Laverna and Jacey, and the need to thrash Scotty, yanked me in opposite directions. Laverna's request smacked me between the eyes, like one of my brother, Evan's, well-aimed snowballs. First things first. My anger could simmer for a while and still be red-hot when needed.

I turned my thoughts to Laverna Jordan as I slid into the driver's seat, latched the door and fumbled for my seatbelt. It was spooky, in a way … almost as if Laverna had known this would happen. But whose mind hadn't gone down this road as soon as the Jane Anne went missing? Laverna had lived with the uncertainty and finality of a son who never returned from overseas, so why wouldn't she have felt the desperate tug of tragedy stalking her family once again?

A knock rapped on the side window, and I jolted, banging my noggin on the car ceiling. I rubbed my scalp and jerked my head to the side to meet Jacey's nose pressed to the glass. Both our eyes wide, my hand released the seatbelt, and it zipped back into its slot. I reached for the door handle, but little hands beat me to it. Jacey opened the door and begged, "Take me with you!"

Before I could open my mouth, Kendall hurried up behind her. "Jacey, come back inside. Gwen's got to go home."

"No!" Her wiry arms wrapped around my arm and held on like a little octopus.

"It's okay," I murmured to both man and child. I looked over the dark head now pressed to my shoulder and into Kendall's frantic stare. "Maybe we could take a little walk."

His eyes darted back toward the house. "I don't know. Olivia's mighty touchy."

Jacey's head swiveled toward Kendall, but she kept her grip on me. "Moo doesn't care about me, and you know it."

"Don't say that, Jay. She loves you. She's just heartbroke over your grampie. We all are. Come on, I'll take you in. Gwen made you some cookies."

Jacey leaned into my side once again. I couldn't stop my arm from going around her thin shoulders and she snuggled into the side hug. "What kind?"

"Peanut butter with chocolate chips."

"You cooked them for me?"

"Just for you. If it's okay with Kendall and Olivia, why don't we take a walk down to the shore and eat some cookies."

"I haven't had lunch."

I shrugged. "Neither have I. We can eat dessert first."

"We could go to Mimi's for lunch first, then have cookies."

"No." Kendall 's gruff retort made the child stiffen. He crossed his arms against his chest, defenses up. "Look, Gwen, don't make this hard on everybody."

"I'm not."

"You'll take me to Mimi's?"

"No." Kendall's light eyes glinted with accusation. "You can take a walk, but only for, say, a half-hour. Oh, and move your car back up the lane."

I nodded. As compromises went, I wasn't going to get a better deal.

"But I want to go to Mimi's!" Jacey whined.

I shook my head. "It's not going to happen today, kiddo, but I say we take what we can get and work on bigger and better things for tomorrow."

She pulled away from me, her dark eyes staring through me. She'd perfected the drop-dead look and I wondered if she'd learned it from Olivia or vice versa.

"Okay," she muttered. "Where're the cookies?"

Kendall scurried back to the step and returned with the bag before Jacey was settled in the backseat. "Remember, a half-hour to the minute. I don't need to be explaining this to anyone," he said. "Your word?"

"You got it." I twisted around to my backseat passenger. "We can keep it quiet, right Jacey?"

She made a lock-and-key motion with her small fingers, and I winked at her as I turned on the engine and put the car in reverse. A moment later we were around the bend. I continued backing until we crossed the entrance to another gravel track I suspected ran to the wharf where Scotty and I had tied up to the buoy the day before.

I pulled onto the left track and was rewarded with our supposed destination in a few hundred feet. I looked out at the sun-drenched stretch of mowed grass to the ledge beyond. *Perfect.* I stopped the car and Jacey was out and running to the wharf before I popped my seatbelt.

I grabbed the bag of cookies and followed more slowly, taking in her small silhouette standing straight as a ruler at the end of the wharf, the empty buoy a cruel reminder as she gazed out to sea ... waiting for her grampie to come home? How much did a five-year-old really understand about death? How much did any of us? We accepted it but, speaking for myself, I never was at ease with it.

I sighed and stepped onto the rough planking. Probably not the best thing to encourage the girl to be keeping secrets from her step-grandmother, but I could look at it as a gift horse or a black mark on a child's soul. I chose the gift horse.

I walked to the end and sat down. Jacey planted her little buns beside me and I was surprised by her trust as she wiggled closer, our legs touching, dangling and swinging over the end of the pier. I knew not to make too much of it. Any port in a storm … and this little girl was in the middle of an emotional typhoon that would change the course of her life forever.

I opened up the bag of cookies and held it out. Her small hand dipped in and grabbed two. She looked up at me as if daring me to reprimand her. At this point, chowing down on a half-dozen cookies wouldn't kill us. It was the least of my concerns.

She downed one in silence. In between bites of the second, she pointed across the water to the rocky shores of Stub Island. "There're people over there."

"Yes."

She shook her head, her ponytail swishing against my

arm. "They shouldn't be there. That's my and Grampie's island."

"I know, but they won't be there forever."

Jacey turned to me and wormed her sticky chocolate fingers into my hand. My fingers gently entwined with hers. "Can we go? You could take me there in the dory."

Your grampie isn't there waiting for you, no matter how much you wish it were so. I glanced at the old wooden boat lying upside-down on the grass. Images of my ill-fated sailing venture flashed and crashed like a lightning storm in my memory. Had I learned nothing from my impulsive stupidity?

"Not today. We promised Kendall we'd come back in a half-hour remember?"

"But—"

"If we don't keep our promise, he won't let us do this again."

"But I wanna go to my island."

"I know you do, but we can't go until they leave. Nobody can go out there until they're gone."

Jacey nodded. "After that?"

"I don't know, but we'll see."

Her small hand yanked out of mine and she pulled away from me. I looked into her upturned face, pale but set in stone—the response of every kid to the dreaded adult "we'll see" panacea.

I put my arm around her but her little shoulders stiffened, resisting the comfort I longed to give. I rested my arm where it was and flipped my other wrist to glance at my watch. "You can sulk if you like, but we don't have time for it. Would you like to send a message to Mimi?"

Her body curved like a spaghetti noodle as she leaned in and looked up into my face. "Are you gonna see her?"

"Yes, as soon as I leave here and, no, I can't take you with me. We promised Kendall, remember?"

"*You* promised."

"Yes, and if I hadn't we never would've gotten the chance to come down here together, so I'm glad I did. Now, do you want me to take a message to Mimi?"

"I can't write you know. I'm only five!"

"I get that."

"I'll just say it and you can tell her."

"Good idea."

"Grampie's in heaven. Kendall said so."

"Yes, I know."

"With your dad?"

I nodded and blinked back tears, and her wiry arms came around my waist and hugged me butterfly tight as only a child can do. A five-year-old comforting me only made me feel worse. I had my father's love and guiding hand into my early forties, and both my grandfathers into my thirties. This little girl had neither father nor grandfather. She'd never again know the blissful security of putting her tiny hand into the comforting power of Luke's strong grip and feeling completely safe.

Jacey shifted her hands to my shoulder and lifted her lips to my ear. "Tell Mimi to come get me. She's supposed to take me school shopping to the mainland. She promised."

"Okay," I whispered back, and planted a kiss on the top of her head. "We have to go back to the house now, but I'll come by tomorrow and tell you what Mimi said."

"Promise?"

"Promise. But you have to be a good girl and stick it out with Olivia and Kendall for a while longer. Can you do that for Mimi and me?"

"Do I have to?"

"Yes."

Jacey nodded. "Okay, if I have to. Suck it up, Buttercup." She gave me a flat little smile very like her grandmother.

"Good girl."

"Can I have another cookie?"

"I made them for you, but you might want to share." I handed her the bag and awkwardly rolled on my knees and got to my feet while my companion jumped up in one lithe movement.

We walked past the car and Jacey tugged at my hand, diverting our feet to a narrow trail winding through a copse of cedars. The shortcut to the house took only a few minutes, but I gratefully accepted the offering of another cookie to assuage my guilt at taking her back to that sad and lonely house.

When I passed her off to Kendall and her sticky little hand let go of mine, I silently echoed her sob as she flung herself back at me and pressed her face into my blouse. I wrapped one arm around her shaking slight frame, stroked her hair and whispered in her ear, "It's okay." Another lie for the present, but I prayed it would be true for the future.

Kendall grew impatient and picked her up bodily. I expected her to fuss but she went limp as a rag doll in his arms. He nodded to me then walked to the house, Jacey's chin on his shoulder, her pale elfin face streaked with tears, those enormous blue eyes fixed on mine.

I waited at the edge of the trees until they disappeared inside the house. I doubled back to the car, failure and guilt nipping at my heels. This wasn't a skinned knee I could kiss and make all better. The BAND-AID® I'd applied was too miniscule for the gaping wound of grief and wouldn't hold for long, so I'd better get busy.

I drove over to Barb's, oblivious to the island's beauty. On this Labor Day, a line of hungry, giddy tourists snaked up to the take-out window. The lot was full, so I pulled up behind cars parked on the sides of the road. I got out and made my decision in a heartbeat. Skirting the crowd, I cut to the backside of the food wagon, rapped once on the door then pulled it open and stepped inside.

Dot Jones cut me off, moved in front of me, her dark scowl and twisted red lips as blatant and barring as a stop sign. I gave her a curt nod and sidled over to get by in the steamy narrow space. "You can't be in here. It's against health regulations."

I could smell the mixture of fried food and a tinge of perspiration from her green T-shirt. We were closer than wings on a fly. Too close, but I held my ground. "I need to speak with Laverna, just for a minute."

"I said you can't be in here."

Nothing wrong with my hearing, but Dot was going deafer on me by the minute. "I know, it's against health regulations, but I need to speak to Laverna."

"She's busy."

"I'm sure, but this can't wait."

"Our *customers* can't wait. *You* can." Her eyes narrowed to slits but that didn't stop the daggers from shooting out at me.

I fought to keep my voice gentle-but-firm, even as hers escalated from annoyed to angry. Had I ever heard her be anything but? "I just need five minutes. Waiting an extra five minutes for a lobster roll won't kill anyone."

"It'll be bad for business. I'll tell her you were here."

"Thanks, but I'll tell her myself."

"What in the world's going on back here?" Laverna Jordan bustled around the soda cooler and pulled up short.

"I told her to leave." Dot's voice was as clammy as seaweed.

"Its okay, Dot. Go tend the window."

"But..." The shorter woman fixed me with that dark stink-eye look she practiced so well.

"You and Cindy can fend them off. I'll only be a minute."

I backed out the door as Laverna pushed past the unmoving Dot and followed me outside. She deliberately shut the door, grabbed my elbow and towed me, none-too-gently, away from the wagon and the chatter of the picnic-table crowd. We hustled down the road, stopping only after we passed the last parked car.

Laverna's stalwart grip fell away, and she turned to face me, a bruise on her bicep looking for all the world like a tattoo of a lopsided heart. Her eyes sparkled with unshed tears. "You been to see my little girl?"

I nodded. "We took a walk and had a little talk."

"How is she?" I looked down, not comfortable with meeting those knowing eyes. My focus lit on her competent hands, a bandage around one thumb—working hands clasped together in a bruising grip. "Olivia got her tied up in knots?"

The anguish in her voice jerked my attention back to her care-worn features. "Not too bad. I think Olivia's pretty much wrapped up in Olivia, but Kendall's there and he's looking out for both of them."

She nodded. "Yup. He told me as much this morning. Kendall's a good friend, but I still worry."

I put a comforting hand on her arm. "Jacey told me to make sure you remember your promise. She expects to go back-to-school shopping with you on the mainland, and tomorrow wouldn't be too soon."

"God bless her!" Tears streamed down Laverna's cheeks. She grabbed her apron and staunched the flow, hiding her face in the dark green cloth … but only for a moment. "Don't have time for this. How'd she seem?"

"She's doing okay. She wanted me to take her over to Stub Island. I don't think it's really hit home that her grandfather isn't coming back."

"It's that way with all of us. I still can't believe Luke's gone." She choked back a sob. "Him and me used to skip school, take his dingy out to Stub Island and spend the day just doing stupid teenaged-kid stuff. Back then there wasn't any house nearby. Luke built that after he married Jane Anne." She shook her head again and muttered. "Suck it up, Buttercup."

"I told Jacey I'd stop by tomorrow and bring her a

message from you."

Laverna drew in a shuddering breath and pulled me into a fierce hug. "Tell her I love her."

I nodded and she stepped back out of the clench.

"It's hard not being able to go see her. But it's been like that since Luke got tangled up with that southern witch. Never seen such a vindictive woman."

I silently agreed but it did no good to trash someone, especially when there were problems the size of Katahdin looming. "Kendall seems to think Jacey's mom will be coming out soon."

Laverna bobbed her head. "Erica called me last night. We're not best friends but we talk more, now that Olivia's in the picture."

Common enemy.

"We never *didn't* get along, but she still has some issues with my boy. Started out good between 'em, but then Cory up and joined the army when Erica found out she was pregnant with Jacey." Laverna rubbed her forehead with a weary hand. "I think he was trying to do the right thing ... get some stability in their lives, provide for his family. I ain't making excuses for him the way he done it, just up and leaving her like that. I think they would've eventually patched things up, but we'll never know. He'd started sending money, writing letters to Erica and Jacey, but he got killed by one of them cussed IED's after he'd only been in Afghanistan two months." She blinked back tears. One escaped and she dashed it away with the back of her hand. Too much heartache and sorrow for one family to bear. "That was yesterday, dead and buried. We've got to take care of today and the living and breathing."

Amen to that. "Erica will come?"

"Yeah, she'll be here tomorrow. She rents a place in Arlington, over in the foothills. She'll take Jacey there, I think."

As a teacher, I knew the necessity of protecting the

children, but I felt a twinge of guilt making sweeping decisions for them, even when it *was* for the best. Something about choosing someone's path, and allowing them no say in the matter, never set right. "Will Jacey be okay with it?"

"If I tell her to do it, she'll do it." Laverna sighed. "Later we can all be together, I hope. I think Erica will be okay with it. She just needs time. We all do." Her voice turned woolly with unshed tears. "It's tough to wrap our heads around Luke being gone. He was always there, you know? None of us will ever be okay with it, but for now, it's whatever works and whatever will get my little Jacey Jane-bug away from that witch."

CHAPTER TEN

I awoke the next day with a headache, people and thoughts crashing like storm-driven breakers in my skull. One individual in particular owned the deepest roar. Mr. Stinson Scott, the younger. For Mr. Candle Island himself, someone with the annoying-but-comforting habit of popping up everywhere, Scotty was nowhere to be found. *Coward!* I figured he was lying low, but this was a new snake-spit-low for any human being.

I'd mentally dumped on him during the remainder of yesterday and through a wakeful night, even though Old Stin had dropped by and confirmed his grandson was busy with the investigation, walking the CSI people through the search and discovery of the body.

I talked with Tasha and found out Scotty wasn't the only one in their crosshairs. A Maine State Police detective was coming to interview Nathaniel today. I felt the family gravitational pull to get on the first ferry to the mainland and go to Bookerton, but what would I do there? Hover around in the background like a demented helicopter-aunt? We were all a little old for that one. The mental image was more than creepy. The twins had promised to call later and there was plenty for me to do right here, with or without Mr. Scott's participation.

I washed up my mug and bowl from breakfast and glanced at the clock. It wasn't a decent hour to visit Jacey, and I didn't want to just show up at the crack of dawn and abuse any good graces Kendall might be willing to extend my way later in the day. But it was well past time for the Candle Island Yacht Company to be up and humming.

The thought came to me in my midnight wanderings. I'd stood out on the back deck while the stars did their slow circle dance over my head, and I thought about tides and islands and boats. Specifically, how did Luke Faraday end up on Stub Island, dry as a bleached mussel shell, without a boat? Nathaniel had no hand in that little escapade, bait knife or no bait knife. Why Scotty had failed to mention the knife bugged me to no end, but we'd get down to it sometime later today, even if I had to turn over every rock on Candle Island to find him.

I suspected he'd saunter over this morning with an update and pretend he had no idea I'd been waiting to hear from him. Two could play that game. As much as I wanted to confront him, I wasn't about to cool my heels sitting around here. Let *him* do the looking for a change.

Thoughts of the Jane Anne had swirled around in my head as I stood out in the black night, the muffled sound of the surf breaking on the base of Blind Man's Bluff. I tried to picture Luke's vessel smashing on the ledges and cliffs, but it wasn't so. There'd been no debris … no nothing. That boat was still out there somewhere. Well, not exactly out there on the water, just MIA, and I suspected it might be found on the one place no one had thought to search—dry land. And where better to hide a boat than in a boat yard? And on an island this size, the likely place to hide in plain sight was under one of those shrink wraps at Vance Jones' business, the Candle Island Yacht Company.

As to why anyone would be stealing an old lobster boat, my wracked brain had come up empty. The only shred of logic I could attach to my theory was the killer needed a place to hide the evidence or conceal the booty. And in spite of Scotty's insistence that Luke slipped and fell, and we needed to "stay out of it" — as long as the island rumor mill, or Olivia, or both, were cranking on Nate as a suspect, I was in my rights to look at suspects on my own.

But I still came up empty. Why would someone bring Luke to Stub Island and kill him? *To steal the Jane Anne.* The answer kept coming back to me like seaweed on the tide. It was a far stretch, even for my mental Grand Canyon leaps, but it wouldn't hurt to look into it and I needed to do something. If I stayed trapped in this house a moment longer, with my thoughts gummed up on top of each other like flies stuck on paper, I'd turn into a raving lunatic. *Might've already happened.*

I strolled out the door without a backward glance, purposefully neglecting to lock it or set the security code. I wasn't going to live in a glorified prison by anyone else's set of rules. I never had before. Why kowtow now, just because I temporarily resided in a rich man's mansion?

I got in the borrowed Beemer, proud of myself and more than a little cocky—a look-Ma-no-hands wing walker going it alone. I hoped I could keep my balance and hold onto the helium-filled confidence long enough to test my theory and maybe find some answers that would take the spotlight off the investigation of Nate.

It was easy enough to pull into Vance Jones' boat building complex with the CIYC logo mounted on my car door. I parked in front of the office as if I owned the place and hurried inside before I lost my self-righteous nerve. I stepped into a honey-lit room, with cedar wainscoting and a porthole-style window to the left. The CIYC logo was displayed on a nautical-looking banner, but a dramatic photo of a yacht in high seas captured all my attention, as I suspected it was meant to, and drew my eyes to the wall-length glass case beneath it filled with trophies. *Subtle!*

A young woman, well dressed and attractive, looked up from her desk and smiled. "Welcome to the Candle Island Yacht Company. How may I help you?"

Very professional. I don't know what I'd expected. Work boots, muddy wood floors, more of a working office, perhaps … like Vance Jones' upstairs study with blueprints spread out and the nuts-and-bolts of the daily operation scattered here and there. My assessment shifted in a blink. CIYC was known for its high-end yachts and its well-heeled clients. This setting reflected both.

The buildings and builders out back were the real heartbeat of the business, but this was all about image, and it worked.

"Ma'am? How may I help you?"

Get it together, Gwen! I cleared my throat to buy time. Now that I was here ... what? "I'd like to see Les Bigelow, if he has a spare moment."

The woman nodded and, in that movement, ran a practiced-but-unobtrusive eye over my person. I'd never seen her before, but I sensed the unfamiliarity wasn't mutual.

She spoke into her phone, her voice low and pleasant as she announced me by name to the invisible person at the other end. A moment later she stood, smiled, and showed me across the room through the door on our right.

I was met by a semi-familiar face seated behind the desk. Marjorie Bigelow smiled and rose. "Thank you, Gail."

Gail promptly exited and closed the door quietly behind her.

"It's nice to see you again, Gwen." Her slender hand extended and slipped into mine. "I saw your niece at the clinic recently. Such a nice girl."

"Thank you." Though we'd barely exchanged more than a few polite comments at a small dinner party earlier in the summer, I wasn't surprised at her friendly response from our prior acquaintance. I was pleased she kept it light, not delving into Tasha's recent broken engagement with one in their social set.

Marjie's poised persona reflected her successful place within the company. She was dressed in cool white blouse and pale blue slacks. Unobtrusive-yet-eye-catching married metals of silver and gold earrings, rings, necklace and bracelets accented her golden tan and, with every carefully colored short blond hair sprayed in tussled place, she was the epitome of the modern career woman exuding grace and class with each nuance and gesture.

"It's nice to see you, too." The chutzpah that had brought me here seeped away in the face of her genuine smile as she withdrew her warm hand and gestured to a nearby chair. I sat and she took the seat next to me, crossing her legs and tilting her head forward.

"We heard you're staying on the island, and teaching as well? Quite an undertaking." Her light eyes sparkled with interest. "I've always admired those who enjoy working with children." Her lips twisted in a wry grimace before she smiled again. "I hope you'll feel welcome here."

"Oh, I do, thanks, but I think the teaching position is up in the air at this point."

"Oh?" Her intelligent face searched mine before her expression sobered. "Oh, yes, Ron told me about Laurel and the baby. Such a shame."

It was said with just the right amount of concern, yet it left a cool aftertaste in my ears. "Yes. I imagine she'll do well to keep busy in the classroom for a while."

"Will you still stay on through the winter, then?"

"Oh yes, I'm committed." I thrashed around in my mind for a way to change topic without sounding like I should be committed to the funny farm. It was one thing to guess Luke's boat was hiding on the CIYC grounds while playing insomniac in my own bedroom; it was another to crash the boatyard gates and come right out with it.

"I'm glad," Marjie said. "We can use more year-round residents, and Vance's lovely home needs to be lived in and cared for. He'd want that, and I can't think of anyone better to do both."

Vance's lovely home? It was as inviting as a cemetery

vault on a gray day. As for staying there, what about Dot and Ron? Again, I felt the underlying coolness settle on my ears. This woman had been friends and worked with my mysterious benefactor. What did she know about Vance's motives and, more importantly, did she know anything about Vance and my father? I sized her up even as I stomped on my curiosity as best I could. Now was not the time to delve into the past.

The woman sitting next to me waited patiently while I endeavored to roll my tangled thoughts up into a neat ball. Marjorie Bigelow was very charming with beautiful skin, might've had some eye work done, but I guessed she was at least a decade older than I, so she could know something from the old days. Ten years didn't make too much difference but, in this case, maybe …

I itched to cultivate our acquaintance but, thankfully, Marjie shifted our conversation back on a professional footing. "But you didn't come here for small talk." She was a natural at putting one at ease, keeping up a lively genial conversation and showing personal interest.

Marjie was a gifted businesswoman but, as she held my eye and smiled, I finally caught what I'd felt earlier—the glint of her personal assessment of me, and I knew we probably wouldn't be getting together for a night of cribbage, or popcorn and a movie, anytime soon. School teacher and a couple of yacht-building moguls? Not necessarily out of the question, but not automatic BFFs either.

What I said next would no doubt deep-six any closer contact, but did I really care? "Right. I wanted to talk with you and your husband about..." I took a deep breath. "It's going to sound crazy, but it's about the Jane Anne."

"Luke Faraday's boat. They haven't found it."

It wasn't a question, and the slight pinch in her forehead above the bridge of her nose was so swift the perfect skin barely puckered and smoothed out before I could be sure. I doubted I'd even seen it. But—

"No, they haven't, but I wondered if—"

The door to the inner office swung open and Les Bigelow filled the gap with his massive square build. He reminded me of a heavyset Roman gladiator with his broad, tough-guy face and gray, curling Caligula hairdo. All that was missing was the armor and sword, but I had a feeling he didn't need it.

He was compelling in an odd way, and he moved like a man who ruled and knew it. His presence filled the room and, for a second, all was quiet except the invisible hum of his radiated power.

I caught a glance that passed between husband and wife. A look that could've been nothing, simply acknowledgement of each other; but my teacher radar dinged loud as the recess bell in the silence, as I recognized the unspoken guilt of a dirty secret when I saw one.

"Gwen McPhail." The acting CEO reached out and engulfed my hand in his heavy grip. He had a working man's calloused palm and a no-nonsense handshake, in spite of the subtle opulence of the CIYC offices. Maybe the show was all Vance, but I suspected both men shared a vision for well-built yachts and the well-heeled lifestyle that went with a successful business. "What brings you to our corner of the island?" Les fixed me with an unblinking stare; not unfriendly, but slightly intimidating.

Their "corner" of the island was more like the cornerstone of Candle Island. CIYC was the unique feature that made this isle more than a speck on a map of the Maine coast. Internationally known, yet CIYC took on only a select number of clients each year, keeping the one-percent social set slavering for this must-have status symbol.

I flicked a glance at my companion, but Marjie had her hands folded, resting on one knee, and her attention focused on her husband. No sense tiptoeing now that I was in the lion's den. "I had a crazy thought last night. What if someone hid Luke Faraday's missing boat in the Candle Island Yacht yard?"

Les smirked. "That's why you're here?"

"Uh ... yes." I brazened it out and drew in a deep breath. "It's a big place, and what's to prevent someone from sneaking in and hiding the Jane Anne in the back with the other shrink-wrapped inventory?"

This time he threw back his head and laughed. The sound sent an obscene hearty echo bouncing off the walls. Les sobered in less than a moment, and his eyes held no trace of mirth. "I apologize, Gwen." He didn't sound apologetic. "But that old tub held together with duct tape and deck screws isn't worth a cent. Luke poured his money in that hole-in-the-water, year after year, particularly this year. We don't throw good money after bad and waste our time with that kind of thing here. Never will, as long as I have anything to say about it." He stopped abruptly, his jaw set like iron. "Did someone put you up to this? Ron Jones, perhaps?"

The last thing I wanted to do was further compromise Ron's tenuous position in his late father's boatyard. I shook my head. "No. Ron had nothing to do with my coming here."

The twist of his heavy lips said he wasn't buying it, so I ramped up my flow of words-per-second which, unfortunately, happens whenever I've overstepped. "No, this is all me."

I sent up a silent plea for inspiration or, at the very least, the ability to make sense with my foot stuck in my mouth. "My nephew, Nathaniel, was out on the boat with Luke when it went missing, and there's some speculation that he had something to do with this whole mess."

"I heard about that. They took him to the mainland."

"Yes, he's going to be alright, but I'd just as soon not have a shadow of suspicion hanging over him while he recovers."

"So, you're here to do what?"

"I thought we could take a look around the boatyard.

Places that might be so seldom frequented someone could get away with slipping a covered boat in unnoticed."

He snorted. "We? I can't let just anyone back there. The insurance company would have my head. Besides, we have a security system. Nobody gets in or out without my people knowing about it."

"Oh, right. I just wondered if maybe someone who knew someone who worked here could get away with something like that." I was sounding like one of those obsessed conspiracy types, but he had me in the corner and I saw no alternative but to keep punching until I talked my way out.

"Nice try." He crossed his beefy arms over his barrel chest. "You want to save your nephew from the rumors? I'm not surprised, but you'll have to look elsewhere."

"Now Les, hear her out." Marjie's gently firm voice of reason hit the wall.

"Excuse me if I'm not sympathetic, but rumors come naturally to your family, wouldn't you say, Gwen?"

I gave him my best narrowed-eye scrutiny. "I don't take your meaning."

"Really. I thought you were far more sophisticated than that. Playing the innocent here won't get you what you want."

"And that is?"

"You tell me."

"I already did."

"Oh, come on! You want to get in here and dig up something to help Ron in his feeble bid to get the boatyard away from me. That little twerp can't even handle a box of tinker toys, and he couldn't handle this place if his life depended on it. He'd run this business into the ground in less than six months, guaranteed."

"Les."

The big man swatted away his wife's caution with an annoyed slat of his hand through the air before he pointed his finger at me and punctuated it with a sneer. "I owe it to

Vance. *We* owe it to Vance not to let that happen. He worked his whole life building this place up to what it is today … one of the premier small yacht-building companies on the east coast. Do you know how many clients are waiting to be considered for a Vance Jones-designed yacht?"

"No." *But I imagine you're going to tell me.*

"We're booked through the next eight years, and that's only the tip of the iceberg. We're coming out with a new design soon that'll have everyone clamoring at our doors."

"But if Vance was the designer … "

Les scowled down at me. "We designed together, Vance and me, right from the inception of the company. Back then it was just Vance and me and a couple of local guys to help with the grunt work."

The words of my father's letter echoed in my mind, but this wasn't the time. Les was on a roll, and I'd be a fool to stop him.

"Too bad Ron didn't inherit his father's eye or brains, but the kid has no skill for anything beyond those cardboard dinghies of his. All he wants is to get in good with the clam diggers and lobstermen. He can hide behind your skirts, but it won't make a bit of difference. Ron Jones is never getting the reins to this place. *Never.*" His full lower lip stuck out to punctuate the faintly petulant tone.

I stood, took a deep breath and held it to let the steam seep out my ears instead of my lips. I'd come in here in a tear and look where it got me. I needed to put some distance between me and CIYC and think. I swallowed the indignation and chose my words carefully. "I told you I wasn't here for Ron. You can choose to believe that or not. I realize how foolish my theory about the Jane Anne sounds, and I apologize for the interruption. Thank you for your time." I nodded and walked to the door but, when my hand touched the cool doorknob, I turned back to the couple in the room.

There is nothing wrong with you, Gwen McPhail.

Scotty's words from the other day hit and knocked the wind out of me. I couldn't slink out like the interfering imbecile Les thought me to be. I was Conner McPhail's daughter. I didn't think like that anymore, but the knowledge resonated within me like a clarion call. When the years pile up, after parents pass on, it's easy to forget that family bond of the old die-trying, damn-the-torpedoes, go-get-'em, blood-is-thicker-than-water way.

That ancient loyalty welled up inside me and I nearly choked on it. *Here goes, Daddy.* "I almost forgot. I recently found old Candle Island Yacht blueprints in Vance's study up at the house. I think they might interest you. He kept some vintage clippings that belong in your company archives." I gestured toward the far wall where a picture of a yacht hung.

A young Vance and Les stood side by side, grinning, as a woman broke a bottle of champagne across the bow. The photographer had snapped the shot perfectly and captured the flying foam and glass bits, forever suspended in mid-air. "Some stuff from the old days, I gather." I closed my eyes as if trying to remember, all the while calculating my next words. It was all-in or nothing, now. "I think it was plans for Frederick Evangelos and Richard Arnold."

"Our first clients."

"And you designed the yachts with Vance?"

Les glowered. "That's what I said."

"And you still use a variation on those same designs today?"

"The uneducated Philistine might think that, but I'd hardly say it's the exact same yacht. We've added several innovations over the years. That's what makes us a leader in the industry today. Now, if there's nothing else." He glanced at his wristwatch and flicked a stone-cold stare my way. "I'm expecting an important call."

Philistine? Huh! I took a page from my student's rhetoric. Uneducated Philistine or not – *it takes one to know one.* "Like I said, sorry to waste your time, but thank you for seeing me."

"It was good to see you again," Marjie said. Her husband disappeared into his office and shut the door. She rose and strode over to me before I could make my exit. "You'll have to excuse Les. He's under a lot of pressure right now, but just because he and Ron don't see eye to eye, I'm sure it'll work itself out."

I nodded. Any platitude I might utter would be a betrayal to my friendship with Ron. "Thanks so much for taking the time to see me. Good day to you."

Good day to you? Was I stuck in the 1800's? I couldn't help the regret welling up inside. I'd booted this whole thing, *big* time. I gave Gail a nod as I hustled out of the building and drove away.

I crawled through the town of Coveside, negotiating the maze of colorful T-shirts and the chatter of tourists still meandering everywhere; but instead of going back to Blind Man's Bluff to reconnoiter, I nosed the car toward Devane's Rip. If Laverna was right and Jacey's mom showed up today, this might be my last opportunity to see her for a while, and a promise is a promise is a promise, especially to a five-year-old.

I turned down Jane Anne Lane and crept along the narrow track, focusing on what to say to a little girl when there was nothing to say that would bring her grampie back. Too soon I pulled into the clearing and sized up the pickups parked next to Olivia's car. One man leaned against the side of Kendall's truck. Kendall's body bent toward the red-haired man, and his mouth moved like a rubber band stretched in several directions at once.

I turned the Beemer toward the garage and parked in front of Luke's vehicle, angling my hood out to make room for more visitors. *More like for a quick get away*, my conscience nagged.

Scotty's truck flanked Kendall's pickup in front of the house. Both men came around the side of the truck at my arrival and stood watching as I got out of my car, Scotty with arms crossed, Kendall with his hands jammed in his pockets.

Neither moved as I approached, although the stern look on both weathered faces said I'd interrupted something. *No kidding!* "Hi, Gwen." This from Kendall. Scotty merely gave me a stiff nod.

"Don't let me interrupt," I said sweetly. "I'm here to see Jacey for a few minutes, if that's okay."

Kendall shrugged. "That's all you'll get. Erica's here. Scotty brought her down from the ferry. They're in there packing up. I don't know what's taking so long. All Erica wants to do is bug out." He swung a sidelong glance at the house then turned back to me with lowered shaggy brows. "Guess I could go inside and see, if you want."

"That'd be great."

Kendall sighed, turned on the ball of his foot, and trudged toward the door to face the firing squad.

I waited until he slipped inside before giving my attention to my tall wordless companion. This wasn't the time or place to have a verbal duel. I bit my tongue and waited in excruciating silence. I was pretty sure Scotty had me beat on this one thing. He was a real Ebenezer Scrooge with his words, and he knew it drove me crazy. Not this time. I'd lock the vault on my own lips and outwait him until doomsday.

"Grampa said you were looking for me yesterday." And apparently, he was also gifted at making me a liar. My eyes widened at his slow-delivery startup of the conversation, and he grinned.

I went nonchalant and shrugged. "I might've been."

Scotty shook his head, the picture of regret. "I got stuck in the investigation, lots of questions."

"Any answers?"

"Not yet."

"They're supposed to talk to Nate today."

Scotty nodded. "Just routine, I imagine."

"Yeah. What are you and Kendall up to today?"

"Just chewing the fat while I wait for Jacey and Erica."

"Looked like more than fat to me, Jack Sprat."

He had the grace to smile. "I'm looking into some things that don't add up."

"What's that?"

"Little inconsistencies."

I take it back. The man *does* have issues with stringing more than two words together. "You mean like everything?"

"Can't say, yet."

"I'll bet. Sort of like that bait knife you forgot to mention."

I watched the tinge of red flush under Scotty's tanned neck and face and his expression went from friendly to shuttered-up-tighter-than-a-summer-cottage-in-December.

The door banging against the side of the house claimed our attention. Scotty's head whipped around. Jacey burst out of the house, raced past my companion, and flung her slender body at me, wrapping her arms around my waist. Scotty raised one rusty eyebrow before I went down on my knees and gathered the little girl close. "This is from Mimi," I whispered, and she buried her face in my shoulder.

"Mama's here," she whispered back.

"I know. That's nice, huh?"

Jacey turned slightly still, leaning against my arm, and searched my face with her somber blue stare. "I guess. We're going to the mainland. Will you tell Mimi?"

"I think she already knows. Mimi's been talking with your mother." I didn't want to say too much, but the woebegone face inches from mine begged for reassurance.

"She has?" A small smile lit up the elfin features.

I hoped I hadn't over-sold the fragile relationship. "Yeah, and she said to tell you she hasn't forgotten her promise to take you school shopping." Not verbatim, perhaps, but a good segue to safer ground.

"We're going to stop by the wagon on our way to the

ferry." The deep voice rumbling above caught us both off guard. I glowered up at him, afraid he'd promised something he couldn't deliver, but Scotty smiled at the little girl, his face kind.

"Really?"

"Really. Your mom said so."

"Let's go right now."

"We have to wait until she's ready," Scotty said.

"You could go in and help her carry out my stuff," Jacey said.

I stifled a laugh. "You could," I agreed.

"Don't want to rush anyone," he muttered.

"Mama's ready to go, but Moo took her into Grampie's den and shut the door."

"So, I probably shouldn't interrupt them," Scotty said.

"No, it's okay. Moo wants us to leave."

"It couldn't hurt to check with Kendall," I offered.

Scotty nodded, looking anything but pleased, although he did immediately stride toward the house.

"Moo was yelling at Mama. I heard her use a bad word." Jacey pressed close to me once again.

"Sometimes when people are sad, they do weird things. They don't know what they're saying."

"Moo knew what she was saying. She talks that way a lot."

"Oh." I rubbed her bony back. "Sometimes people say things they don't mean." I felt like a traitor defending Olivia, but what could I say? "Have you ever been to your mother's house?" Safer topic. *I hope*!

"Yeah, Grampie and I went in the winter. There was lots of snow and we all slid on a purple sled down the big hill in her backyard."

"That sounds like fun."

"I guess. And she's got a cat."

"What's its name?"

"Cleo."

"I like cats."

"Cleo doesn't like me."

I had a feeling this kid would never take it easy on anyone, but there was something about Jacey that made you want to hug the stuffing out of her, all the while debating the issues of life. I snuggled her close. "I imagine Cleo will love you once she gets to know you."

"Maybe, at least she's better than Maggie. Maggie only likes Olivia."

"I noticed that."

"Cleo is Mama's cat. I want my own kitten."

"Something to think about."

"Grampie didn't like cats."

"Yeah. I don't think Scotty likes cats, either. It might be a guy-thing. What do you think?"

And speak of the devil. Both Scotty and a thin young woman, her dark hair pulled back into a Jacey-style ponytail, emerged and headed toward us.

Jacey's back was toward them. She shook her head and said, "Logan was in my K-4 class and he has three cats and he's a boy."

"Huh! Well, I guess that blows that theory. But your mother's here."

Jacey turned but remained leaning against me. "Mama, can Gwen come with us?"

Erica Faraday's light eyes narrowed. With her father dead and her stepmother giving her nothing but grief, the last thing Erica needed was a stranger hanging around.

I stood and reached for Jacey's hand. She tucked it in mine and looked up from her mother to me. "I'm Gwen," I said. Erica frowned. "Jacey, you're gonna be busy with Mimi so I'm going to say good-bye for now."

"But . . ." Jacey whined.

"Maybe your mom will give me your address and we can write to each other."

"I can't write, you know."

"I remember. We can draw each other pictures, how's that?"

"Can we, Mama?" I released her hand but she didn't relinquish mine.

"I'll give it to Laverna. Come on, Jacey. We gotta go." Uttered through lips as tight as a clam shell at low tide, and terse enough to make Laverna sound like a magpie.

I gave Jacey a little nudge forward. Scotty had stowed her bags in the bed of the truck and opened the passenger's door. I caught his eye as I looked past Erica.

Jacey turned and faced me, her blue eyes accusing. "Will you be here when I come back to the island?"

"I plan to be. Maybe someday you'll come to visit me, and you can meet my cat."

"You can come to visit me and meet my cat, too."

"Sounds good."

Jacey flung her arms around my waist one more time in a fierce hug before she flitted over to her mother and Erica boosted her up into the cab.

I stepped back as doors slammed and Scotty started the engine. I waved when they drove away. "Suck it up, Buttercup," I murmured before I cut across the yard to my own ride.

"Gwen!" Kendall's hail stopped me mid-stride. He rushed over, his eyes red-rimmed and bright in his haggard gray face. He didn't look good. "Have you heard anything?"

"About what?"

"You know, about Luke's boat or, well, anything?"

I shook my head. "No. I'm always the last to know anything."

"I thought maybe your nephew might be remembering stuff."

"Nothing important, as far as I know. A police detective's coming over to talk to him today."

"Today, huh."

A dog yipped and we both jerked our heads toward the

house. Olivia, clad in a pastel flowered robe, stood on the doorstep with Maggie in her arms.

"I'd better go."

"Do you need anything?" I asked.

"No, I think we're good, but I might stop by later and see what happened with your nephew."

"Sure."

"Kendall!"

"I'll see ya." He jogged back to the house.

I hurried into the car and, by the time I drove down the lane, they were back inside. My last glimpse in the rearview mirror showed a closed door and a house that looked lifeless and abandoned. I wondered how long it would be before that impression became a reality. I couldn't see Olivia staying on the island. The only thing holding her here would be Luke's service and getting her affairs in order, which probably meant liquidating her assets.

As brutal and unflattering as the thought was, I didn't think Olivia would take offense at the prospect of taking that last ferry ride off Candle Island and stepping onto the mainland and into the next chapter of her life.

CHAPTER ELEVEN

I went home and did what I always did when I was waiting. Some people pace. I bake. I made my favorite chocolate cake—comfort food, but also something that didn't take long to prepare so I'd be ready to give Scotty my full attention when he returned.

The cold kitchen smelled like warm chocolate when the phone rang. I answered on the first ring, pleased to hear my nephew's voice sounding less hoarse. "Hey, Gwen, the detective just left."

"How'd it go?"

"Okay, I think. The guy just asked the same questions everybody else has asked, and that was it. He kept coming back to the phone calls and the radio, but I wasn't much help."

"Well, they already know he talked to Olivia."

"Yeah, multiple times, and to a couple other boats on the radio on our way to Blackwall. And I remembered the dude's name he talked to on our way home was Ken ... I think."

My antenna went up. This was something new, or at least I didn't remember hearing it before. "I didn't know he talked to Kendall."

"Yeah, but they already knew that. It's the time *after* that, that matters! I heard the phone and the radio when I was sick, but I don't know who Luke talked to, or if he talked with anyone. I don't think he answered either one. He was passed out at the wheel, and we were drifting, I think. I'm not even sure of what I used to think happened anymore. It just gets more messed up in my brain every time I go over it. I wish I could remember more about the boat leaving, but I can't get it straight in my head." Frustration buzzed over the line.

"Did he get into anything about Luke turning up on Stub Island?" I danced around the knife issue and hoped Nate would tell me what I didn't dare to ask outright. How often does that happen? That's why subtlety is for the dead … or deadly patient.

"No, not really. I didn't know anything firsthand about that, and he was super tight-lipped about the investigation. I tried to ask him something, but it was all one way. He asked the questions, and I gave him whatever answers I could. The guy left his card and I'm supposed to call if I remember anything else."

"Do you think he'll be back?"

"Not unless I can figure out what happened. I'm such a *loser!* I might've been able to stop all of it. And maybe I could have, and that's why I'm blocking it out of my memory. That's what's bugging me. I ought to know what happened to Luke, or at least what happened to the boat."

A hundred aunt platitudes threatened to tumble out, meant to soothe his survivor guilt, but I held back, knowing they wouldn't help. Instead, I went with the cautious truth. "You might never remember, but sometimes when you don't focus on the lost memory it surfaces on its own. Maybe try giving it, and yourself, a rest."

"Yeah, I get that. How's Olivia doing?"

His question slapped me across the face like wet laundry in a sudden gust at the clothesline. "About as well as can be expected."

"I feel bad for her. I'm thinking maybe I ought to come out and see her."

"Oh, no. I think it's best to wait. She's had family coming and going." Okay, that was a sugar-coated stretch, but he swallowed it.

"Yeah, I hear ya. I'll come to the funeral and talk to her then."

Oh boy. Our Nathaniel wasn't foolish enough to get tangled up with Olivia on the rebound, was he? A combination of survivor guilt and a what-might-have-been wave of nostalgia could make for a toxic combination for a chronic Casanova. For the first time since this all went down, I hung onto the hope that Olivia still blamed Nate for Luke's death. It wasn't a kind thought; light on compassion and heavy on self-preservation—make that nephew preservation.

"Let me know what's happening." Nate's voice held a note of weariness.

We'd all be better when this was behind us, but I didn't see that happening anytime soon. "You, too," I said, unwilling to lie to him. He didn't need to know about the bait knife or the rumors or anything else for now. Doesn't everyone have a little of the Czarina in them when the family honor is trampled in the streets or, in this case, the piers?

We said good-bye and I headed out the door just as Scotty pulled up the driveway in his pickup. A walk first to clear my head would've been nice, but his arrival was a relief. I didn't expect us to agree on anything, but it would be good to shove the theories back and forth, if only to let the prowling thoughts out of the cage in my skull and free them for a time.

He nodded and came around the hood of his truck. "You going out?"

"No. I was going for a walk while waiting for you."

"Then let's go."

"I've got chocolate cake cooling in the kitchen."

Scotty grinned. "Bribery?"

"If I thought it would work, yeah, but you're gonna tell

me everything anyway."

"Confident. I like that." Somehow, our feet started moving and we walked down the driveway together, the breeze threaded with clear cool currents as the sun played hopscotch with the clouds.

As much as I enjoyed the fine day, determination dogged my every step. I wasn't about to stroll in silence. "When were you going to tell me about the knife?"

"I've got a message for you from Dot."

Talk about avoidance! He had an unusual and annoying flair for tact. More like a fine fencing tactic. But this total-oblivion move? It must be bad news for my straight-shooting companion to boot-stomp the subject. "Do they think Nate had anything to do with Luke's murder?"

He stopped mid-stride. I took an extra step and whirled to face him, stumbling slightly on the steep pitch but I held my ground. He snaked out a quick hand on my arm to steady me. "Whoa, hold it."

"You're not going to distract me from the truth. If you didn't want to tell me, you shouldn't have come."

He dropped his hand from my wrist. "Point taken but, for the record, I *did* come to tell you what's going on."

I couldn't help but notice he didn't use the word truth, but I'd give him a chance for now. I crossed my arms and waited.

"But first, I really *do* have a message from Dot. I saw her down at the lunch wagon when I dropped off Erica and Jacey."

I hated myself for getting dragged into his diversion, but a little detour wouldn't hurt. "How'd it go with Laverna?"

"Good, I guess. Lots of tears, but I took them all down to the ferry landing and they were sitting there talking when I left. And Dot *did* give me a message for you."

"I got that! Go ahead, Gunga Din. Spill it."

"She said to tell you, 'Never in a million years.' " He arched one auburn brow and it disappeared for a second under the shade of his baseball cap. "She may have used a more colorful response, but that's the gist of it."

So, Dot had gotten my note. What did I expect? A girl day of just the two of us hanging out on the deck, gabbing, eating ice cream and braiding each other's hair like some kind of preteen slumber party? Never gonna happen. But if she wouldn't come to me, I'd find a way to take my idea to her.

I shrugged one shoulder, turned back to his side and we started walking again.

"Sorry."

"Did she tell you what it's about?" He knew. Of course, he knew; Dot was his cousin.

"In a Dot-rant kind of way."

As we neared the bottom of the hill, I gestured toward her simple white cape cod, old-fashioned and beautiful.

"Houses. I got that much. You might just have to let it ride for a while," he said.

"Spoken like a wing-walker-wannabe. I'm letting go of that albatross if it kills me."

"Understood. Now, what do you want to know?"

That's why I could never stay mad at Scotty. He might bob and weave in every conversation, but he stayed in the ring. "You talk to me about keeping secrets. What's up with Nate and the bait knife? And don't leave anything out, because I know more than you think."

That last part was pure bluster and, as we passed Dot's house, Scotty chuckled. "I'll bet you do. Far as I can tell, the bait knife has nothing to do with anything."

"Say that again?"

"In spite of what you've heard, Luke wasn't stabbed to death."

"But—"

"*But* is just it."

"But the investigation is calling it a suspicious death?"

That stab in the dark earned me a quick sharp look from

those serious blue eyes. "From what I saw firsthand, and what I gleaned during my interview, the knife wound was likely self-inflicted when he twisted and fell. It caught him in the shoulder."

"So that's not what killed him."

"No, I wouldn't think so. When I found him, he had a nasty bloody contusion on his temple. He must've gone down hard and hit a sharp rock at one of the worst possible spots. The poor guy never seemed to be able to catch a break. Grew up dirt poor. His father drank. He worked hard, made his way, then his wife got cancer." Scotty shook his head.

We stopped and looked out over the thin sandy crust of Eyelash Beach to the ocean beyond, alive with sparkling sunlit waves. My companion took off his cap and rubbed his forehead before he settled it back in its usual spot. "Luke couldn't handle seeing Jane Anne in such a bad way. He spent a lot of time out on the boat and browbeat his daughter to do the heavy lifting. Erica came back to the island to take care of her mom, but she blew out of here and took the last ferry to the mainland the day of her mother's service. Far as I know, Luke didn't see her again until she showed up with the baby. Story goes she hit Luke up for money, then disappeared again. She came back maybe two years ago, left Jacey with Luke and his new bride, and went off to study massage therapy or some such thing. Now she's back for her dad's passing. Tough going."

The sad family history of the Faraday clan was all well and good, but it was water under the bridge. "I hope Jacey and Erica and Laverna can build a happy life now."

"And Olivia, too."

What is *it with Olivia and the men around here?* "Olivia will land on her feet, trust me."

Scotty snorted.

"Hey, snigger all you like, She's a survivor."

"You got that right."

"And I wouldn't be surprised if she's the one who

started all this hoopla about Nate. First, she said he caused the boat disaster. Now she says he killed Luke."

"With the bait knife?"

"According to her, Nate was using it that day on the boat."

"If you told that to a dead fox, he'd jump up and kick you in the teeth."

I flung myself at him, Jacey-style, and wrapped my arms around his waist in a brief hug but stepped out of the embrace before his arms came around me.

"That makes no sense, you know." I blinked back tears, obviously closer to the edge over all this than I should be.

He shrugged one shoulder, but I recognized the steely guarded look. His brow furrowed, calculating how much to tell me and how much he could get away with keeping to himself. I loved his loyalty but, tears or no, it was all-in time for both of us. "But Nate's still not in the clear?"

"He probably is, but he was maybe the last one to see Luke alive and they'll keep coming back to that, if they don't get a concrete lead on something more substantial."

"*Maybe* he was the last one to see Luke alive, but not likely."

Scotty swatted away a buzzing horsefly and scratched the back of his neck. "If dead men could talk, eh?"

"Nobody's talking except the gossips."

"Since when does Gwen McPhail listen to the sour grapevine?"

The heat rose in my cheeks. He was right. If it was just me, okay; but when it was one of mine being picked apart by mean-spirited scavengers, well that was a different kettle of fish.

"It'll sort itself out, and those who have nothing better to do than talk will find something else to chew on quick enough. They always do." Scotty sounded just like his grandfather, but the platitude was a comfort.

I sighed and started walking back up the hill. Scotty fell

into step at my side. "You're probably right, but have you heard anything about the Jane Anne? You'd think people would be all over that."

"Oh, they are. Some of the islanders like nothing better than spinning a good yarn, and this has all the makings of a tragic fishing tale."

"What are they saying?"

"Nothing that makes any sense."

His gait was still slow, arms relaxed at his side, but when I flicked my eyes over to his profile, his jaw was as rigid as the rock cliffs of Blind Man's Bluff. I nodded. "They're still saying Nate scuttled the boat."

I could feel his eyes on me, but I quickened my steps as the gravel road slanted up, and kept my face pointed toward our destination.

"Some. But like I said, it doesn't add up. Nate wouldn't have taken Luke to Stub, then come back, scuttled the boat and tied himself to the whistle buoy. It's too strange even for a fish tale."

I sucked in a deep breath as the climb up the hill intensified. "What if the boat isn't out there?" I flung my arm toward the small wedge of ocean sparkling between the spruce branches. "What if it's here?"

"Here?" Scotty's hoarse voice triggered the memory of Les Bigelow's scoffing tone.

"Well, maybe not here-here, but on dry land somewhere."

Scotty touched my arm, and we stopped in the ring of the driveway and faced each other. "Where'd you hear that?"

I'm not the only one with that theory? Huh? "I thought it up myself."

Scotty's touch fell away but the tension still held between us. "Is that the newest rumor?"

"You could say."

"No, I couldn't say, but *you* could. Didn't I hear something about chocolate cake?"

"You did. Come on. You've got plenty enough time to spill it while I frost the cake."

I preceded him into the mansion, and he was aggravatingly silent as I clattered the bowl and spoon and he sat at the kitchen table. Just when I was about to crack, my companion spoke. "There's talk Nate ditched the boat at a secret location because, when things cool off, he'll marry Olivia and get all of Luke's property, including the Jane Anne."

I spread the butter cream frosting on the cake with a violent stroke of the knife and snorted. "Then he swam to the buoy and faked his sickness."

"I didn't say it was true, and I didn't say I believed it. There're more holes in that version than buckshot in the stop sign at the end of my road."

I placed a hefty slice of cake in front of him and poured a tall glass of milk.

"We've danced around the maybe's long enough. Consider this a bribe for the whole truth." I lowered myself into the chair across from him, suddenly spent, my smaller portion of cake and milk already begging me for seconds before I took a bite. The heck with dainty. Mindless stress-eating had to be good for the soul on occasion.

Scotty tucked into his cake, making me wait, but I did the same, trying once again to penetrate the blackout of vanishing boats and a body on an island with no means of arrival.

"There has to be someone else involved," I blurted, then downed my outburst with a final swallow of ice-cold milk.

"Powerful good," Scotty said, but he nodded. "Luke."

"Luke, what?"

"I've been thinking Luke did it for the insurance money."

"You mean he sunk his own boat on purpose?" I sounded like one of my kindergarten students and probably looked like one, too, with my eyes bugging out. I'd never considered the possibility that Luke was the culprit of his own misfortune.

"It happens. The Jane Anne was worth more on the bottom than it was afloat. Olivia was high maintenance, and he had the little girl, too. That's a lot." He rested both elbows on the table and cupped his chin in one hand.

I narrowed my eyes and stared into his blue gaze. I tried to wrap my head around Luke masterminding this tragedy. "You think so?"

"It may not make a whole lot of sense, but it makes more sense than anything else. Think about it. That's why Luke took out Nate that day and not Kendall, so no one would know."

Why did everyone assume Nate was so easily duped? Not so … and neither was his aunt! "If that's true, and I'm not saying I buy it, how did Luke get rid of the boat?"

"He probably hid a skiff on one of the islands. Took the Jane Anne there, picked up the skiff before he scuttled the lobster boat."

"So, where's the skiff now?" I asked.

"We always come back to a missing boat, don't we?" He scrubbed his fingers across the side of his jaw. "Maybe he scuttled her right off Devane's Rip, rowed back home and swam over to Stub. There's some deep water right off that island."

"Pretty risky to do it within sight of the shore, and his clothes were dry, don't forget. I think there had to be someone else involved."

"I've gone over that again and again in my head, but I don't think Luke would trust anyone not to talk, especially Olivia or Kendall. They'd spill their guts in a second."

"I don't think Luke would scuttle the Jane Anne," I said. "It's his dead wife's namesake and he lives on Jane Anne Lane. You told me once Luke was a belt-and-suspenders guy. That says to me he's not the kind who could trash one of his most prized possessions."

"That's what would make it the perfect crime. No one would suspect him because he loved that boat. And if he hadn't fallen and died, he probably would've gotten away with it."

"I still say he didn't do it. He was too attached to it and the memory of his late wife."

"You're forgetting he's got a new wife now, who likes the high life and would've liked nothing better than to be rid of the Jane Anne. Since he got tangled up with Olivia, Luke's been like a different person. Moody, mean even."

I thought about Olivia, Luke, and Kendall's three-way argument I'd stepped into the other day when I stepped off the ferry. Were they fighting about getting rid of the boat? The fragments I remembered fit in with Scotty's scenario. Maybe my companion was right about the whole thing, but something still didn't feel right to me. "If it's true, why was Luke hiding out on Stub? Why didn't he just go overboard at the buoy and get rescued with Nate?"

"My guess is he wanted to make sure Nate didn't see anything suspicious."

"So Luke planned to turn up later and arrive back home, no questions asked?" I shook my head.

"I know. There are a lot of holes in my theory. Too bad your nephew can't recall what happened to the boat, but I think that's the way Luke planned it. He slipped him a Mickey Finn, gave Nate something to put him out of commission."

Lights exploded in my brain like a summer thunderstorm. Food poisoning and knocking boat motors. Nathaniel did remember something, and just maybe it was enough. "You mean he *tried* to give Nate something. Luke gave Nate some homemade chicken soup for lunch, but Nate didn't like it. He said it was too salty so he poured it over the side when Luke wasn't looking. But that doesn't mean anything because Nate saw Luke eat the rest of the chicken soup. The only other things Nate had to eat or drink didn't come from Luke." Tuna fish sandwiches, food poisoning, and guilt swirled around in my conscience.

"So, what're you saying?" Scotty leaned back in the chair and laced his fingers behind his head.

"Nate said he thought he heard a smaller motor, one with a knock in it, do you remember?"

My compatriot nodded.

"What if someone else came aboard and pushed Nate overboard?"

"Why?"

"That's the big question. We figure that out and we've got it solved, but first we look for a small boat with a knock in the engine."

Scotty whistled between his teeth. "That describes half the boats on the island."

Rats! "Okay, maybe we need to backtrack and see if we can find anyone who saw them before the boat went missing."

"The buoy where we picked up Nate isn't in a real high-boat-traffic area. I don't like to think it, but that's another reason I suspect Luke did it for the insurance money. No witnesses. There was no call for him to be out that way, especially if he was heading home. And that's supposedly what he told Olivia when he talked to her."

"Luke talked to her when they were in Port Blackwall. Last contact," I said.

"Yeah, she told you that, too?"

"Don't sound so surprised. I imagine she told her troubles to whoever'd listen." *And aired her suspicions about Nate!* "We bonded on the wharf during the search."

"Last contact," Scotty murmured.

"But was it? Nate remembers the cell phone ringing later, but he doesn't recall Luke answering and he thought he heard a radio call about the same time. Maybe Kendall?" I threw it out there hoping Scotty would see a connection I couldn't quite grasp.

Scotty muttered something I didn't catch. "Nothing solid to go on after Olivia's call."

"Are you thinking *we* need to retrace their steps from Port Blackwall?"

"Thought I might just make the trip to Crossjack, see if anything turns up."

"Sounds good. I'm ready."

Scotty chuckled but his brow remained furrowed. "I'll just bet you are."

I grabbed a sweatshirt and jacket. I threw a few snacks and a couple of water bottles into a backpack and trailed Scotty to the door. He held it open for me and made a point of turning on the security system and locking up. "You don't have to do that."

"Yeah, I do."

I'd expected a little more lip, but he was silent on the drive to the boat and, once aboard the Semper Paratus, he kept his remarks to casting off and getting underway. We skimmed over the roughening waters and made good time on a following sea. I studied the man at the wheel. With my mind and loyalties firmly fixed on my nephew, I hadn't given much thought to Scotty's stake in this. I didn't think he and Luke were particularly close, but they were both islanders to the core. That made them family, in a sense, and it must hurt to think of a brother not only gone, but gone wrong; going out in such an underhanded way.

As I watched his tanned arms steer us around a cluster of three small islands, I wondered if Scotty was doing this to disprove his distasteful theory and clear Luke's name of any suspicion. I wasn't sure how it would pan out or where it put us. I took comfort in the knowledge he wouldn't pin any trumped-up charges on Nate, and, at the end of the day, we might be coming at this from different angles but we both were searching for the truth.

Nevertheless, as we pulled up to the big pier at Port Blackwall, I wasn't confident we'd find the truth here or anywhere. We tied up, walked past the Coastguard slip and up the gangway. I wondered if Scotty had been stationed here during his military career, but he barely glanced at the square brick building that housed the Port Blackwall coastguard station. The flags snapped smartly overhead, but his gaze remained totally focused forward as he strode by at a good clip.

I had to hurry to keep up while we wove in and out of foot traffic. The tall ship scene was nearly over for the season, but today the quay still teemed with tourists. The Amerigo, the resident windjammer, was loading up for an afternoon sight-seeing cruise. Its signature pirate flag and sunset-red sails made it easy to spot when it skimmed across the waters.

I tugged on my companion's sleeve, and he slowed but didn't stop. "Maybe someone from the schooner saw something. They might not even be aware of the significance of what they witnessed … two guys in a lobster boat, but they're always cruising around out on the bay."

Scotty shook his head and resumed his long-legged pace. "You can bet the cops, Marine Patrol, and the Coast Guard have been up and down the shore checking the whereabouts of the boats during that time, talking to the captains. Besides, I can't see them taking the Amerigo over that way. They mostly have a pretty set routine when they go out, except if they spot a finback or a minke. Then they might deviate a bit."

Whales. I hadn't thought of that. There'd been more whale traffic around this August than usual. Maybe a humpback surfaced and wrecked the boat … *Yeah, right, and then spit Luke out on Stub Island Jonah-style?* I was glad I'd kept my lips zipped on that one.

I was getting crazier that a loon by the minute. *Just listen; don't talk.* Not sure I could pull that off. "Just a thought," I murmured as we stopped in front of Crossjack Marine, and he opened the door for me.

I strode in and nearly crashed into a pyramid of cans stacked shoulder high in the middle of the floor, a hand-lettered sign with much too much small writing advertised something about a surplus paint sale. It might as well have been a novel and, without my cheaters, the content was lost on me. Scotty's gentle hand on my back guided us around the hazard. His hand dropped away as I continued past the aisles of life jackets and boots, marine paint, rope and cables, five-gallon buckets of who-knows-what, quarts of oil, and various and sundry parts and tools.

It smelled like a man's store. I know how sexist that sounds, but I've never been one to enjoy the scents of grease and gasoline and machine oil ... just saying. If that makes me a wussy girl, I'm not going to lose any sleep over it because, at the end of the day, I know how to change a tire, jump a battery, and can still change the oil in my car ... if I have to.

Scotty was at my side as soon as we reached the counter. "Hey, Perry, how's business?"

"Good enough. What can I get you?"

"Wondered if you had any info about Luke Faraday."

"Do I look like a newspaper? That's all anybody's yapping about today."

"I heard he was in here the day he went missing."

"Sure, same as a dozen other guys."

"What'd he want?"

Perry Bickford had the face of a hound dog, complete with flapping jowls and sagging eyes, and yet I didn't suspect he was any older than I. He had a touch of silver at his temples, and his unnatural jet-black hair was combed back into the 50's greaser style. The Elvis look didn't really go with his straight-from-the-pound expression as he frowned at my companion. "Can't say."

It took a second to make the connection, but the annoyed glower emanating from his opaque mud-puddle eyes clinched it. Old Stin's voice stirred in my memory — *Heard it's not the same over there since Andersen's girl barged her way in and took the wheel. The girl's alright, but they say that one she married wouldn't know a grapnel from a guppy.* This must be Guppy Guy.

Scotty gave Perry a stiff nod. "Understood. Luke was telling me he had problems with his engine ever since the season started. He couldn't get the help he needed over to Hanover Point. He figured it might be farther to travel, but you guys would know how to fix him up."

I flicked a glance at the man at my side. He was leaning one hand on the counter, for all the world settled in for the long haul, just hanging for the afternoon shooting the breeze. I'd never seen Scotty hang out anywhere, but it was a convincing act. And he'd made it sound like Luke had spoken with him about the Jane Anne just a few days ago. Knowing my compatriot, I didn't doubt he'd talked with Luke, but *when* was totally up for grabs. "Not a lot of guys in the business who know what's what anymore."

Generic in the extreme, but when I saw Perry run a palm over his dark mane as if he were polishing the chrome finish on a classic sports car, I gained new respect for Mr. Stinson Sullivan Scott. *Not overplayed ... well done!*

"That's so." Perry's jowls quivered in a teeth-baring grin. "Luke was having trouble with his engine that day. He'd been in and out of here the last week or so, but this wasn't like the problem he had with it the first time."

"He buy a part?"

The grin turned into a grimace. "I'm not in the business of airing my customers' private dealings."

Oh, come on, Guppy Guy! Getting all doctor/patient confidential over a boat part? Seriously? Scotty might be able to talk around Guppy Guy, but it looked like my companion was backing him into a corner and Perry was getting a bulldog face on. We were likely to come away with nothing. "Did Luke have anyone with him?" I asked.

Perry puffed out his drooping cheeks and narrowed his eyes as if he just noticed me. "You mean the young guy with him? Nice looking, in a pretty-boy kind of way."

Scotty's steady hand came to rest on my forearm. I didn't shake it off; I just chose to ignore it.

"Yeah, my nephew."

"Thought as much. Picked up on the resemblance right off."

How nice. Smarmy as well as disagreeable. "Thank you." I tried to hold in the sarcasm, but a little splashed over. Not the time for putting an egotist in his place. "And?"

"He told Luke he thought the part he got the other day wasn't put in right. He sounded like he might know what he was talking about, but he didn't get in more than a few words before Luke bit his head off."

Nate hadn't mentioned this encounter. Was it just a head-butting guy thing or something more?

"The young guy doesn't have much of a spine, does he?" Perry broke through my thoughts like a baseball shattering a picture window. "He apologized right away, and Luke backed off. Told your ... nephew, was it? to go out and walk around, see the sights, whatever, and meet back at the boat in a half-hour."

Charming man. Scotty's grip tightened on my arm, exerting just a warning pressure. Mr. Scott needn't worry. I recognized a pompous little twit when I saw one. I'd do my best to follow my own advice with my students: *don't lower yourself to his level. He isn't worth it,* but my family pride said otherwise as I clenched my hand into a fist.

I turned my head away from the odious shop owner, stared at the far wall and focused on putting the timeline together. In spite of his superior attitude, what Perry said lined up with Nate taking in the food vendors at the Pirate Festival.

"What'd Luke buy?" Scotty tried again. "Seems like her nephew talked him out of buying anything."

I turned my attention back to the man behind the counter. Perry grunted. "You got that right. Luke went over to the parts aisle." The owner jerked his thumb toward the back of the store. "Stood there for maybe fifteen-twenty minutes and, thanks to pretty boy, left without nothing."

A cool breeze blew in, rattling the sales signs as the door opened.

"How's the paint sale going?" I asked.

"If you're not buying—"

Scotty towed me away from the snotty response just when I had a snotty comeback on my lips. "Thanks, Perry." His voice came low in my ear, "Let it go."

We pulled up short a second later. "Vickie, good to see you. How's your dad doing?" Scotty addressed a stocky woman, her tanned face careworn but her eyes bright as the sun on the water. Dressed in jeans and a yellow T-shirt, her graying-blond ponytail slotted out through the back of a Crossjack Marine cap, she exuded an air of efficiency.

"Hey, Scotty." She hunched one shoulder. "You know how it goes. He's got some health issues with his heart, and now we're looking at diabetes."

"That's tough going."

"Tell us about it," Perry brayed from behind us.

Vickie ignored the outburst. "Did you find everything you're looking for?" Her eyes darted to our empty hands, then quickly back to our faces.

"I wondered if you saw the Jane Anne anytime after Luke stopped by that day it went missing."

"I don't know, but Perry would."

"We're all set," Scotty said. I took a small sidestep to get around Vickie, but she smiled and held up her hand, pointing toward some invisible place outdoors, effectively stopping my exit.

"I'm sure there's some scuttlebutt, don't know how true it is, but you know how it is being at the end of the pier. If you don't see it, you hear about it. Perry, can you come here a minute?"

I stepped back beside Scotty, and it was my turn to exert

a little pressure on my friend's forearm. A blowhard like Perry wasn't going to take it well if he thought Scotty was going behind his back to get info.

"What's up?" Perry was all smiles as he wrapped his arm around Vickie's wiry shoulders, but his mud-brown eyes glared at us.

"Didn't Dennis say he thought he saw a boat that looked like the Jane Anne over by North Larkin?" Vickie asked.

God bless her, she knew how to grease the skids with this surly brute.

"A lot of rumors going around," Perry stalled.

"Yeah, I know, but guys always tell you things they won't tell me." She set him up perfectly. "Seems like Dennis and Andy said they saw a boat hauled out the day after Luke's went missing. They did a double take because they thought it looked like the Jane Anne."

"Wrong color, from what I hear," Perry said.

"You tell the cops?" Scotty inquired.

"Nothing to tell. One old lobster boat looks pretty much like another. Someone hauls out a boat and puts it in storage or whatever, it's nothing to me."

"That'd be Dennis Bernier?" Scotty asked.

Vickie gave an almost imperceptible nod, but Perry looked right through us as the door opened and a couple of guys clomped in, in rubber boots. "We got customers." Perry stomped away.

"Dad's health has been hard on all of us, especially Perry," Vickie said. "I have to be away a lot running Dad to appointments and staying over to his place nights, so my husband has to manage the business on his own. It's a job-and-a-half, especially in summer. He's been getting into buying salvage." Her hand dipped toward the roadblock of paint cans.

Scotty nodded. "Good to see you, Vickie. Give your dad my best."

"Thanks, Scotty. See ya."

CHAPTER TWELVE

"Luke didn't scuttle the Jane Anne. He painted it with some of Perry's surplus gray and passed it off as a different boat." I stated the obvious, at least it was blatantly obvious to me.

"Maybe." That was the best I could get out of Scotty on the boat ride back to the island, and all he left with after he dropped me off at home.

"But you *are* going to look into it. You know this Dennis guy?" I queried.

"We have a passing acquaintance, but I can see by the gleam in your eye you already expect too much. I'll talk to Dennis, but North Larkin is just the tip of the iceberg. If, and it's a *big* if, the Jane Anne did get hauled out, it could be halfway to California by now."

"True." I flashed back to my crushing meeting with Les Bigwig at CIYC. "But maybe they stashed it close to avoid being seen by too many curious eyes."

"Maybe."

I let the *maybe* haunt me until the next morning. By that time my brain was itching with a case of *what-if* hives. Only one thing would cure it—some straight answers.

I wouldn't get anything out of Scotty, at least not for the morning, so that left Kendall Jones. He'd talked with Luke on the radio that fateful day. In spite of Scotty's theory that the Jane Anne's disappearance was a one-man job, I disagreed. Kendall knew something. And if he didn't exactly know, as Luke's best buddy, he likely knew more than the rest of us.

I closed my eyes and pictured Scotty and Kendall talking by their trucks yesterday in Olivia's driveway and, call me a skeptic, they hadn't been just shooting the breeze. Scotty wanted me to think he was as cool as the waters off Candle Island but, like Devane's Rip, he had currents of suspicion running deep inside him. I was convinced Scotty had interrogated Kendall, after a fashion, but had the police even questioned the man? Huh! My eyes flapped open. *Maybe* I was on to something.

I stared out the deck doors into the fog-shrouded backyard while I punched in his number. I waited for Kendall's voice while PM wove circles around my ankles. Phone balanced on one hunched shoulder, I picked up the scrawny gray-and-white cat and he purred like the Beemer's engine as he draped over my other shoulder.

Aren't cats supposed to lower stress and blood pressure? It wasn't happening for me. I finally disconnected on the eighth or ninth ring. By that time, I'd lost count. The delay kicked in my conscience and out dribbled a growing pool of uncertainty. Maybe I should sit tight and leave well enough alone but …

I didn't want to do what I was about to do, but I couldn't stop myself. I put down my pet and he followed me out the door, halting on the step and holding up a disdainful paw at the mist-covered stair.

"It's an island day," I crooned to him before I got into Vance's car and drove off. The fog thickened as I descended from Blind Man's Bluff, so I turned on my lights and slowed down. Good thing, too, because a second later Ron's Bosox-Red pickup backed out in front of me.

I tromped on the brakes and slewed in the gravel but, mercifully, the truck stopped its backward path and sped off, disappearing into the morning vapor and leaving me to wonder if I'd imagined the whole thing.

I drove with a bit more caution over the island roads, the familiar sights of Peaslee's Pond and the heath obscured from view by the low clouds' cotton mesh. I turned onto Fossett Road and, before I could think twice about turning back, committed to taking the track down Jane Anne Lane to the Faraday place.

Without Jacey as an excuse, coming here didn't make a whole lot of sense, even to me, and visiting Olivia? She wasn't likely to buy it. *I should've baked something.* Of course, if Kendall had answered his phone, I wouldn't be coming unannounced, but even though it was a half-baked plan, my gut told me it was my best option.

I pulled in next to Kendall's truck, relieved to find Olivia's car missing. Luke's pickup was parked over by the garage. Maybe I could slip under the radar, in and out before she returned.

I hurried toward the house, but a shout from the nearby gambrel garage stayed my hand mid-knock. I turned. Kendall leaned out the side door and beckoned me over. With each step through the shifting mist, he looked scruffier than ever with four days' beard growth, bed head, ripped jeans, and a gray T-shirt with a Texas-shaped stain on the front. But he grinned and, with a rag in his grease-stained hand, held the door open for me. "Gwen, I was coming to see you today."

"I must've gotten the vibes and saved you a trip."

He shut the door, and the large space hummed with the buzz of the overhead fluorescent lights. The garage smelled of lawn equipment, dried grass, oil and grease. A couple of outboard motors and boat paraphernalia were scattered around, but the tools hung in an orderly fashion from a large pegboard on the wall. On a workbench were parts of something Kendall was dismantling. It looked like a water pump, but I wasn't sure. "Don't let me disturb you," I said.

"Oh, this is nothing." He flung his rag on top of the

project. "I brought it over from my place. I was just messing around to pass the time."

I nodded. Wasn't that why I was here? Neither one of us was used to sitting still.

"You got news?" He propped one lean hip against the bench.

"The detective came and talked to my nephew yesterday."

"What'd he say?"

I wasn't sure if Kendall was referring to Nate or the detective. "Not much on either score. Nate said the detective was tight-lipped, only asked questions and never answered any."

"Huh, makes sense." He scratched his graying stubble. "What'd your nephew say?"

The question wasn't out of line, but the high-voltage intensity of his light blue stare unnerved me. Of course, he wanted this solved. By his own admission, he and Luke were like brothers. Did Kendall believe Nate was responsible for the tragedy? I tried not to let the loopy thoughts in my brain spaghetti out of my mouth. "Not much. He doesn't remember anything, and it's eating him alive."

Was it my imagination or did his tense body ease. "Well, there you have it." He sighed. "We'll probably never know what went on out there."

Did I detect a note of relief in his tone? I took a deep breath and let it all out. "He *did* say you called Luke on the radio."

Kendall swung his head back and forth at an angle, like a swimmer with water in his ear. "More like Luke called me to ream me out. The Jane Anne was skipping, having engine problems again, and he blamed me. I thought I'd fixed her up once and for all on Friday, but she must've had something else go south. The boat was a floating catastrophe, but Luke wouldn't give her up."

It was now or never. *Dig it up or leave it alone.* I was

always handy with a garden spade. "Was that what you guys were…" *how should I put it* "discussing when you came to pick me up at the ferry on Friday?"

"Uh . . ." Kendall closed his eyes. "Seems like a million years ago. You heard that, huh?"

"Sorry, it was hard not to."

"Yup." He stretched his neck like a heron in what I now recognized as a familiar Kendall Jones' tic. "We were going at it, but it wasn't the first time. I was so used to it, I didn't really think of it as an argument. More like a debate."

A rose by any other name. *Sounded like an argument to me.*

"Olivia hated that boat, thought it wasn't safe. She was right, but Luke would never admit it."

This was leading somewhere, but it could lead to him never speaking to me again. Thin-ice topic. *Tiptoe.* "Was Olivia desperate enough to try to force Luke to get rid of the Jane Anne?"

"Maybe." There was that word again. "But wanting to, and being able to make it happen, are two different things." He ran his gray fingers through his thin hair. It helped get rid of the bed head, but left the 'do lank and as dull as my grandmother's ancient moth-eaten raccoon coat. "Luke would never give up that boat. Never happen. Olivia didn't know a thing about the boat or about the water. Didn't want to. Oh, she rode on the Jane Anne a few times in the beginning, but it got old fast. Can you picture her with that manicure of hers, handling bait or hauling traps? She was as different from Luke's first wife as winter and summer."

Who was winter and who was summer? I had a pretty good idea.

He kicked the toe of his sneaker at a dead leaf that must've blown in with me, snubbing it against the cement floor. "Olivia wanted out. Luke knew it. Everybody knew it."

Luke and Olivia's marital problems might have played

a part in this tragedy, but I was with Kendall. I couldn't picture Olivia chipping a nail, let alone engineering a boat scuttling. She might seem the type for that sort of revenge, but she wasn't the type to actually pull it off. She'd never get her hands dirty; it was too much work.

Olivia was a dead end, but the man in front of me had to know something. "Why do you think Luke didn't take you out with him on Saturday?" A little convoluted, but as least I got it out there. *Finally!*

Kendall shrugged. "You saw it yourself. He was mad at me. That was Luke, cutting off his nose to spite his face, and I just happened to be the nose this time. He always got over our spats, but he wasn't over it on Saturday."

For a man who knew something, Kendall was frustratingly calm. I dropped the bomb. "If he'd taken you with him, maybe none of this would've happened." Not exactly how I'd wanted to say it, but *boom!*—there it was.

I felt a twinge of guilt. I should've phrased it differently so he wouldn't be feeling guilty, too. Turns out the concern was all mine. Kendall pulled a red bandanna out of his back pocket and wiped his nose. "No, don't you ever think like that, Gwen. I hear what folks've been saying, but it's not your nephew's fault. None of it. If it's anyone's fault, it'd be Luke's." He reached out a grease-stained finger and swiped it under his eye, leaving a telltale silvery smear as he derailed a tear.

Was Scotty right? "Do you think Luke engineered the whole thing? I mean, not his death, but the missing boat so he could..."I couldn't bring myself to be so crass as to use the words *cash in on the insurance* when speaking ill of the dead. I took the safer, hopefully more sensitive, route. " ... make Olivia happy?"

Kendall frowned but nodded his head. "Could be. You know, it very well could be." He stood.

Did his back look a little less bowed? *Just wishful thinking.* "What would he have done with the Jane Anne?"

"Made it disappear."

"But how? I wouldn't think he'd've had the heart to scuttle it."

"I wouldn't have either, but to keep Olivia? Maybe. It was make-or-break time for their marriage, and it was either the wife or the boat."

"Nothing's that simple."

"This was, cut and dried from the day she came to live on the island. It was the boat and all that the Jane Anne represented. Competing with a first wife who still held a place in Luke's heart, living on Candle Island day after day, taking care of Jacey, being tied down to a blue-collar working life ... none of that's Olivia."

"She must've known that when she married Luke."

Kendall shrugged. "When you fall for someone, everything looks golden. Life on a coastal island can sound like paradise, but Candle Island ain't no Hawaii, and it didn't take long for Olivia to figure that out."

Tell me something I don't know.

"But Luke was a good guy, down deep, and Olivia knew that, and I think she really loved him."

"Would Luke have chosen Olivia over Jacey?" I asked.

Kendall pulled on his chin. "Now *that* I don't know. Would've been tough on him, either way."

He perked up his head and I heard it, too—the hum of an engine, tires crunching on gravel.

I should've baked something.

"Olivia's back." Kendall's tone was dead neutral. *Strange.*

"Well, I'd better run along. I just wanted you to know about Nate and the investigation."

"Why don't you stay and visit with Olivia? The pastor came over once, but most everyone else has stayed away. 'Course part of that's Olivia. Down to the pier, she as much as said Laverna and her friends weren't welcome, and that's about everyone on the island. I'm surprised she made an exception for me, to tell you the truth."

He massaged his forehead. "She's in a bad way. She even turned away a visit from a couple of older ladies from the church, and that got around some quick. Said she didn't want to listen to their sugar-coated sympathy."

"Then what makes you think she'll want to see me?"

"You're different, Gwen."

Different in a good way? I didn't think so.

"Kendall!" Olivia's southern-accented fishwife cry was like fingernails on a chalkboard to my guilty conscience. No sneaking out now. I had no sugar-coated sympathy, but Olivia was a grief-stricken widow. How hard-hearted could I be? I turned and opened the door with Kendall nearly on my heels. "Better let me go out first." He pressed by me, smelling of coffee, grease, and some other chemical scent. Maybe turpentine?

I didn't want to break it to him, but the Beemer with the CIYC logo was parked out there. A dead giveaway. This had been a bad idea from the moment I left the house. Why hadn't I listened to myself?

I rubbed my face with my palms and pasted on a smile. Nothing to do but brazen it out, but what I wouldn't give for a plate of fresh-baked brownies to use as a shield. "Olivia." I stepped out of the safety of the garage and into her line of fire. She stood beside Kendall, the glint in her eye one of feminine assessment. Even with a home-baked offering, Olivia Faraday wouldn't be fooled or pacified.

While her mental gears turned and her eye took in my maroon-and-gold Bookerton Bobcats' hoodie and faded jeans, I did my own woman-to-woman critique. For a mourning widow, Olivia looked well, far better than the man at her side. She wore ecru slacks and a teal silk blouse with an off-white fuzzy, maybe Angora, sweater casually draped over one arm, not quite concealing a pricey handbag.

Not a smudge of blue eye shadow or red lipstick was out of place. Her hair had that fresh glowing sun-kissed breezy look. Her fingers reached out and, as I took them in mine, her jeweled rings flashed in spite of the lack of sunlight. The golden bracelets on her wrists softly clinked, and her proximity emanated eau de beauty parlor.

She was probably getting ready for the memorial service. Looking like a million bucks would be a top priority, and one way Olivia could set herself apart from the island mourners. Although she'd always set herself apart from them, so why would this tragic time be any different?

The thought quickly morphed into personal paranoia … Nate attending Luke's funeral. Olivia looking like this, needing comfort and a shoulder to cry on. Bait knife or not, it had all the makings of an island soap opera with my nephew as the unwitting fall guy.

"I'm so glad you came." Her breathy voice accentuated her drawl. I'm sure I gaped as she squeezed my fingers and finally let go. "I hope Kendall hasn't been boring you with his fix-it-up project of the day. He's practically taken over Luke's workshop."

Kendall snorted and, with ill grace, pushed past me and disappeared into the garage once again.

"Don't pay any attention." Olivia fluffed her hair with a practiced gesture. "He's just in a mood because I've decided not to have a service for Luke, and he wasn't consulted. I learned the hard way. I can't trust Kendall with even the simplest thing. He'll always screw it up."

I didn't think my eyes could pop out any farther, but I was wrong. "No service?"

She gently blotted away a tear from the corner of her eye, at least I think it was the start of a tear. "I decided it would be too sad for me, *and* for Jacey, of course. Better for her to remember her grampie as he was, full of life and laughter, lifting her up in his big, strong arms."

"That's considerate." *I guess.* "And it really *is* your decision, yours and Erica's."

"Erica couldn't make a decision to save her soul. She'd

be happy to have me take care of everything for her."

"She doesn't know yet?"

Olivia shook her head. "I decided just this morning. The pastor called and it was suddenly all too much. I'm this far away from a breakdown." She held up her thumb and finger and it looked to me like they were touching. I hope that didn't mean she'd gone over the edge, but chatting it up with me seemed like a warning indicator of weirdness.

I kept it generic. "It must be overwhelming, but maybe Erica could help you with some of the details."

"You don't know the girl. Why do you think Luke and I had Jacey? She's incapable of making adult decisions. But I've decided I'll have her pick up Luke's ashes. She can throw them out with the tide if she wants. That would be the most fitting memorial."

Harsh!

"Luke was her father, she ought to do something, but Erica just wants this all to disappear and she certainly doesn't want anything to do with the island."

And you do? Not the time to be catty. "You might feel differently later on."

Olivia slowly shook her head. "I'm not the type of wife to carry ashes in my handbag. I have my Luke in my heart. That's all I need. But I'm so tired of all this, I could just scream. I want to talk about happy things, do you mind?" I could've sworn she batted her eyes at me, but maybe I imagined it. "Won't you come in for a moment?"

She tossed her head toward the house, and the blond strands fell magically back into place as I fell into an uneasy step beside her. This went beyond weird and straight into the twilight zone. "Sure." I should've baked something. At least then I could stuff my face and wouldn't have to talk so much.

Turns out I didn't have to worry about the talking part. Olivia had it covered. "I went to Coveside and had my hair and nails done at the Coffee and Coiffure. I try to go to the mainland when I need to have it colored, but over the past week I've let myself go. You understand."

I fought the urge to finger comb my hair, sure that the misty day had turned it into a frizzy-sphinx flashback to the eighties. Why bother? I was totally out of my league, and if that's what Olivia needed to feel good about herself, I was happy to oblige. "It looks nice," I murmured.

"I thought it would help keep me sane if I got out of the house and mingled with other people." As we stopped at the door she flicked a finger back toward the garage. "I mean someone besides Kendall and Luke's family. People who can talk about normal things. I've been so cooped up here, almost like a prisoner, I swear, and it's enough to drive a person crazy."

I automatically nodded as she opened the door and her little dog came tearing out, yapping around our ankles.

"Magnolia, honey, did you miss Mama?" Olivia scooped her up and hugged her to her cheek, cooing to the frenzied, squirming, licking ball of white fur as she led the way into the house. It was warm inside, and close; almost like a sauna, but she was, after all, not from around here. And yet she'd been standing outside for the past ten minutes sans sweater. Her perfectly accented outfit and makeup told the story. Beauty knows no pain, and certainly doesn't surrender fashion to any weather condition.

I slipped off my sweatshirt, emphasis on *sweat,* in this room.

Olivia twitched as a shiver seized her body. "It's just like winter out there today. I can't bear the thought of snow." She sighed dramatically, set down her purse on the table and gestured toward a chair. "Would you like a cup of tea or coffee? I'm sure I could dig up something for you. It's been so difficult to even think of eating, or doing the mundane things around the house. I know it's a mess. I apologize."

I glanced around the large kitchen. It was beautiful. Even with the gray day, the butcher block counters, off-white cupboards, and delft-blue-and-white tile splashback gleamed with a cozy inner glow. The elevated table and chairs were cherry and sat taller than the nearby window, an indication of new furniture. A few dirty dishes sat in the sink, and some white fur skated across the blue-tiled floor as I stepped toward the table, but it was a well-kept home. What'd I expect? I'd heard Pam Dutton came in once a week to clean for them.

"I'm fine, thank you, unless you'd like me to get you something." I glanced toward what looked like a brand-new gas range, pristine with no tea kettle in view.

"No, I couldn't bear anything. The island's so stuck in the dark ages with strangers sending all their leftovers to me. As if that could take away my pain!"

So, I *shouldn't* have baked anything. I fell into clover on that one ... once in a row. As I turned toward the table, my eye caught several boxes and a couple of large black trash bags stashed against the wall by the door.

"I haven't been able to eat at all. I'm too emotionally distraught. We can just sit and chat." Olivia slipped into a high kitchen chair and stroked the dog, but her eyes and those of her dog didn't miss a trick. She nodded toward the boxes. "I've had Kendall helping me clean out some of Luke's things, and some of Jacey's stuff that Erica refused to take with them."

I studied my hostess with growing amazement. I'd figured Olivia wouldn't be sticking around the island, but this woman not only didn't let the grass grow under her feet, she ripped up the lawn, grass seed and all, on her way out of town. "That must've been tough on both of you."

"You probably think I should wait a while. Most folks do."

I tried to school my features into a benign expression as I hung my sweatshirt on the back of the chair and sat. "I think everyone handles grief differently. There's no right or wrong."

"You should tell that to Kendall and the island gossips.

Worse than a bunch of magpies, each and every one of them. Of course, you know exactly what I'm talking about. Look what they did with our Nathaniel. Dragging his reputation through the mudflats like that. It was downright shameful."

Our Nathaniel? Selective memory time! Olivia had been the head cheerleader on *that* smear campaign, but fortunately she had one foot out the door, and for Nate's sake, I was glad to see her go. "He's a big boy. He can handle himself, and the truth will come out. It always does."

"I suppose you're right, but it hurts to hear the things they're saying about both men. Thank goodness, they've found the body so I have closure. The investigation won't last much longer."

"But they didn't find the boat, yet." These were the happier things she wanted to talk about?

"Sunk. It was older than Noah's Ark. Luke bought it used, decades ago. Can't you just see my poor Lukey trying to get the boat back home and then having the engine blow and having to abandon ship? He must've swam all the way to Stub Island, wanting to get home so badly." She stifled a sob.

What about leaving Nate on that buoy miles away from Stub? I settled for something less sarcastic. "What about the bait knife?" I shouldn't have asked at a time like this, but with her flip-flop on Nate I wanted to know where we stood.

"Luke always kept one over there." She gestured toward the outside. "Up in the tree near that horrid little Pepto-Bismol™-colored camp. He hid it up high so Jacey couldn't get her hands on it."

"So," *just to be clear* "the investigators don't think it was the knife Nate was using on the Jane Anne?"

"Oh no. Where would you get that idea?"

Where indeed? I shook my head.

"I can't for the life of me figure out why Luke had it, but I told the man who came to question me all about the camp and the knife. He was a nice young gentleman. He apologized for having to talk with me. Of course, I didn't know much, and a lot of it was the grief talking, but I told him what I thought. I think Luke must've rested on Stub to get warm and gain his strength. I believe he was going to swim across the rip when the tide was right, but he must've been delirious, or had hypothermia or something. He was so close to me that last day, and I never knew. He could've hollered for help, and maybe that's what he was going to do when he slipped and hit his head." She sniffled and bowed her head into the little dog's fur.

"I guess we'll never know all the details."

When she looked up again, her eyes showed no trace of tears. "That's why I want to get off the island and visit Nathaniel in the hospital. I know he must be feeling almost as low as I do. It'll help us both to commiserate, and maybe we can find some closure."

I thought you already had closure. I didn't bother to correct her assumption that Nate was still in the hospital.

"I just feel so bad, responsible really, for allowing Nathaniel to get on that old boat. And for nearly losing his life. I hope you don't hold it against me, Gwen."

"It's the farthest thing from my mind, believe me."

"Oh, I do." She reached across the table and gripped my hand, the diamond on her ring catching the overhead light and shooting rainbows across the kitchen wall. "I have nightmares about it. I haven't had a good night's sleep since they disappeared. I'm hoping that will all change when I leave tomorrow."

Tomorrow? *Shocker!* "I hope so, too." I disentangled my fingers and rose slowly to my feet. "I'm truly sorry for your loss. I'll keep you and Jacey in my prayers, and I wish you well in the days ahead."

"I may be seeing you."

"Yes, I'd thought of that. We'll see." I didn't sound sympathetic or particularly encouraging. I sounded like the schoolteacher I was but, short of acting like a crazy woman, it was the best I could muster. "I really should go. I'm sure you have a lot of things to take care of before you leave."

She stood and shifted the little dog to ride in the crook of her arm. "Oh, Kendall will take care of any loose ends for me." She smiled. "He's a little lost, now that Luke's gone. I'm afraid when I leave he won't know what to do with himself. He was always showing up and inviting himself to dinner ... well, any meal, actually. He sort of attached himself to us, like we were his family. Neither Luke nor I had the heart to turn him away. Sometimes it got to be a bit much, especially for Luke. He used to call him bloodsucker."

Careful, dear. When Peter talks about Paul—or Luke talks about Kendall, I learn more about Luke than Kendall. I hadn't known him, but I wasn't sure I would've liked him. "I know he's heartbroken. Kendall told me he thought of your husband as a brother."

She snorted and the dog growled. "More like a rival. The two of them were always competing, although Luke didn't really care. He had everything he wanted. And you didn't hear it from me, but my Luke had everything Kendall wanted. I thought about giving Kendall some of Luke's tools, but I know that's the last thing my husband would have wanted. Once I leave, I'll hire a caretaker to look after my interests and the place. How about your man, Scotty?"

I swallowed hard. If I didn't leave soon, she'd be inviting me to her and Nate's wedding and asking me to cater it. Maybe that was a bit harsh, but Olivia's steel-magnolia personality was steamrolling over me. I needed to leave now, or we might not part on such cordial terms. "Yes, I believe he looks after a lot of summer properties." Delivered prim as a turn-of-the-century boarding school head mistress.

Olivia put her hand on my wrist. "Could you ask him to stop by today?"

"I can give you his phone number."

"Oh no. I think it would be better coming from you. Remember, I'm leaving tomorrow. I plan, first thing, to contact a real estate agent on the mainland, but I don't know as I can unload this until next summer. I won't take just chump change for all this. Would you?"

I was beginning to think sugar-coated sympathy would've been better on my psyche than this. "It's a lovely home and a beautiful location." I edged toward the door. "I'll leave Scotty a message." I had my hand on the doorknob almost home free.

"Thank you. Oh! Please don't tell Nathaniel I'm coming by. I want it to be a surprise."

"I wouldn't dream of it." That woman was delusional ... or bonkers ... or both. I slipped on my sweatshirt and, in that moment, she blindsided me. Olivia rushed forward and wrapped me in a hug, her neck extended carefully to the side to keep her hair from getting crushed.

The dog whimpered and growled. I wanted to, as well, but I kept silent. I accepted the clinch and said good-bye again before I slipped out to the BMW, desperate to go, even if it meant skipping out without saying good-bye to Kendall. Turned out, he'd already left.

I drove off with traces of coffee and coiffure clinging to my sweatshirt. I opened the windows wide to blow away the foreign scent and drink in the chilly air. At the main road I turned toward Coveside. The town still had its share of tourists bobbing in and out of the fog, but the number was markedly fewer now that summer was officially over.

I didn't want to admit we had anything in common but, like Olivia, my life had been held hostage by the recent tragic events. I bought some groceries and pulled into the parking lot at Barb's before leaving town. I wanted to get Jacey's address before I forgot. Never make a promise, especially to a five-year-old, that you don't intend to keep.

I didn't know if anything Olivia said about Erica had a grain of truth to it. I suspected it was mostly jealousy talking, but Jacey could use a friend right now, even a recent one like me, while she settled into her new life and new school.

My mind replayed those moments right off the ferry when I'd talked with Luke about his granddaughter and he'd voiced his need to protect her from me, a stranger, if I was teaching instead of Laurel. How twisted life had become in less than a week's time. I'd been thrust into Jacey's life and Luke had been yanked out.

I might not know much about Luke Faraday, and I might not like what I *did* know, but he did love his granddaughter and she was going to miss that love.

I saw Dot's signature maroon cap of hair bobbing at the window and stood like a squirrel in the road, uncertain how to play this. Go to the window and encounter Dot? Go to the back door and encounter Dot? I had a feeling it was a lose/lose for me either way, so I stepped into line and waited, using the time to carefully craft a non-inflammatory remark but, knowing Dot, even a "Nice day," would set off a spark at best. Most likely a stick of dynamite.

Sure, we had that little bugaboo-thing between us of her late husband leaving me the mansion in his will, but I didn't get her over-the-top hatred. I stepped up to the window. Looking past my nemesis, I glimpsed Laverna in the back. *I should've done the back door thing.*

"What's your order?"

"Hi, Dot. How are you?"

"Oh. It's you!"

As if she was unaware of my arrival the moment I drove into the parking lot in her late husband's car. But it worked for me. Denial and manufactured surprise beat open ranting any time. "I'd like to speak to Laverna, if she's got a minute."

"You aren't here to see me?" She pressed her nose mosquito-close to the screen so I could see her pores and mole through the mesh.

"No, not unless *you* want to talk." Not really the timing I would've chosen, but I *had* written the invitation, and since when did Dot ever want to talk with me? *Carpe Dottie.*

"Talk! Is that what you think this is?" Her squawking turned the heads of those around me. "I can't believe what you've done now. I didn't think it could get any worse, but I should've known you'd never stop until you stole every cussed thing of mine. You won't be satisfied until you get the very last egg in my refrigerator."

She was right. Make that *rant,* not talk.

I felt like a DIY home plumber trying to stop a busted pipe leak with my bare hands, but I took my shot when she came up for air. "What are you talking about?" I kept my voice low.

"You think I don't know? You sneaking around behind my back? It wasn't enough to take my home, now you're trying to get the boatyard away from Ron."

Loonier than a bin! "No, I'm not."

"And you know the worst part? He thinks you're his friend. Two-faced backstabber."

"I never—"

"Oh, Miss Sweetness-and-light, don't try that on me. I went to school with Gail's mother."

Gail? I might be wing walking here, but I was totally off balance and about to take a header, *big* time.

"I know everything. How you drove my husband's pride-and-joy BMW, parked in Vance's spot and waltzed in there like you owned the place. Well, my boy is too tender hearted to see what's going on, but you better believe I'm not."

Ah, Gail, the receptionist at CIYC. I kicked myself out of the brain clouds and went on the offensive. "Understood." *Loud and clear.* Actually, loud and clear enough for everyone here to get it. I wondered where Ron got his tenderhearted nature. Must be from a long-lost ancestor.

"Ron and I had words this morning, thanks to your interference. Trying to turn my own flesh-and-blood against me." Her words caught on a sob.

Ron's red truck pulling out in front of me earlier. It

made more and more sense. "I'm sure it's just—"

"Shut up! It's *all* your fault!" She wasn't just ready to pounce, she was in it for the brawl, the nastier and bloodier the better. If she had her way, Dot would use this lunch box stage to paint me into a corner and, if she couldn't do that, she'd at least color my reputation with as many islanders as were in ear shot.

Come on! "You had words over me?"

"You were part of it. You and that Shaunessy girl he married. All them Shaunessys are no good. They're a lazy tribe."

Pick on me, okay. Ron's sweet wife? Uh-uh! I fought to keep my voice pleasant. "Not Laurel. She's a wonderful teacher and a Jones now, your daughter-in-law."

Dot ignored my plug for a little truth and sanity. "Ron would choose her over me, even choose her over the shipyard. He said that to my face."

Good for him! I sent up a quick SOS for checking my temper. *Keep it civil.* "Ron's stepping up, trying to be a good husband and protector. Traits he learned from you." It was a stab in the dark of a semi-compliment, but it didn't cut Ron, Laurel, or me any slack.

And it obviously didn't scratch her conscience or her motherly loyalty either. "Says he and that new wife of his 'need their own space.' He's moving out, and don't think I don't know who give him that advice and put him up to it."

I nodded. I'd own that one. "I might have mentioned something along that line."

"It's all because of you coming here. You've ruined my life. Now he's leaving me." Her rant slowed as she stripped the tears from her cheek with a rough hand. "Ron's all I have. Where will they go? Frank Shaunessy don't want 'em, he's made that plain enough. He'll never forgive his daughter for marrying my son."

Like you forgive Laurel for marrying your son? I tried to switch direction. "Maybe things will change when the grandchildren come along."

"*What* grandchildren! She just miscarried their first, and maybe there won't be another."

Way to keep it positive. "Give it a little time. Ron's upset, but he'll come around."

"He won't. Only reason he didn't pack up their stuff was they ain't got nowhere to go, yet. "

Providential? This was my shot, and I should take it. It couldn't be any clearer than if it was a window without a pane of glass, but maybe that was just me. I squinted through the screened square at Dot's face, the mottled skin nearly matching her hair color. "They could come to the mansion."

"No!" Her trembling voice rose to a shriek. "You are not taking my son."

Let go and let it fly. Now or never. "I wouldn't. I couldn't. But did you ever think of living in the mansion and making it into two separate living quarters?"

"You'd like that, wouldn't you! Making a home for my son in what should be *my* home."

"No, if you'd just listen a minute. You could live there, too. I'd move out."

It went deathly quiet for a second. No murmuring and muttering behind me. A gull shrieked overhead, and the woman behind the screen drew in a loud shuddering breath. "Where?" Her small eyes narrowed to slits and her lips compressed beyond her usual lemon-sucking look to a tight alabaster line.

Good-bye wing; it's all-or-nothing time. "Maybe you could let me stay in the old homestead until I find something.

"The cottage? I knew it! I knew you wanted every lick of what I own, and I won't be paying you rent to live in my own home up on the cliffs."

"Dot, what in the daylights is going on? They can hear you all the way to Mulroon Point." Laverna flashed a dark look at her employee, then at me.

Dot Jones ripped off her apron, flung it to the floor,

pushed past Laverna and slammed out the back door.

Laverna never missed a beat. "Cindy, come tend the window." She beckoned me toward the back with a blur of her hand.

I nodded, stepped out of line, careful not to make eye contact with the disgruntled patrons behind me, but I didn't hurry around the trailer. I wanted to give Dot plenty of time to vacate the premises.

Laverna had the door open and motioned with an impatient jerk of her head. "Get in here. I gotta cook while we talk since I'm one person short."

Thanks to me. "Yeah, sorry about that. What can I do?"

She pushed Dot's apron into my hand. "Put on a hat and an apron and start stuffing crab rolls. Six of 'em, nice and full, no skimping."

"Gotcha." I quickly washed my hands, slipped on my predecessor's accoutrements and got to work. It could've been fun, but my co-worker's smoldering glances and set jaw stopped any flippant comments. I worked in silence, except for Laverna's terse directions, and had three orders up before she finally pulled back her iron curtain peeve.

"Is it true?" Laverna demanded.

"What? Ron and Dot?"

"You think I care about that bull?" She shook her head and turned from the fryer to glare at me. "I'd believe almost anything of that southern witch, but to not have a memorial for Luke, that's low, even for her."

From the fryer into the fire on this one. Dot I could take, even on my worst day. Laverna? I was no match for her even on my best day. I tried to put a good spin on it, but it had already spun out of control long ago. "She thought it would be hard on Jacey."

"That's what she's saying? Bull! She *never* intended to do anything. It's not right! Luke deserves some type of tribute, at least a few kind words from his friends. This is low, even for her."

"Yeah, but she's leaving soon." I tossed it over my shoulder as I passed Cindy a couple of grilled red-hot dogs smothered in onions."

"Leaving?" Laverna grabbed hold of my wrist. "When?"

"Not sure." Pretty sure I shouldn't have told Olivia's business to anyone, particularly Laverna, but it was out now.

"I shouldda seen it. I seen her come out of Anna's shop this morning, strutting around, all glitz and glitter. I thought she'd got all painted up for Luke's funeral. Shouldda known. She got rid of Jacey. She got rid of Luke. She's movin' on."

I couldn't fault her logic. The door fanned open, and Dot barged in, locking eyes with me. I pasted on an innocent smile, but neither one of us bought it.

"What's she doing in here?" Dot barked.

"Working," Laverna retorted. "You left me short-handed."

"Just taking a break." Dot's eyes never left me.

I whipped off the apron and hat.

"Could've fooled me. You back on now?" Laverna demanded.

"Yeah." Dot's glower left me with the hat dangling from my fingers as she tied on her apron.

I set the hat on a case of soda, sidled past her, but Laverna grabbed my wrist on the way by. "We'll talk later."

"Okay. I came by to get Jacey's address. Thought she might need some cheering up."

Laverna nodded, tears in her eyes. "Thanks." She squeezed my hand before she let me go.

I stepped out into the dank air and took a deep breath. "Two strikes, eh, Gwen?" Old Stin sauntered up, carrying the two-hotdog basket I'd just prepared, one dog half gone.

"You heard all that?"

"I'm old, not deaf! Impossible not to."

I sighed. "You might want to stay away from me, then."

Old Stin tipped his head back and roared.

CHAPTER THIRTEEN

Call me a wimp, *which is only slightly better than 'Olivia's tool.'* I couldn't bring myself to leave a message demanding Scotty put in an appearance at the Faraday place to placate Olivia before she left the island. Instead, I left a somewhat chirpy-worded sentence for him to call me back or, better yet, stop by.

I spent my downtime stress-eating a lunch-and-a-half of calories and roaming the cold rooms of my mausoleum. I tried to divert my attention by mentally constructing a wall here, a door there, converting the library into bedrooms, the conservatory into a kitchen/dining area. There were plenty of design options and it could be a beautiful thing, but it wasn't *my* thing. It would have to be Dot's, Ron's, and Laurel's.

I hoped once her rage settled back into its usual simmer, my proposal would, if not resonate with Dot, at least percolate into some way she could turn this into her idea, and we could get on with it. *Why does everything have to be so hard?* Because, by and large, people prefer it that way. We refuse to get along. We fill our mental tanks with slights, envy, and conflicts, real and imagined—the emotional equivalent of rocket fuel to power us through another day of judging others.

Cynical! Time to move on to something better, but my mind simply shot over to Luke's death with the velocity of a paperclip zipping up and sticking to a car crane magnet. I was just like Olivia, telling me she wanted to talk about happy things but meandering over unresolved issues. *This isn't good!* I didn't like the mental comparison between either of these two women and myself, but if the apron fit . . .

I put on a pink Candle Island cap and an anorak to shed the fog that had now become a blowing mist and got out of the house. Instead of doing the smart thing, walking over to the cliffs and staring off to sea from Blind Man's Bluff, my feet turned out the driveway and down the hill. I told myself it was because I couldn't see the ocean view in fog like this, but I knew where I was going—straight into trouble.

I walked at a good clip, all the while sorting facts in my muddled brain. The version of Luke's death Olivia fed me this morning was pure fantasy. If she needed to believe the fairy tale that her hero was swimming the Atlantic Ocean to get back by her side, that was her prerogative; but, seriously?

Nevertheless, Luke leaving Nate at the buoy didn't fit with any of it. Why did he just drive the Jane Anne away from a man who was sick and in the water? Okay, Nathaniel was on the buoy, but it was still surrounded by water. If Nate was drugged as the patsy, for what purpose? So Luke could ditch the Jane Anne and save his marriage? To cash in on the insurance to keep his bride in the manner of living she demanded?

These were all patched-together theories from everyone else. What did I believe? Nate was suffering from food poisoning. Couldn't prove it, but I'd own my part of the pirate's revenge with my tuna sandwiches, if I had to. Luke couldn't have known Nate would get sick. *But Olivia had!* I did a mental gasp as I pictured her pale distorted face inches from mine under the lights on the pier that first night. What had she said? *Luke told her Nate was seasick.*

I clenched my fist and stopped mid-stride. There was something fishy here. Nate wasn't sick until they were on their way back from Blackwall. Olivia couldn't have known that, could she? I felt I was onto something, but maybe I had the timeline messed up in my head. I needed to think about it. I started walking again, head down, seeing nothing save the blur of wet shiny gravel under my feet.

What was the deal with Olivia and Nate? She blames him for her husband's death then wants to jump into his arms for comfort? How sick is that? What were the chances she'd know the guy her husband hired on the spur of the moment? Did Olivia have a say in hiring Nate? I didn't think so. Nate hadn't mentioned it.

But Nate getting sick after they left Blackwall, after Olivia had spoken to Luke on the phone, was a breakthrough … I hoped. Maybe she was just mixed up and grief stricken, but it pointed to Olivia talking with Luke on the cell somewhere enroute to home port.

Nate said he'd heard Luke's phone and the radio, but by that time Luke had passed out at the wheel. Maybe someone drugged the wrong guy. If so, Luke had no part in it.

Could it be as simple as Kendall had said? Luke was so angry at his long-time buddy, he chose Nate at random, an able body showing up at the right time in the wrong place?

Luke wouldn't have scuttled the Jane Anne. I didn't know him, but all that I *did* know pointed to a man with deep emotional attachments to his late wife, and that included the boat still bearing her name seven years after her death. He hadn't changed it to the "Olivia," and that spoke volumes.

Had he painted it gray and hidden the fact from Olivia? I thought about the guy from Crossjack Marine and the rumors of the Jane Anne sighting, but that's all they were right now … rumors. Depending on what Scotty found out—and I needed him to come back with one tangible piece of evidence to get this thing unstuck from the doldrums—some of these jagged-edged pieces had to go together.

How had Luke ended up on Stub with no boat? There had to be an accomplice, and *not* the boat-hating Olivia. That left Kendall or someone I didn't know.

I glanced up as the aura of glowing headlights bore down on me. A familiar pickup emerged from the wall of mist and stopped alongside. A rusty-haired head poked out the window. "You stare at it long enough, maybe you can get it to magically change places with the house on the hill."

I looked back at the old Jones' cottage, the unconscious object of my scrutiny. Heat burned in my cheeks. "Hop in, I'll take you home … unless you've already moved in down here."

"Ha! Ha!" I swatted the arm leaning out the open window before I skipped around the hood and got in the passenger's side. I was relieved to note the driveway was empty. Ron's truck was nowhere to be seen, and Dot must still be working at Barb's. No activity, no eyes to catch the longing in mine ... except for the man sitting next to me.

The engine was running but he hadn't started up the hill. "Well?"

"Grampa filled me in on all the gory details at Laverna's."

"It wasn't pretty."

"You gave it a shot."

I shrugged, drooping from the moisture in the air and my morning of defeat. I looked into his blue eyes and caught a twinkle so like Old Stin's. But what was charming in the elder Scott could be annoying in the younger version. He was enjoying this! "Maybe it's a long shot, but it doesn't have to be," I said.

"I don't take your meaning."

"You could help that shot-in-the-dark hit the target."

"It's more like a Hail Mary." His eyes took on their usual guarded look.

"You're Dot's cousin. You could help her, and Ron come to the right decision here."

"And that is?"

"Move back into the big house and let me rent their

cottage, at least for the time being, and see where it goes."

"Hardly an even swap. If they're going to rent to you, you ought to rent to them."

"Hey, don't complicate it."

"Complicate it? It's more knotted up than a buoy rope caught in a propeller. I couldn't possibly make it worse."

"That's just it! You could make it better."

"Where'd you get *that* idea?" He scratched his jaw and shook his head. "Nope, don't answer that, forget I asked. Wouldn't touch it with a ten-foot pole. Why can't you just stay put for the winter and leave well enough alone?"

"Ron and Laurel need their own place."

"And that's *their* problem."

"It wouldn't be if I hadn't taken Dot and Ron's home away from them."

"Last I heard you didn't take it, Vance left it to you in his will."

"Yeah, well, he made a mistake, and we are *not* going to be held hostage by a dead man's bully agenda."

"Why is this so important to you?"

I gestured toward the little white cape with only the chimney and part of the roof poking through the fog, the tops of the spruces pointing up like ghostly sentinels. Scotty put the truck in gear and drove slowly away.

I couldn't put it into words. I wasn't sure I wanted to because, while I might talk about other people holding onto fantasies and fairy tales, it takes one to know one, as my students would say. This cottage was my fantasy, and totally unrealistic when I thought it through in the harsh bright sunlight. But wrapped up in wisps of fog and morning mist and evening starlight, it held the once-upon-a-time mystique of a dream that could have a happily-ever-after ending.

Never happen? *Never say never.* That's why I was stuck in this fantasy and wouldn't let go.

"You gonna tell me?" His voice was soft and slow.

I'd rather he think I was naïve than crazy, wouldn't I? I

looked down at my hands, fisted in my lap, and unclenched them. "Doesn't everyone at some point dream of a little home with a garden and children? I've had it all—a house and my flowers and my kids. I'm blessed. God is good. Life is good. Unexpected, but good." My heart thumped, but it thumped with a lighter beat now that I'd let the fantasy take wing in the real world.

"But this is your future home?"

Pragmatism reasserted itself, and with it came a resolve to keep my feet grounded in the gritty reality of life. My life. "Probably not, but it's the home of my heart, and I know that ought to be enough for me."

We pulled to a stop in front of my present home of cold brick. I glanced over at my friend and pretended not to flinch under his scrutiny. "What'd you find out from Dennis?"

He smiled; I suspected as relieved as I at the change of subject. "He may have seen a boat like the Jane Anne put on a trailer."

"Painted gray?"

He put up his palm. "Don't get excited. I said 'may have,' and that's as close as it gets. The boat he and Andy saw was painted in camo colors. He said it looked more like a do-it-yourselfer's duck-hunting blind than a lobster boat. That's why he took a second look. It didn't have a name on it. It was all spray-painted over, except when the guy hauled it out, it was white below the water line."

"Did he talk to the guy who hauled it out?"

"Yeah. He called out the window when the guy pulled up off the ramp in his truck. Said he wasn't too friendly. Muttered something about inheriting the boat from his crazy uncle and parting it out, then drove off. If it was the Jane Anne, we can't be sure."

"Did you show him a picture of Luke?"

"It might surprise you to know I'm not in the habit of carrying a picture of Luke Faraday in my wallet."

He wasn't telling all he knew. "What are you thinking?"

"Before I found Dennis, I ran the timeline in my head. Depending on when Luke died, he might not've had the time to paint his boat, trailer it, hide it on the mainland, and get back to Stub on a different boat. Besides, Dennis knows Luke as a passing acquaintance. Luke wasn't the one with the boat."

"He had a partner."

Scotty nodded. "Kendall."

I'd come to the same sad conclusion. "Yeah. What are we going to do about it?"

"Nothing."

"But—"

"But nothing … for now. We need to think on it. We've got no proof and nobody's going anywhere."

"I've been thinking about the timeline, too."

"Why am I not surprised?"

"I think Olivia called Luke *after* they left Blackwall, after Nate got sick, because she mentioned it to me. She accused Nathaniel of causing the loss of the boat because he was inexperienced, got seasick, and couldn't help Luke. That was when she blamed Nate for everything."

"She could've been confused about the timing of the phone call. She's had a lot to deal with the past few days."

"I thought of that, but now that she's changed her tune about Nathaniel … "

Scotty cocked one eyebrow; his face shadowed under the darkened bill of his hat. "Since when?"

"This morning. We might not have as much time as you think, oh wing-walking one. Might be time to let go of the thinking stage and stagger out to find the proof. Olivia's leaving the island tomorrow and she wants you to go over there and interview for the position of caretaker of her estate."

"And you know this how?"

"I might have been over there earlier talking to Kendall, and I ran into Olivia."

"Funny thing, since that's her house and she lives there."

"It's not what you think. Olivia invited me in for a chat."

He took off his cap and exposed the furrows on his tanned forehead. "And what did you two chat about?"

"Not much. She seemed to be suffering from selective memory, or maybe complete amnesia. Hard to tell. Let's just say, Nate's no longer a person of interest in Luke's death, but he *is* a person of interest in Olivia's future plans."

"You're kidding."

"I wish. Olivia plans to go visit Nathaniel when she leaves the island so they can commiserate in their grief and find 'closure.' Her words, not mine. Funny thing is, I was worried about Nate coming to Luke's funeral and getting tangled up with Olivia. Now there's not going to be a service, but the black widow could still be spinning a tangled web for me and mine."

"Heard about Luke not having a memorial. You've had a busy day." Scotty put his hat back on his head, got out of the truck and came around to my side. I didn't make a move when he opened my door and he finally nodded and shut it with a muttered. "And the day ain't over yet."

We drove in silence over the roads to Devane's Rip. As we turned down Jane Anne Lane, my driver killed the engine and turned to me, his face as impassive as the stones on Cobb Beach. "What'd you and Kendall talk about this morning?"

"Nothing much. He asked about Nate and his interview with the detective. Kendall was pretty cool about the whole situation. If he was involved, he's taking it well."

"Kendall has always marched to his own drummer, even as a kid growing up, but he's basically a good guy." Scotty shook his head. "I can't wrap my head around him being involved in this, but none of it makes a lot of sense and Kendall *is* the king of confusion." He turned his face away and stared out the water-streaked windshield. The soggy trees dripped with a dull tin ring on the roof of the cab, and the mingled smell of the damp spruce and the tide snaked in his open window.

Rats! Was I the only reason we were sitting a few hundred yards away from a ticking time bomb that threatened to obliterate even more island relationships, or would Scotty have eventually come here without my insistence? *Eventually.* I was more into *right now.* I was lower than snake spit on this one, but I couldn't leave it like this. "I forgot he's your cousin." *Isn't everyone your cousin?* "If you don't want to do this, I understand."

"You understand, but you're not going to stop digging even if I say 'quit,' " he muttered.

I shrugged one shoulder, trying to dislodge the guilt, but it didn't budge. Scotty leaned toward me, rubbed his cheek and his hand lingered on his chin. I swallowed hard. "I can't imagine leaving it buried. It won't make things right, and sooner or later someone's going to dig it up and it'll only have gotten more rotten by then."

"What you mean is it'll stink to high heaven. It already does." His low tone came out as harsh as a crow's caw.

I nodded and glanced out at the wet distorted green curtain beyond the truck window. He took my hand, and I swung my eyes back to his.

"If this whole thing—the search, Luke's death, Nate's rescue—could've been avoided, I need to know. Lives were at stake. There's no excuse for needlessly putting your people in danger." Scotty squeezed my hand and let go. A second later he started up the truck, put it in gear and gunned it down the lane and into the Faraday yard. All vehicles were present and accounted for; there'd be no postponing the explosion.

Scotty hopped out and opened the door for me. We walked together to the garage, its artificial white light blaring out the windows like a neon sign. Kendall met us at the door. Scotty nodded as we entered the chilly workspace. "Olivia's been waiting for you."

"I'll get to her. Wanted to talk to you first."

"What's up?"

"I spoke with Dennis and Andy Bernier today." Scotty's voice was slow and deliberate, like a bullet straight out of the gun that wouldn't stop short of its target.

Kendall lowered his pale eyebrows and frowned. "Those names supposed to mean something?"

"They're the guys who saw you haul out the Jane Anne at the North Larkin boat landing the other day."

"What are you talking about?" His face turned to rubber, lips a thin colorless band, mouth stretched wide and eyes to match.

"The day of the search for Luke when I was waiting on you." Scotty never took his eyes off his cousin. "You left me on the boat. Said you'd be back in a bit. Told me you were going to get one of your jury-rigged contraptions that would help locate the Jane Anne, but you were gone for hours. I went to your place, came here, made the rounds of the island on the boat. I couldn't find you. I found Gwen. We found Luke's body, but I never found you."

I don't know what I'd expected from my companion, maybe a hand on the shoulder, not a fist to the gut; but Scotty was no wing walker. He let it fly and took a step closer until the two cousins were nose to nose.

Kendall spun away on the ball of his foot and retreated to the work bench. He leaned on one elbow and stretched his neck from side to side and the silence stretched between them.

"That's because you were off spray-painting the boat like some fool juvenile delinquent."

"No." Kendall spat out the denial. "You got it all wrong. You don't know what you're talking about, Scotty."

"Maybe not all of it, but if we go to that piece of property you own on the mainland in Clement, you telling me I won't find the Jane Anne there, vandalized like a blasted relic from the Army? Let's go! Show me I'm wrong."

I had a feeling neither man knew I was there. I ached for both of them, for Scotty because his heart had to be breaking, and for Kendall because he was as twitchy as a rabbit caught by a toe in a trap of his own making.

Kendall shook his head. "Not everyone went off and became a big man in the Coast Guard, Scotty. Some of us just lived here day to day, hand to mouth, and got along the best we knew how. Don't you come back here and try to tell me how I ought to be living my life." While Scotty's accusation had been delivered without emotion, Kendall's surly charges were laced with savagery as he bared his teeth.

"I don't give a flying leap if you decide to live in a bird's nest out on the point, smoke weed and wear purple pajamas. You lived your life pretty much just the way you wanted, thumbing your nose at everyone else. You took a man's boat and it cost him his life." Scotty's jaw was set in iron and his right hand, clenched in a white-knuckled fist, rested against his thigh.

"No!" Kendall spewed the word as if it was torn from his gut.

"Then take me to your place in Clement. Show me I'm wrong and I'll leave it alone."

"I can't."

I wanted to bolt out the door. I shouldn't be here, eavesdropping on this private death of a lifelong friendship. I should do something, say something; but there was nothing to say.

Scotty continued coming at him like he was stalking prey—calm, steady, relentless. "Why?"

"It's not what you think. It wasn't supposed to go down this way. If Luke had just stayed asleep, none of this would've happened." Kendall straightened and his words came faster.

"This is all on Luke?"

The mist blew in, along with a smattering of dead leaves

as the door behind me slowly opened and silently closed. Olivia floated in like a ghost. She stopped beside me and her cold fingers crept over mine and grasped them in a painful death grip.

I glanced over. Her makeup stood out in an obscene clownish slash of color on her chalky features. She didn't spare me a glimpse; her eyes were fastened on Kendall. He showed no sign of awareness at her intrusion. He reached out toward Scotty's stiff torso, as rigid and unyielding as only a military man can be, and Scotty gave no quarter, no softening of his posture as Kendall's hand fell short and skittered back to his side, his fingers curled like a dead man's hand.

Kendall's Adam's apple bobbed as the words fought their way out. "In a way. Tell me you didn't see how Luke had changed lately. He was pre-diabetic. Did you know that? He had high blood pressure and an ulcer, but he never told anyone. He never accepted it himself. Thought he was Superman, but he was a heart attack waiting to happen. He couldn't give up the life … never would."

Kendall shook his head and his thinning hair flopped back and forth with the force of the movement. "He was hell-bent to die out on that boat. I offered to buy him out on time. I couldn't come up with the big bucks all at once, but I was good for it." His mouth twisted in a painful grimace, causing the stubble to bristle out on his sharp chin like quills. "You know what he did? Laughed in my face! Fifty years of friendship chucked down my throat until I choked on it." He choked back a sob in the telling. "Luke couldn't see it, but Olivia could. She and I did this to save him for his own good."

"Try telling *him* that."

"He wasn't supposed to wake up. It was supposed to be like a blackout spell. Let him see how bad his health was, get rid of the boat while he was out, then rescue him and move on." He was pleading now.

"But you couldn't get rid of the boat, could you?" Scotty ground out each word. "Kendall Jones, always the collector. You might've gotten away with it if you'd scuttled the Jane Anne, but you never could pass up junking and repurposing it into *more* junk. It got a man killed, Kendall, and sent another to the hospital."

"Oh, no. Don't you pin that on me. I knew exactly where to find Nate. I pushed him overboard right by the buoy, and it was me who pointed you in that direction as soon as the search began. And, Luke. Luke slipped and fell. I had no part in that." He clasped his hands together but I could still see them shaking; or was the trembling I felt coming from the woman beside me?

"Except for the fact that the poor guy was drugged out of his mind and stashed on an island. Can you imagine what was going through Luke's mind when he came to on Stub? If he was coherent enough, he must've known something bad was going down. He wasn't stupid."

Olivia moaned. Her grip loosened and she crumpled down beside me. My hands clutched at her little blue jacket but caught only air as she melted into a puddle of designer clothes and misery at my feet.

"Olivia!" Kendall shot forward, dropped to his knees and cradled the limp woman, stroking her brow. Scotty spun around to the drama unfolding behind him. She moaned again but it was more like a mewling as she stirred.

"This has been so hard on her." Kendall looked up at me with teary eyes, then back at the fainting victim. "Olivia? You alright?"

Her body writhed like a snake, and she lashed out and slapped Kendall across the face. The report of flesh connecting with flesh startled me, and I jumped when she grasped the bottom of my jeans. I recovered enough to reach down in time to grab one of her arms as Scotty and Kendall supported her rise to her feet.

Olivia immediately sagged into Scotty, but I noticed she

wasn't so weak that she couldn't push Kendall away. "Let's get you into the house," Kendall murmured.

Olivia's body might still be woozy, but her speech was razor sharp and cut deep. "You, you killed my Luke! Stay away from me!" She pressed herself into Scotty, her fingers digging like claws into his forearms.

"You want some water?" Scotty asked, all the while half-carrying, half-leading her to a stool on the other side of the work bench. He got her situated but she still clung to the sleeve of his blue flannel shirt. I couldn't help but notice he stayed close enough to support her, should she have a relapse.

I would've had more sympathy for her if she'd gone down like a ton of bricks and whacked her head like an honest-to-goodness real Maine woman. *If* Maine women fainted, which of course we never would, even if we have to jam our boots deep in the mudflats of life to remain upright. Olivia may have fainted for real, not sure if she faked it for the men, but the way she slithered down my leg like it was a lamppost and oozed onto the floor with a ballerina's grace and barely a hair out of place, raised my hackles instead of my compassion for a member of my own gender.

She flicked a quick look in my direction, her eyes aglow with ... vengeance? anger? hatred? I couldn't be sure, in that strafing glance, until she turned and focused on Kendall. "How *dare* you! Come in here and pretend to be my friend, pretend to be my *husband's* friend. It wasn't enough to eat at our table and have Luke constantly bail you out, was it? I was such a fool! Did you think with Luke gone you could step in and take his place? I should've known you'd make a play for me and all that was Luke's. You lying, two-faced murderer! Go crawl back under your rock and stay there!" Her voice trembled and a wail keened around the cavernous space like a banshee.

"Olivia, I know you're upset but—"

"No! Don't you *dare* talk to me. Get out!"

"Olivia, please! You know I'd never hurt you or Luke."

"I *don't* know you, and you obviously don't know me! How could you think I'd ever take up with you in the *first* place, let alone after you've killed the love of my life." She buried her face in her hands and sobbed.

"You'd better step outside, Kendall." Scotty's low voice of reason couldn't penetrate the hysteria in the room.

"No, you got it all wrong, Scotty." Kendall's voice rose to a fever pitch. "This was *her* idea all along. Olivia was the one who asked *me* to help her out. It was all to save Luke from himself. We did it together to save him from himself, can't you see that?" Kendall wiped his dripping nose kindergarten-style and, with his unshaven upper lip, achieved similar results.

"Stop it!" Olivia screeched. "Liar!" She held her hands over her ears.

"Outside, Kendall. *Now*." Scotty's voice cracked like a canvas sail catching the wind.

"No. You've gotta believe me."

Scotty stepped toward his cousin, but Olivia held on tight. "Don't leave me."

"Get him out of here, Gwen."

I nodded, too stunned to speak.

"And Kendall, you know you got nowhere to go," Scotty said.

I put my hand on Kendall's arm and he slatted it off. "I'll go, but this ain't over!"

I followed him out into the drizzle. As soon as I latched the door behind us, Kendall rounded on me. "You believe me, don't you, Gwen? I'd never do anything to Luke. *She* did it. She slipped some type of sleeping pill/drug cocktail into the soup she made. He was just supposed to pass out and stay out for twenty-four hours. And it *did* work, at first." He ran a hand over his weary features. "I called him on the radio to make sure he was out, and when I boarded the Jane Anne, it was all going good, just like we planned. The only glitch was your nephew was still up and at it, so I left him on the buoy."

"No you didn't!" I clenched my fists at my sides, trembling with the force it took not to slap him as Olivia had done.

"I made sure he was okay before I left with Luke. Then I took Luke over to Stubb and put him in Jacey's little camp. Nobody was s'posed to get hurt. I was coming back to rescue him, but you beat me to it."

He sagged against the side of the building but I couldn't muster up any pity for him, only loathing that someone could twist loyalty and friendship into such a perverted pretzel of a hangman's noose.

"We didn't beat you to it because there *was* no rescue. Luke was dead by the time we found him. You can't drug someone and not expect bad things to happen."

"But I didn't drug him. I told you, Olivia did. She had some old medicine of hers she used along with sleeping pills. She swore it wouldn't hurt him."

And she knew this how? I couldn't go there with the man in front of me thrashing like a slimy fish caught in a net.

"You've gotta believe me. Can't you see? I did it all for Jacey. She needed Luke." Kendall reached out and plucked at the sleeve of my anorak. I stumbled back a step, out of his grasp. He stretched his neck stork-like and his rheumy eyes met mine. "And ... and I wasn't gonna keep the Jane Anne. I was gonna fix up the boat and give it to her someday. I did it for her."

"But you did it."

CHAPTER FOURTEEN

The crisp sparkle of the September morning shimmered on the flat ocean and mocked my sleepless night. I'd been over on the cliffs of Blind Man's Bluff, staring out at the start of a new day, trying to pray but failing because I didn't know what to say. Now I stood in the shadow of the mansion, head tilted back, taking in the bright blue sky and puffy clouds.

Looking up, I could almost convince myself yesterday had never happened, but that made me sound just like Olivia. She and Kendall were gone from the island, for good, I suspected. Like a canary, Kendall had sung enough verses to seal his fate, regardless of who else might've been involved. Olivia, on the other hand, was more like a mockingbird, swearing Kendall's version of the events never happened. The proof that Kendall did it was damning for him; not so, for her. Olivia was either a gifted actress or totally innocent. As far as I knew, she hadn't been charged with a thing.

I walked with heavy heart and heavy feet down the lane to my favorite ledge and the small clearing. The early sun's rays filtered through the towering spruce and lit the small clearing, turning the tiny goldenrod petals to incandescent lemon. I resisted the urge to sit on the rock and mope. Instead, I trailed into the sunlit idyll and set to work picking the wild blooms.

I had a nice bouquet of fall asters, goldenrod, and black-eyed Susans by the time my ear caught the rumble of an approaching vehicle. I whipped out the length of dark green ribbon I'd stuffed into my sweatshirt pocket and tied the stems together with a little bow for added flourish. It definitely wasn't florist quality, but it held an island charm, and I didn't think Laverna or Luke would mind.

I smiled at the thought; not because it wasn't sad, but because, in this place, the stillness, the beauty, and the comforts of home, never failed to fill my heart with its peace. I stepped out onto the gravel track just as Scotty's truck rattled by. It stopped a second later and reversed fast enough to send me scurrying back into the bushes.

"You're safe," he drawled through the driver's side open window. The one person I didn't want to run into this morning until I finished my errand, but my heart went out to him. He looked worse than he had during the search.

"I'm sorry," I murmured. I stumbled out and put my empty hand on the window opening.

His rough calloused palm covered mine. "You didn't do anything. Kendall's in it up to his eyeballs. It doesn't matter whether or not Olivia sucked him into it. He's a grown man. He knew what he was doing." Scotty shook his head. "The autopsy may shed some light on Kendall's version of things, but if I had to guess, I'd say Olivia covered her tracks well, and he'll take the fall for the drugging and all of it."

I nodded. There was nothing left to say.

"You picking a bouquet from the home place?"

I hesitated, tempted to bluff my way out of my true mission, but pulled in by his haggard face and the need to bring some measure of comfort. I decided to Scotty it. He was the king of drawing me into ordinary conversation and pulling me out of my troubles. Maybe I could work it in reverse. "I wish. Dot's got some beautiful phlox and golden glow and bachelor buttons down there, but I didn't think she'd appreciate me stealing her posies, and I didn't want to stir up a hornet's nest today."

"Since when?"

This ordinary conversation tactic was harder than I thought. My hand slipped away from under his and went to my jean pocket where Jacey's angel rock waited, a reminder of my promises, quickly made but oh-so-difficult to keep. Was this a different hornet's nest lurking just around the bend? I sensed it, but that feeling was only based on yesterday's unraveling of my childish dream of the innocence of island life.

The silence stretched, and for once, I couldn't for the life of me come up with a remark, smart or dull, to fill it.

Scotty gave me a slow grin. "What are you up to this morning, Miss McPhail?" He chuckled, so I heard it before his bat ears picked up the hum of another truck approaching. Laverna Jordan pulled her small pickup directly behind Scotty's and kept the engine running. The semi-glare of light in the windshield did nothing to soften the stab of her dark glare and curt nod.

"I gotta go."

I hurried around the back of his tailgate and slipped into the passenger's side of Laverna's truck. "What's Scotty doing here?" she asked before I could latch the door.

"I'm not sure. He just showed up a few minutes ago."

"You tell him where we're going?"

Her terse tone was no different than it had been when she called me last night. I'd honored her wishes and told no one of our morning mission. The total secrecy she demanded chaffed, but I chalked it up to Laverna being Laverna. I tried to ignore the tweak on my conscience from the tug of disloyalty to the man whose truck pulled up the hill and disappeared at the top of my driveway. "No, but I *do* think he'd like to come with us if he knew."

"I can't.' She said it so low I strained to hear as she put it in reverse. In the uncomfortable silence that choked the cab, I stifled the urge to turn on the radio, and instead admired her backing-up skills as she wasted no time negotiating Blind Man's Bluff Lane, executed a quick turn at the bottom of the hill in Dot's driveway, and sped away.

Neither of us said a word as she fast-tracked the island roads and whipped onto Jane Anne Lane. Instead of driving to the Faraday house, she took the fork leading to the wharf. She finally slowed as we traversed the small strip of mowed grass and jounced beyond into an overgrown rutted area, the tall weeds and bushes clacking and ticking against the moving truck body.

Laverna halted behind a copse of spruce. She wasn't taking any chances of being spotted, but I didn't think she needed to worry. Everyone was gone from this place, except maybe the crime scene guys. I imagined they'd take a look around Olivia's house, but like Scotty, I doubted they'd find anything incriminating.

Olivia's words from the other day played over in my head like the broken-record-act they'd done throughout the night. *I learned the hard way, I can't trust Kendall with even the simplest thing. He'll always screw it up.* At the time, I thought she was talking about the decision not to have a memorial service for Luke. Now? The churning acid ball of revulsion in the pit of my stomach said it was something much, much worse.

"You ready?" Laverna fixed me with a hard stare.

"I think so." I followed my companion out of the truck in the direction of the shore. We tramped through the tangle of tall grass; beach rose, their thorns snagging on my jeans, their rose hips as big and bright as cherry tomatoes; unyielding steeple bush; and goldenrod spreading its rich spicy scent around us as we bruised it with our passage.

When we made it to the ledges, Laverna nodded toward my simple bouquet. "That's nice."

"Thanks."

"Set it down on the rocks and give me a hand here." She turned back to the undergrowth. I lay down the bouquet and followed a step behind, puzzled by the detour and, frankly, the over-the-top secrecy. But as we zeroed in on a lone cedar up the shore, I saw the soft blur of dull aluminum tucked away in the shade of the old tree. "Luke always left a skiff here." She stopped at the bow of the overturned boat. "I imagine he needed it to sneak away from that creature he married."

We flipped the boat over and collected the oars lying protected underneath. It wasn't a pretty portage as, with stutter steps, we carried the boat down to the shore and I silently marveled at the sheer strength of the woman on the other side of the skiff. I was no weakling, but in the presence of her easy power and grace, I felt like I was.

We lowered the boat onto the wet rocks of a small cobble inlet, and my companion turned to me. "You okay without a life jacket? We're only rowing over to the island."

I lifted my eyes to the oasis of rocks and evergreens floating in the sunlight across the churning channel.

"I'm fine." My response was automatic, but my mind was freaking out ... just a little. This had all the makings of the near disaster with my sailing foray in Ron's boat and me nearly ending up in France. I had more confidence in Laverna's skills than my own, and *mostly* trusted her knowledge of the island dangers and mores, thank goodness.

"Don't forget the flowers."

"Right." I hurried back to the ledge and retrieved my slightly limp bouquet. I hoped it held up better than I was. I'd thought we were just going to a secluded spot on the shore, maybe down by Laverna's place, where she'd say a few words and I'd throw the flowers in the water. Just a small, but hopefully fitting, tribute to her old friend. But standing on this shore, I admitted I'd mentally filled in these blanks to suit myself. She hadn't said any of that last night. Then again, she hadn't mentioned anything about trespassing on Olivia's property, rowing across Devane's Rip, or hanging out at the crime scene, either.

She waited, perched on a ledge, with the boat in the

water, holding it steady. I beat feet over and laid the flowers on the backseat while she got in, light as a fairy, and settled at the oars. I clung to the boat and walked it out along a sloping ledge, giving us as much distance as I could from the shore, before I gave a shove and jumped aboard.

Before I clattered onto the seat, Laverna was already pulling at the oars. I watched her muscular back and arms work with the measured precision of an Olympic athlete.

"I can take a turn if you'd like."

Laverna shook her head, astute enough to realize mine was, if not a token gesture, a totally inept one. "The tide's about slack so it's no problem."

I swiveled my head toward the rocky shore of Stub Island, its spruces standing sentinel, the morning sun glinting silver off their needles as a pair of gulls wheeled overhead. So beautiful, yet it had been the setting for such an ugly ending to a man's life. Perhaps we could restore a sense of peace here in Luke's memorial; not only for Laverna, but for Jacey as well. Her little camp should be a place of happy memories, and I prayed she'd be able to return here with her grandmother someday soon. Not for closure. I couldn't stomach the word since Olivia had dropped it with such contrived emotions, but perhaps for a new and better start.

We skirted the island shoreline before Laverna angled us in and the bow grated on the ledge, the same place Scotty had beached the Zodiac less than a week ago. I worked my way past our oarswoman to the prow, leaped out and hauled the skiff up.

Laverna boated the oars and got out slowly, clutching my bouquet in one hand. "Better tie 'er to the spruce. We won't be too long, but you never know." I secured the rope around the scarred trunk and she head-gestured toward the path. "Thought we'd go up to Jacey's little hide-away first."

I waited for her to step past and lead the way, but she hung back, her head turned in profile to me as she gazed toward the open sea. I took a tentative step across the ledge and caught the blur of movement behind me as she followed, and we walked in single file on the path through the trees to the camp.

I heard her choke back a sob when I stopped within sight of the pink door. The place seemed forlorn, with its graying shingles and faded Jolly Roger flag. I looked down at my feet planted on the yellow-lichen-mottled rock and couldn't seem to move them forward. Instead, I stepped to the side and waited for her to enter.

My flesh felt chilled in the shade of the spruce. I was reluctant to go inside but refused to look around and behind me, down the rock-strewn slope where Scotty had found Luke's body. Laverna, too, hesitated, standing beside me, silent tears coursing down her cheeks. "Maybe we should just go back to the shore and lay the flowers on the tide," I said.

"No." Her cold hand engulfed mine in a painful grip. "I have to do this."

Apparently so did I as we walked hand-in-hand to the shelter. The door creaked when she pushed it open, but the interior waited in quiet welcome. Whatever the CSI people had done out here, they hadn't left it harmed in any way and, thinking of Jacey, I was grateful for that. A shaft of sunshine through the window lit the floor, painted the same girly shade as the door; a spool table and two chairs sat in the center of the small camp. A vintage one-piece wooden student's desk resided under the window with a more modern plastic kitchen set on the far wall.

Luke had built shelves that were covered with shells and painted rocks with googly eyes, sea glass and feathers, a homemade wooden boat, a buoy in Luke's colors—treasures collected from a little girl's travels with her grandfather. I blinked back tears as Laverna blew her nose.

"Didn't know if I could come here on my own but I had to do it, so thanks for coming."

"You're welcome. Thanks for asking me." I took the

angel rock out of my pocket, its polished surface silky-warm between my fingers. I placed it carefully on the table. "I thought I'd leave this here as a tribute to Luke and his love for Jacey. And one day, when she comes home, maybe she can show me how to glitter the halo. I didn't really know Luke, and this is going to sound foolish, but I love Jacey."

"I know you do." She squeezed my hand even harder before she set it free. "And she took to you right off. That's why I asked you to come. I want you to look after her."

"I thought you were going to the mainland to be with her and Erica in the off season."

"Maybe. I closed the lunch wagon for the season. Early, I know, but I made the decision yesterday. Dot wasn't happy, but she never is."

"So, you're leaving?" I scrutinized her care-worn features but she didn't meet my gaze.

"Yeah. I can't stay, not right now. Too much has happened."

"For what it's worth, Jacey's going to need a familiar face and the security of you being there for her."

"That's it. I haven't made up my mind to go over to Arlington and see them."

"I didn't mean to live *with* them, but maybe close enough to be a part of her life."

"I'd like that but..." her voice caught. "How can one person destroy so many innocent lives?"

I shook my head. I wasn't sure if she was referring to Kendall or Olivia, but in my mind they were both equally guilty.

"Kendall's a good man," she murmured. "He loved Luke. It's ... it's that witch Luke got tangled up with! Everything she touches, she poisons. Kendall will go down for this, mark my words, and that creature will never have to even break a single fake fingernail. She'll walk away scott-free."

"You don't know that."

"No, I don't, but look me in the eye and tell me you haven't thought the same thing." Now her gaze bored into mine with the furious intensity of a blast furnace.

"Maybe."

"She'll get away with murder."

I refused to believe it and shook my head. "Nobody ever gets away with anything forever. My father always said 'you haven't seen the end of it yet.' "

"Yeah, the axe will fall on the judgment day, but by that time I'll be dead, and I won't care."

I had no wise words of comfort, only an aching heart for the broken hearts of a little girl and this strong woman.

"But she's not gonna poison my little Jacey Jane-bug. No way I'll let her hurt my little girl." Laverna picked up the angel rock and clutched it to her breast.

"I don't think Olivia will want anything to do with Jacey. I mean, she didn't exactly shine as a step-grandmother. And she never kept it a secret she didn't want the responsibility of caring for a child, even when Luke was here."

"It'd be just like her to try and ruin our lives and stick her interfering nose into my family business."

Where was all this coming from? We'd come to pay tribute to Luke, not exhume the hate Olivia had left buried here. "Maybe she'll go to jail for her part in all of this."

Laverna placed the rock back on the tabletop, but traced the white stripe encircling the top of it with her forefinger. "I pray to God it'll happen, but if it's true Luke left everything to Jacey, she'll be coming after us."

"Oh. I hadn't thought of that." Deaths aren't final. I'd learned that the hard way. The living were left behind to clean up the mess and deal with the fallout of a dead man's last will and testament. If Dot Jones and I were any indicators of a quick painless way through, Laverna was right to be concerned.

"Far as I know, Luke had a will drawn up when Jacey

was born. He was pretty low after Jane Anne died and he had that blowup with Erica. He came to see me one night, about a week after the birth of our granddaughter. Erica hadn't even let him know she was expecting, so when I got the news I thought he had a right to know."

She rubbed her large weather-beaten hands over her compressed lips and looked away for a minute. "It could've been so different. Luke said he wanted to make things right with Erica, and left all his property, everything he had, to Jacey. Course he sent the news via a lawyer. Don't know what ailed him, but, for all he was a brave man, Luke was chickenhearted when it came to dealing with woman problems, and look what it got him. When Erica got the news that way, she was less than impressed."

Laverna swallowed hard and her voice turned husky. "Who would've thought Luke's will would even come into play while Jacey was a child? That's what Erica thought. She came out here when Jacey was just a little bug about two-months-old, lit into her father about pretending to care about her and the baby. Luke gave her some cash and she left. Neither one of them was happy. Especially after Luke went south for the winter and showed up here in the spring with Olivia." She shook her head. "Biggest mistake of his life but, far as I know, he never changed his will for her. Probably thought he had plenty of time. And he would've, if she hadn't killed him."

This wasn't exactly the quiet memorial I'd imagined, but Laverna wasn't ready to close the door on this with a bunch of wildflowers and a prayer. She might be trying to talk herself out of getting involved with Olivia, but she'd already thrown her heart in the ring, and though it was bloodied and trampled at the moment, she'd get to her feet and fight off anyone who tried to touch her granddaughter. She couldn't deny her tigress gene. She just hadn't acknowledged that yet.

"I want you and Dot to take over Barb's, maybe name it

something different. Never really took to the name when we bought it, but my husband favored it."

"What?" Talk about a piano-dropping-on-your-head change of topic.

"I want you to take over my wagon."

"I got that part." Where was this coming from? Neptune?

"And I know it'll be hard on you, but I need you to promise me you'll keep Dot on the payroll. She's the best crabmeat picker on the island."

"So, I've heard." This was getting more far-fetched by the moment.

"We've known each other since God invented dirt. I can't leave her high and dry."

"Why not just let Dot manage the business for you?" *Please!*

"She couldn't hold it together for a day, and she'd have every employee quitting after ten minutes of working with her."

She sounded like Les Bigelow's assessment of Ron's business acumen. I still bristled at his caustic derision, but in Dot's case, Laverna was on the nose. Still, Dot and me working together? Jumping up and down on a bee's nest would be less painful. I threw out my best defense. "I'm a teacher and a mainlander."

"Don't matter. You got a good head on your shoulders, and you're quick. I saw how you handled yourself in there the other day when Dot walked out in a huff. You've already got it down." She shrugged one shoulder. "You may not be from the island, but folks won't hold it against you for long, now that you've come over for good."

Some of them will. But she knew that and didn't care, and since when did I need to have the approval of the crowd? "I don't know what to say."

"You can think about it. That's why I closed down for the season. I didn't want to make you jump in before you were ready, but if you ask me, you're ready now."

"Huh!" *Blast*! The idea had dropped into my brain like a seed and had started to spread its roots. Maybe this was my next life—away from teaching and into the food service industry? Crazy, but appealing.

"Huh is right! I need you to step up, Gwen."

"But why me?"

"Because if Olivia comes after Jacey, I've got to make an awful choice."

"Living on the mainland?"

She cracked the ghost of a smile.

"Don't know as I can handle living on the mainland. Too many people and too many places to go, but I'll do anything for my granddaughter. I've lost my husband, Leroy, and my son, Cory. Jacey's all I got left."

"But you won't lose her. You and Erica are getting along okay, or did I miss something?"

"Erica's not the problem." Laverna drew in a shuddering breath. "It's Jacey. When she finds out her Mimi killed her Grampie, she'll hate me forever."

My eyes bulged and I sucked all the air out of the small room, trying to fight the shock and mental hypoxia clouding my thoughts. "What?" I whispered.

"I can't bear to see that hate in those blue eyes of hers."

I swallowed my confusion and struggled to make sense of her confession. "What are you talking about? You had nothing to do with Luke being drugged and Kendall taking the boat."

"No, I didn't, but I came here. It was during the search, right after I run into you and Jacey at Pop's ice cream stand. Got me to thinking about Luke, so I came down here and rowed over in the skiff, just like we done today."

"But why?"

Her lips compressed into a grimace, and she shook her head. "I don't know. You got me to thinking about family and what was important. And Luke and Jacey were my family, at least before *she* came on the scene. I was feeling so helpless and alone. I didn't really expect to find him here. I just wanted to be alone for a little while. Luke and I were sweethearts in school. T'warnt nothing serious, but I still have a soft spot for him." She tapped her fist against her chest.

"But you found him here?"

Laverna nodded. "I opened the door to Jacey's camp to sit a while, and there he was ... on the floor."

"I don't understand. Scotty found him outside on the rocks."

"I know, but he was in here. Could've knocked me over with a feather. He was livid, kicking and squirming, all tied up with duct tape. I got the bait knife and cut his wrists loose. He ripped the tape off his mouth and started swearing. Then he grabbed the knife from me and cut loose his ankles.

"I tried to talk to him, calm him down, but you know Luke. He was always a bull of a man. He had me haul him to his feet, and I had to hold him up to keep him from falling. I made him sit on the table for a few minutes, but he wouldn't stop muttering."

Weirder and weirder. I tried to wrap my head around what it meant, but the stream of words kept coming. I don't think she could stop them, even if she tried; and out poured all the hurt and pain she'd kept hidden the past three-and-a-half days. It must've been a lifetime to her. I put my hand on her arm and she grabbed hold of it.

"Finally, I got through to him, told him what was going on with your nephew on the buoy, and the Jane Anne missing, and the search. He scooped up the tape and staggered out the door, face as red as a lobster. I tried to hold him back, but he made it to the shore and flung the ball of tape into the rip before he turned back to me. I asked him what was going on, and he was all over Kendall, ripping him up one side and down the other. I should've left him to it, but I couldn't. I told him Olivia was behind all of it."

She squeezed my hand in her punishing grip until both our knuckles turned white. "Never seen him so mad, right livid! And he grabbed onto me and shook me 'til my teeth rattled. Told me he was done with people hurting Olivia, especially me. He cussed me out and accused me of making up lies about his wife.

"About that time, I was fit to be tied. I didn't think about him being drugged out. All I could think about was Jacey. I didn't want her in that house anymore, with Luke right crazy and that witch poisoning both of 'em. I threatened to take her, get custody of our granddaughter.

"Something inside him must've snapped. He dragged me up the rocks like he was a rabid wild thing. I tried to get him to let me go, but it was like he couldn't hear me. I fought him and shoved him away to get loose. That's when he fell and hit his head."

Laverna sobbed and I pulled her into a hug. "I tried to revive him but he was dead. I thought he broke his neck. I didn't know, and I didn't know what to do. I came back to the island, crazy, not sure who to tell. But before I could decide what to do, you and Scotty found him. I'm glad it was you and not some stranger. That's all I could think when I heard the news."

She gently stepped out of my fierce clutch. Her cheeks wet, eyes red, Laverna bowed her head. "Then, God forgive me, I kept mum on account of Jacey and what we just talked about. I didn't know all the ins and outs about Kendall then. And now?" She sighed. "I been trying to play it safe to keep my granddaughter."

Wow! It all fit. The bruise on her bicep, her sudden desperate attachment to me, the timeline that neither Scotty nor I had figured in—Laverna's part in it.

"Say something, Gwen."

I was in sensory overload, but it was nothing compared to the woman in front of me, strangling the last bit of life out of the wilted flowers. "You don't have to play it safe to be safe," I said slowly, each word being tweezered from my brain with tremendous effort. "Playing it safe can be risky. You can get stuck in one place and eventually run out of air. You think Jacey will blame you for Luke's death? No one can say for certain, but I don't see her doing that. And you said it yourself ... Olivia might walk away from this and go after Jacey to get Luke's property." I thought of Olivia greedily making plans to put the property on the market. Could it be property she didn't own? The implications were staggering.

"If she gets away with it, there's nothing I can do."

"But Luke was tied up." The brain that was in quicksand suddenly pulled free and flew at the speed of light, and my words struggled to keep up with the catapulting thoughts. "Nobody knows that but you and the person who wanted to make sure Luke never made it off Stub Island alive. Think about it. Kendall's story was that he was coming here to pretend to rescue Luke. I'm not really sure how he intended to make that scenario believable, but if that was his plan, that means Olivia *never* planned to rescue Luke."

Laverna stood before me, tall and straight now, an aura of calm radiating from her. Perhaps she'd passed all the mental torment to me and was now free. But it wasn't true. It would come back to haunt her in the dark hours and lonely moments; we both knew it. "Could've just been insurance. Kendall used the duct tape in case Luke came to before he got back here to pick him up for the rescue."

"Yeah, but how were they going to explain it to Luke?" She was being the rational one, but my mind exploded like a roman candle. Had the plan been to scuttle the Jane Anne and let both men drown? Thank goodness Nate hadn't been drugged. Was that what changed Kendall's mind? Or was it as Scotty said ... he couldn't pass up adding the Jane Anne to his collection of stuff.

I certainly didn't buy his 'I'm fixing the boat up for Jacey,' because if Luke was going to be rescued alive, that never could've been an option. A sudden white-hot thought flashed above the rest. "Maybe Olivia didn't know Kendall stashed Luke over here, and when she found out he'd deviated from the original plan, she freaked and came over and tied him up so she could figure out how to salvage the situation that was about to blow up in her face."

"Too bad you don't have the duct tape."

Laverna's tan face blanched white as an albino, and I spun around to face our interloper. "Stinson Sullivan Scott!" Laverna spat out the name like a curse.

"It would've been circumstantial evidence in the case against Kendall and Olivia."

"You have no right to be here!"

Instead of leaving, Scotty stepped into the camp and laid his hand on my shoulder. The room suddenly got a whole lot smaller, but Laverna held her ground.

"You followed us," I said.

"Guilty as charged."

"Why?" I looked up into his guarded blue gaze.

"Just a hunch there might be trouble."

"There's no trouble here," Laverna said. "We were just leaving." She picked up the flowers and advanced, and Scotty stepped back and held the door like a gentleman. The three of us walked the path back to the ledges. Scotty's Zodiac was beached next to the skiff. I wondered why neither of us had heard it, but my ears *had* been filled with louder things.

Laverna put her arm around me and exerted the slightest pressure as she began reciting the 23rd Psalm. I joined her in a hushed voice. The wind had picked up and soughed through the branches, carrying the healing tribute out across the waves. She flung the flowers into the water and the wavelets carried them toward the horizon, where water blended with sky. Scotty's slow deep voice rode just above the wind as he said a prayer for the living and thanked God for Luke's influence on our lives.

At the final amen, Laverna slipped away from me and crushed Scotty in a fierce embrace. "You gonna let me handle this on my own?"

He nodded. "Just don't leave it buried too long. Somebody's bound to dig it up someday. Sooner you talk to the cops, the sooner they have what they need to convict."

But what about this woman?

"I don't trust it to happen."

"You won't know if you don't come forward."

"It's gonna take everything I've got."

I wasn't sure if she meant guts or her relationship with Jacey. Either way, she saw it as a phenomenal risk. Who wouldn't?

EPILOGUE

I'd just gotten off the phone with my niece and nephew. Nathaniel was getting stronger and back to his usual self. So far, Olivia hadn't put in an appearance, or maybe she had yet to track him down.

I hadn't talked with Scotty since we left Stub Island and he followed us in to shore. Laverna had pooh-poohed his offer to tow us to Luke's wharf. Instead, she rowed us back to the rocks with enough grit and strength to combat the turn of the tide.

She'd driven me home and assured me we'd stay in touch. I wasn't so sure, but I prayed she'd find the courage to make it through to the other side of this emotional canyon. I'd moped around the house yesterday, and this morning I hadn't done much better except I'd made a fish chowder. I was debating on whether to take it over to Old Stin's for the common sense and wisdom I knew he'd serve up to put this past week into perspective, but I hadn't convinced myself yet.

Thoughts of my old friend propelled me to the mailbox he'd given to me. I opened it and found an envelope from a lawyer, forwarded from my house on the mainland, as well as a set of keys with a sticky note that simply said. "Lunch wagon. Both sets. I didn't give any to Dot."

Great! So much for giving me time to think it over. It wasn't enough to have the house-thing and the yacht-company-thing between Dot and me. Now I had Barb's between us as well.

I stood there, staring off into space, as Scotty pulled up in his truck. He got out and strode in front of me, pointedly looking at the items in my hands. I held them like the scales of justice as if weighing the pull of the past in one hand and the revelations of my potential future in the other.

"Heard Laverna's talking to the cops. Thought you'd like to know."

"Yeah. I hope it works out for her."

"Me, too. You feel like taking a walk, or do you prefer to stay here holding onto whatever it is you've got there."

I felt the flush in my cheeks. He couldn't possibly know what I was holding, but it wouldn't surprise me that he did. "Is that a wing-walker dig?"

"Might be." He grinned.

I slipped the letter in my back jeans pocket and the keys in my front pocket and looped my arm in his. "Where are we going?"

"Jumping right off the wing. And if we do this right, you just land on your feet down the road and might end up in the home of your dreams."

"Home?"

"House … home." He flipped his hand palm up.

"Small distinction."

"Big one, to those who know the difference."

We started walking down the hill. Scotty chuckled. "This is probably the biggest mistake of my life, but can't have you hanging onto a house when you need a home."

The End

Did you miss book 1, Blind Man's Bluff? You can get it here

"May God grant you always…A sunbeam to warm you, a moonbeam to charm you, a sheltering angel so nothing can harm you. Laughter to cheer you. Faithful friends near you. And whenever you pray, Heaven to hear you."

Dear Reader,

Thank you for coming to Candle Island with us! We love to stand on the rugged Maine cliffs, engulfed in the sounds and power of the Atlantic wind and surf. We're blessed to live in a place where we can hike to secluded beaches and lonely headlands.

Gwen's adopted island holds a special place in her heart and ours … but in the real world, we all have our "islands" of family and friends. We don't need to swim an ocean or climb a cliff to find adventure and to discover our purpose. It's all about daring to try, jumping out of our comfort zone and, like Gwen, letting go of the wing strut and walking without fear into today's sky toward tomorrow's horizon.

Dreams and goals may change with the years, but we wish for you new dreams and the imagination and determination to live them out. Regardless of our age or circumstances, or maybe because of them, the Cuffe sisters believe today is our best day ever to live life without a doubt or worry. Imagine the possibilities and open your heart to the opportunities. Make a day you'll treasure!

We hope you enjoyed your time on the island with Gwen and her friends. We've included a couple of her recipes below, as well as the prologue for **Emerson Rock**, the next book in the Candle Island Cozy Series, and live links to our other books and social media. Looking forward to hearing from you!

Best regards,

Sadie & Sophie Cuffe (real life sisters forever!)

Anadama Bread
Ingredients:
2 cups milk
¾ cup water
4 tablespoons butter
2/3 cup cornmeal
1 tablespoon salt
½ cup molasses
2 packages dry yeast
5-6 cups flour

Combine milk, water, and butter in saucepan and bring to boil. Shut off heat. Add cornmeal and stir. Cool to lukewarm, pour into mixing bowl, and salt, molasses, yeast, and 1 cup of flour. Beat for 2 minutes with electric mixer.

Gradually add balance of flour, stirring by hand until dough is free from sides of bowl. Place dough on floured board and knead for 8-10 minutes.

Let rise in greased bowl until doubled in bulk (about 1 hour). Punch down, divide in half, and place in greased bread pans until double in bulk.

Bake at 375 degrees for 50-55 minutes.

Peanut Butter Cookies
Mix together thoroughly:
½ cup shortening
½ cup peanut butter
½ cup white sugar
½ cup brown sugar
Add: 1 egg, ½ teaspoon vanilla and beat well
Stir in: 1 ½ cups of flour, 2 teaspoons baking powder, pinch of salt
Form in balls, place on ungreased cookie sheet, press down with fork, sprinkle with sugar if desired. 375 degrees

10-14 minutes, makes 3 dozen.

Emerson Rock
Book #3 in the Candle Island Mystery Series
Miss Appropriated

I rolled over in bed, but the annoyance stuck with me in the form of claws kneading in my hair. "PM, leave me alone," I murmured to the persistent cat, just before his small body tensed … and so did mine. A distinct clunk thumped from somewhere above our heads, then dead silence. My cat was here with me, so who else was in the house?

"It's nothing," I whispered. I slipped out of the covers and grabbed the flashlight from the nightstand. I edged toward the door in the dark and waited. The mausoleum I called home was noiseless as a held breath, and I discovered I was holding mine.

No restless Atlantic wind rattled the branches at the window. No moonlight brightened the hallway before me. The gray and white cat tiptoed to the open door and stood staring at nothing, just like me.

"I'm being paranoid," I whispered again, spooked by the sound and the silence. My mind went down to the front door and its pain of an alarm system. Had I set the alarm? Maybe. I couldn't be sure. I wasn't always the most reliable when it came to cyber security or techno in general.

"I imagined it," I told the cat, but neither one of us believed me. I leaned into the hallway and heard it, the furtive scuff of footsteps overhead. I cocked an ear upward toward the uncarpeted third-floor office. Someone was up in the room where my late benefactor, Vance Jones, had kept his own counsel, surrounded by his triumphs and his obsession of designing million-dollar yachts for the filthy rich.

I hefted the baseball bat sitting against the bedroom door frame, ready for this very purpose. In theory, it seemed like a solid move. I'd used the old Louisville Slugger over the years; once to repel a stray dog from my garden, and once to rout a stranger who was trying to get into my car while it sat in my own driveway. If I was honest, my dubious success on both occasions came from yelling at the top of my lungs like a mad woman. This was decidedly different.

I should hide out in the bedroom and call the cops. But Candle Island didn't have a police force. I could call the caretaker I'd inherited, Stinson Scott the younger, but by the time Scotty got here, the culprit would probably have skipped. The choices flitted through my mind like a bat on the hunt, as I negotiated the dark hall. I hesitated for just a second at the stairway and looked up into the nightlight's dim glow on the landing.

I needed to know who was here and why. The thought of someone getting away "Scott free," with whatever they were doing up there, bugged me. It wasn't happening on my watch.

"Stay here," I whispered to the cat who was nowhere to be seen.

I tucked the flashlight in my red-and-black plaid pajama pants pocket and, on bare feet, crept up the stairs. I hugged the near banister, hoping if someone popped their head out of the doorway it would take them a moment to catch the movement below. I don't know what I expected, but nothing happened. I made it to the landing undetected, as easily as if it were the middle of the day.

I had a feeling it was about to get a lot more interesting. A fleeting thought crossed my mind of slamming the office door shut and imprisoning the interloper until help arrived, but since I hadn't called anyone, no help was on its way … although the person inside that room wouldn't know that.

I considered it for a few deep breaths and liked the idea. They say if you point a gun you better be ready to pull the trigger. The same was no doubt true of a baseball bat. Could I crack it into someone's head? I grimaced, not so sure on that score. This was more doable, I hoped.

I slipped up close with my back flattened against the outside wall. The sound of drawers opening, and papers riffling was loud in my ears, adding a treble slide accompaniment to the bongo drum of my heartbeat. The door opened out, but I had to cross the opening to grab it. I rehearsed in my mind, springing across the open doorway, grabbing the handle, slamming it shut and wedging the bat under the knob. I'd've felt a little better about the plan if the bat was longer. My eyes told me it was long enough to jam into the door and the edge of the top post of the landing, but maybe at a point much lower than the doorknob and maybe at only a slight slant to accommodate the placement of the landing balustrade.

The murmur of voices upended my plans. More than one person was in there, and they were headed toward me. It was too late to reconsider. It hit me what a fool I was as I leapt across the wooden floor, jerked the door toward me with my left hand as I twisted my body out of the way.

The door banged with a satisfying slam. I jammed the bat end up against the railing and slapped it down with my palm against the wooden door. It wedged tight for maybe a blink before the door blew open. I was still bent with my hand on the bat handle. The solid door hit me full force on the top of my head and dropped me like an old dead birch in a hurricane.

I saw stars but fought the urge to curl up in a fetal position. I lay on the landing as they charged out, stepping over my body. Two figures highlighted by the nearby nightlight. Both clad in black, both wearing ski masks.

I heard the intake of breath above me and a guttural "No!" I tried to place the voice but it was cut-off by a rough "Shut-up." They bounded down the stairs, heedless of the noise now that their nefarious night foray had been discovered.

The alarm blared as they bolted through the front door. I *had* remembered to activate the alarm, but the thought brought no comfort. I raised myself on a shaky elbow, fished out my flashlight and tried to urge myself to run down the stairs and see their get-away car. My fifty-plus body said it wasn't going to happen. Instead, I lay like a beached whale, the alarm edging my headache up the Melzack/Torgerson pain chart past ten with each screeching pulse.

I groaned, rolled over to my knees and got up. On rubber legs, I staggered into the office, flipped the light switch and doused the flashlight. In the harsh brilliance, blueprints, orders, notes and papers littered the shiny bamboo floor, but beyond the mess stood a hole in the battered kneewall of Vance's scarred maple desk. I wobbled closer, my fingers rubbing the egg forming under my hair.

I flumped into the vintage wooden desk chair. It accepted my weight with a familiar creak. In spite of my big head, I leaned under the desk to get a better look. A narrow wooden panel had been jimmied open to reveal an empty space about the size of a shoebox. I had a feeling it hadn't been empty for long.

I leaned back against the wooden slats and stared. It had been there in front of my eyes all this time, and now it was gone. Goose egg aside, I'd find out what it was and who had taken it, or my name wasn't Gwen McPhail…

Author Bio

The Cuffe sisters live on the edge of the Atlantic, where the sunrise first touches the shores of the USA. They know rural and island life, and the unique flavor of Yankee characters—tough and salty as their wave-pounded rockbound coast, and just as solid and unpredictable. Privileged to be raised in a large extended natural and Spiritual family, much of their childhood was spent in the churches of Five Islands and Georgetown. The rural church remains a major force in their lives.

They run a small farm Downeast and bring Jane-of-all-trades know-how to their novels, writing squarely to the hearts of real women who aren't twenty-something, who don't wear a size two, and who prefer boots and flannel to high heels and the LBD.

Other books by Sadie & Sophie Cuffe
A Woman Like Me 4-book set
A Mustard Seed Book #1 – A Woman Like Me
Wheat and Tares Book #2 – A Woman Like Me
The Bittersweet Harvest Book #3 – A Woman Like Me
Kernel of Wheat Book #4 - A Woman Like Me
Blood Brothers 3-book set
Arrow That Flies Blood Brothers book 1
Long Road Home Blood Brothers book 2
Grasping the Wind Blood Brothers book 3
The Wainwright Family Saga 3-book set
The Seekers Book #1 Wainwright Saga
Faith in the Shadows Book #2 Wainwright Saga
The Heart Knows Book #3 Wainwright Saga
Hard Country
Lonesome Whistle
The Runaways
The Burning Ocean

Patchwork
Hearts of Seven Pines
Maine White Pine Cone Conspiracy
Massachusetts Mayflower Mayhem
The Balsam Bride
Hard Country
Christmas at Mercy's Gate
Birds and Breadcrumbs
Take a Peak
The Hidden Path
Sea of Tranquility
Cinnamon Sunrise
The Golden Spoon

Follow us on Facebook, Amazon, or contact us directly at
sscuffe@yahoo.com

Bless you!